Praise for the Red Carpet Catering Mystery Series

"The Red Carpet Catering series delivers a buffet of appealing characters, irresistible movie-industry details, and tantalizing plot twists. As delicious as a gourmet meal—and leaves you hungry for more!"

Susan O'Brien,
Agatha Award-Nominated Author of *Finding Sky*

"Movie lovers, this is your book! Engaging and high-spirited, Penelope Sutherland never expected that catering for the cast and crew of a top flight movie would lead to...murder. Great fun."

– Terrie Farley Moran,
Agatha Award-Winning Author of *Caught Read-Handed*

"With a nice island flavor, a nice puzzling mystery and a great cast of characters, this was a very enjoyable read."

– *Dru's Book Musings*

"A fast-paced cozy easily read and enjoyed in an afternoon...with Simmons' picturesque writing style you can almost taste the salt in the air. Take a vacation and join Penelope."

– *The Reading Room*

"Such a fun book..The characters are very likable and the writing is very well-done. Think of it as a cozy behind the scenes."

– *Booklikes*

"Delicious! A great read written by someone who knows the behind the scenes world of filmmaking   ."

Scott,
eries

MAR 13 2018

"This series is so well done that you will feel as though you have just gone to a friend's house to visit for a few hours."

– The Reading Room

"Loved this book! The characters are well-drawn and it's cleverly plotted. Totally engrossing...I felt as though I was actually on a movie set. The author is well-versed in her setting and she is able to keep the reader in suspense. I can't wait for the second book in the series."

– Marianna Heusler,
Edgar-Nominated Author of *No End to Trouble*

"Much of what makes this such an enjoyable new mystery is the background information on both catering and movie-making. Equally compelling is just how seamlessly author Simmons works Penelope into the investigation...this is a fun new series for readers who enjoy their theatrical showbiz mysteries with a culinary twist."

– Kings River Life Magazine

"A fun mystery on a movie set and delightful chef with delicious sounding food....Shawn Reilly Simmons has a flair!"

– Penn State Librarian

"With a likeable cast of characters and an inside look at the movie industry, this was an equally entertaining and engaging debut."

– Dru's Book Musings

"Simmons has given us quite a good beginning to a new series; she manages to create characters that are both believable and likable, while weaving in small tidbits of movie-making and what is involved in catering food to a movie crew. I look forward to reading the next in the series. Highly recommended."

– Any Good Book

MURDER
IS THE
MAIN
COURSE

**The Red Carpet Catering Mystery Series
by Shawn Reilly Simmons**

MURDER
IS THE
MAIN
COURSE

A RED CARPET CATERING MYSTERY

SHAWN REILLY
SIMMONS

HENERY PRESS

MURDER IS THE MAIN COURSE
A Red Carpet Catering Mystery
Part of the Henery Press Mystery Collection

First Edition | May 2017

Henery Press, LLC
www.henerypress.com

Trade Paperback ISBN-13: 978-1-63511-203-0
Digital epub ISBN-13: 978-1-63511-204-7
Kindle ISBN-13: 978-1-63511-205-4
Hardcover ISBN-13: 978-1-63511-206-1

Printed in the United States of America

For John & Patricia Montgomery,
my grandparents

ACKNOWLEDGMENTS

As always, first and foremost, thanks to Matt and Russell for their constant love and encouragement. I really couldn't do all that I do without them by my side.

I'm honored to be a member of the endlessly helpful and supportive mystery writing community. From my Malice Domestic family to the Dames at Level Best, to my Sisters in Crime, my Mystery Writers of America pals, and my Crime Writers' Associates in the UK, I have so many writing friends near and far that I never feel alone, even when I'm typing away in the dark well before dawn.

And as always, thanks to Ildy Shannon, my first reader, to Colleen Shannon, a great source of support, and to Stephanie Reilly for always believing in me.

This book takes place in Indiana, where I'm originally from, where my family has lived for many generations, and where I used to visit my grandparents every summer. I have lots of wonderful memories of those trips back home, and of spending time with my aunts, uncles, and cousins. It was nice to remember all the fun we had together while I was writing the book.

Special thanks go to Kendel Lynn, Art Molinares, Rachel Jackson, Erin George, and everyone else at Henery Press. Over the course of four books, I've experienced nothing but support, enthusiasm, kindness, and encouragement. I'm truly grateful.

Finally, I'd like to dedicate this story to readers. Not just readers of my books, but all readers, everyone who enjoys a good story, loves books, and makes reading part of their lives.

Love,
Shawn

CHAPTER 1

Penelope eased the door to the walk-in freezer open with the tip of her boot, then caught the edge with her hip before it could swing closed again. She inched inside the narrow metal space, balancing boxes of frozen chicken on her arm, a chill seeping through the sleeves of her chef coat. Her shoulders ached from the long hours she'd spent cooking the day before for the cast and crew of the new movie she was working on, a reboot of the classic tale *The Turn of the Screw*.

Penelope crooked her elbow into the corner and flicked up the light switch. She heard an electric buzz, then a glassy pop as the overhead bulb lit for a second then snuffed out. When she stepped forward, the spring-loaded door swooshed shut behind her, leaving her in complete darkness. Penelope closed her eyes and counted to five, hoping they'd adjust to the darkness, but it was just as black when she opened them again. She took a tentative step forward and elbowed aside the plastic flaps suspended from the ceiling that held in the frigid air whenever the door opened. She tried to remember where there might be some empty spots on the shelves.

Penelope slid a box of chicken wings onto a shelf on her left and was relieved when it stayed in place and didn't come crashing back down on her. She shifted the remaining boxes onto one arm and ran her hand along the plastic shelf. While she was searching for more room, she thought about going back out to the kitchen and looking for a flashlight or a replacement light bulb. She stepped into the middle of the walk-in, reaching out her hand to find the opposite wall.

Something heavy brushed her shoulder when she reached the center, then twisted away. Penelope froze. The object bumped her again, harder this time, and the boxes dropped from her arm. Reaching out her hand, her fingertips brushed across thick cotton fabric. Her heart thumping, she backed toward the door, slipping between the flaps and feeling behind her for the red release button under the light switch, the one that made sure no one would get trapped inside the freezer with no way out. Penelope thought about what it would be like to be stuck in there, slowly freezing to death with no one on the outside able to hear her yells.

There was no sound except a whispered rubbing, the creak of something being pulled tight. Otherwise the silence was overwhelming, a metallic buzz that filled her head and made her breathing sound like a freight train rolling through the small space.

Penelope slapped the release button with a numb palm and pressed her back against the door. Light from the kitchen poured in, momentarily dazzling her, and revealing a blurred outline behind the plastic of something suspended from the ceiling in the center of the freezer. She rubbed her thumb against her fingertips, remembering the roughness of cloth under them, and willed herself to calm down.

Penelope backed into the kitchen and watched the freezer door swing closed, the rubber edges sealing back together. The urge to leave and find someone else, anyone else, to help her deal with what was happening was overwhelming. She looked around the deserted kitchen, then out the frosted glass of the windows at the fresh snow that had fallen the night before. Everyone she knew who might be able to help was either upstairs in the inn asleep, or very far away, back home in New Jersey.

Penelope cleared her throat and pulled open the walk-in door again. A pie-shaped wedge of light sliced into the blackness and she leaned in to pull apart the heavy plastic flaps, keeping the toes of her boots as close to the door as possible.

Two bare feet twisted in mid-air, the skin tinged blue around a man's toenails. Penelope willed herself to take another step, pushing the door open as wide as it would go. She slid a box in front of the door to prop it in place, the coolness encircling her as it mixed with the warmer air of the kitchen. She parted the plastic flaps, looking up into the man's face, her worst fears confirmed. Penelope hurried to him and grasped his arm, feeling icy flesh beneath her fingers.

"Oh no, Jordan," Penelope said, choking back a sob. Her first instinct was to throw her arms around his legs and help him down, but when she saw the rope cutting into his neck and the unnatural color of his cheeks, she knew she was too late to help her new friend and owner of the kitchen she was working in. Chef Jordan Foster was dead.

Penelope stared at his face as she backed out of the walk-in. Her heel caught on the box and slid it aside, the door easing shut once again. Penelope pulled her phone from her back pocket and dialed 911, an unfamiliar trembling overcoming her as she held it to her ear. When the voice on the other end assured her an ambulance was on the way, she hung up and dialed the movie's director, who picked up after a few rings.

"Go for Jennifer."

"It's Penelope," she said, her early-morning voice sounding hollow in her ears. She stared at the walk-in door, irrationally imagining Chef Jordan strolling out and flashing a toothy grin, catching her in a prank.

"Morning. Crew call time is at nine. You're not going to be late for breakfast, are you?" Jennifer asked, sounding distracted. Penelope knew she was often up hours before most of the crew, working on script rewrites or viewing the dailies in her suite before submitting them to the producers back in LA.

"Jennifer, something's happened to Jordan," Penelope said urgently. "An accident, in the kitchen downstairs."

"An accident?" Jennifer asked. "Is he okay? Wait, why is he here so early?"

"I've called an ambulance. They're on the way," Penelope said, hedging.

"An ambulance? Penelope, what's happening?"

Penelope felt the rush of tears she'd been choking down since finding Jordan rise to the surface. "Jennifer, Jordan's dead. I found him," she cried.

"No. He can't be," Jennifer whispered. "I'll be right down."

CHAPTER 2

Penelope was propped on a stool near the windows in the inn's kitchen. Images flashed through her mind like a stack of gruesome flashcards: Chef Jordan's feet twisting just above the floor, the blue tint of the skin around his toenails, the unnatural puffiness of his face, the look of panic, or maybe it was sadness, in his eyes.

"You okay, ma'am?"

The room around her came back into focus and she sat up straighter.

"You looked gone there for a minute," the EMT said gently from his place outside the walk-in door. "Give me a shout if you start feeling faint."

Penelope nodded quickly and he turned his attention back to his partner, who was inside the freezer with Jordan's body. She stared at the yellow lettering on his back that spelled out the ambulance company, the dark blue uniform shirt taut across his shoulders, his pale thin fingers resting lightly on his belt. He shook his head once or twice as he spoke with the tall female police officer, who'd showed up at the same time as the ambulance crew. She scribbled in a spiral notepad, fraying at the edges, the diamond ring on her finger sparkling under the bright kitchen lights.

"What's happened?" Jennifer was suddenly standing in front of Penelope, her long brown hair spilling over her shoulders. The police officer's head snapped up from her pad at the sound of Jennifer's voice.

Penelope rose from the stool and met her gaze. "Where have you been?"

"I came as fast as I could. I had to get dressed," Jennifer said.

Time had slowed down for Penelope. It felt to her like hours had passed already. "I called 911 as soon as I found him," Penelope said, nodding toward the walk-in. "The police, EMTs, they all came."

Jennifer searched her face. "I can see them, Penelope. I'm asking you what happened to Jordan."

"Oh, right," Penelope said, gathering herself. "Like I told Officer Collins—"

"Excuse me," the policewoman interrupted. Penelope hadn't noticed her approaching, but now she was right behind them. "If I could ask you to step over here please, ma'am?"

Penelope hooked a thumb at her chest. "Me?"

"No." She gave Jennifer a quick nod. "It will be helpful if you don't talk with each other until after I've gotten your statements. The sheriff will be here any minute."

Jennifer stared at her, confused. "I don't have a statement. I just got here, I have no idea what's going on."

"I'm sorry, you are..." Officer Collins flipped to a fresh page in her notebook.

"Jennifer Carr, the director. We're staying here, all of us, the cast and crew, at Jordan's invitation. He's one of my oldest friends. We grew up together. Please, tell me what's going on." Jennifer's forehead creased with worry. Penelope looked away quickly, fearing a fresh round of tears coming on.

"I'm sorry, Ms. Carr, we're still investigating and I can't give details." The young officer's expression shifted from stern to comforting in a matter of seconds. "Your patience is appreciated. We're here to help, I promise."

"Fine." Jennifer walked away, pulling her phone from her pocket.

"No calls either, if you don't mind," Officer Collins said.

Jennifer held her phone out to show her she wasn't calling anyone, then slipped it back in her pocket.

Officer Collins turned her attention to Penelope and lowered her voice. "Ms. Sutherland, can you tell me again what time you got to the kitchen?"

"Just after four thirty," Penelope said. She gazed at Officer Collins' shiny diamond ring as she jotted more notes.

"Do you always start work that early?"

Penelope brushed her cheek with her hand. "No. Sometimes. It depends on the day."

Officer Collins nodded and chewed her bottom lip. Her hair was pulled into a tight bun, the blonde strands blending with her porcelain-colored skin. "And just to confirm, you didn't see anyone or anything suspicious when you got downstairs?"

"No. I mean, besides Jordan being here so early. Why are you asking...it's a suicide, right?"

"We investigate all unattended deaths. I know this is hard, but they're standard questions," she said, a bit quickly, like she was reciting from a manual.

"Have you found something that makes you think it's not suicide?" Penelope asked, instinctively lowering her voice.

An expression passed over Officer Collins' face, a brief second that made Penelope pause, stop her mind from turning in circles, and focus on what she was saying. "Too soon to say," Collins said simply.

"I can't think of anything that was different, Officer Collins." Penelope said, carefully considering her words. "It was the same delivery guy that comes every week. I met him out back in the lot like always, only for a few minutes. He didn't come inside, just stacked everything on the porch, then left for his next stop. I logged in the delivery, and was putting things away before opening the kitchen up for the day. I went in the freezer and the light went out. Chef Jordan was—"

Officer Collins raised her pen in the air, cutting her off gently. "It's okay, you've told me this part. When the sheriff gets here you'll have to tell it again." She placed her cool palm on the top of Penelope's hand. "I'm sorry for what you've been through, that you had to see what you did."

"Thank you, Officer," Penelope said, taking comfort in her gesture.

"You can call me Edie."

A man in a fleece-lined leather jacket stepped through the back door, gave Edie a quick nod, and strode to the walk-in. A star-shaped patch on his sleeve indicated he was the sheriff of Brown County, Indiana. He spoke quietly with the EMT, his shoulders rigid and his expression serious.

Edie squeezed Penelope's hand once more before going over to speak with Jennifer, who stood with her thin hip propped against the countertop.

Penelope watched them talk in low voices, Edie taking more notes and Jennifer bobbing her head in response to the questions, flicking her eyes to Penelope a few times. When she was finished, Jennifer rejoined Penelope and Edie went to speak to the sheriff.

"When Jordan didn't answer my text last night I should have known something was wrong," Jennifer murmured. "He always responds right away."

"When did you text him?" Penelope asked.

Jennifer pulled out her phone and checked the time on the message. "Just after midnight."

Penelope thought for a moment. "The last time I saw him was late afternoon. He must have come back over here after he closed the restaurant last night. I was already in bed."

"How did he seem to you?" Jennifer asked.

"Fine. He brought over some canapés for us, the ones we served before dinner. We talked briefly about this morning's delivery, how he wanted his items put away. He wasn't getting much. It was mostly stuff I'd gotten for us. Then he said something about a special table coming in for dinner, someone he had to prepare for."

"Do you know who he was expecting?" Jennifer asked.

"He didn't mention a name, but it was some kind of press. A reporter maybe?"

"There's only one paper in Forrestville," Jennifer said. "He could have been talking about someone from Indianapolis or Bloomington. Or any website anywhere, for that matter."

"He wasn't specific. He just said he wanted to be sure they had a memorable dinner," Penelope said.

Jennifer nodded distractedly, then threw a quick glance over her shoulder at the sheriff. "Well, no one has contacted our publicity office from any local press, so whoever it was wasn't here to see the set or cover the movie, as far as I know."

Penelope watched the sheriff stick his head inside the walk-in, but he made no further move to go inside.

"Are you okay?" Penelope asked.

"Yeah," Jennifer said automatically, then reconsidered. "I mean, no. Of course not. I'm having a hard time believing Jordan would hang himself in his own freezer."

"It's hard to imagine anyone doing that, especially a good friend," Penelope agreed.

"No, I mean, I can't believe Jordan would kill himself at all. He didn't believe in suicide."

"Well, under the worst circumstances, none of us can really be sure—"

"No, you don't understand. There was this girl, a friend of ours, back in high school. She ran away, then committed suicide after her parents found her and brought her home. She made it all the way to Chicago, was crashing on someone's couch. Jordan was really upset about the whole thing, started an anti-suicide campaign for the students."

"Wow," Penelope said. "Well, that was a long time ago now."

Jennifer shook her head and folded her arms. "He wouldn't do this. It's hard to find a more upbeat person than Jordan."

"Was he depressed? Worried about anything?" Penelope asked carefully.

"Not that I know of," Jennifer said.

Penelope sat back down on the stool, her legs feeling heavy. "Jennifer, if you don't think he could have killed himself, then the other answer is that someone came in here and killed Jordan."

"I mean," Jennifer considered, "I can't believe that either."

Penelope thought. "Who would want Jordan dead? What could he have done to make someone do that?"

"No one would. Everyone loved him," Jennifer said, relenting.

Penelope thought for a moment, trying to piece together the answer. "There are lots of stresses that go along with owning a big business like this one," she said, circling her finger in the air, indicating the inn and the adjoining buildings.

"Sure. We all have stress," Jennifer agreed. "But things are good. The movie is financed. Jordan's investment in the film is solid. No more crowd-funding or begging for production money from friends and family."

"But that's just your part. There could be family problems, money problems...maybe he had a health issue you didn't know about," Penelope said.

Jennifer shook her head. "He owns this beautiful newly renovated inn. This place and the restaurant are a dream come true for Jordan and his family. And business is good, from what I understand. It's just..." Jennifer's voice broke. "Why build your dream business and then kill yourself?"

Penelope shrugged and Jennifer turned to gaze at the framed photographs hanging in rows on the wall next to the back door. They were mostly of Jordan, a few from his culinary-school days, others in the various kitchens he'd worked. Penelope's favorite was the one of him surrounded by his four kids, his long arms draped over his wife's and oldest daughter's shoulders. They'd just cut a velvet ribbon stretched across the courtyard, the opening day for his restaurant, Festa, and the Forrestville Inn. His expression was hopeful, happy.

As the sheriff and Edie finished conferring and approached Penelope from across the room, she sifted through the different conversations she'd had with Jordan over the past six weeks, searching for any clue to why he might have decided to take his own life, but she was unable to pinpoint anything.

The sheriff eyed her chef coat just below her shoulder where her name and *Red Carpet Catering* was stitched in red. "Ms. Sutherland, I'm Sheriff Bryson, Forrestville PD. Officer Collins has already asked you some questions, but I have a few more. You found Chef Jordan?"

Jennifer stopped gazing at the pictures and turned her attention to them.

"Yes," Penelope said, taking in his tired expression and red-rimmed hazel eyes. He looked younger than she'd originally judged him to be now that he was up close. His cheeks were lean and rubbed red from the cold.

"And you're part of the crew here from Los Angeles?" He directed his question at the top of Jennifer's head as she studied her boots.

Jennifer nodded at the floor, then looked up. "That's right. But I'm originally from Forrestville."

"Hmm," he said, giving Edie a quick glance before continuing. She scribbled in her notebook, her cheeks flushing.

"I've already told her all of this," Jennifer said flatly. "Jordan and I are old friends."

Sheriff Bryson grimaced. "How long since you've been a local?"

"I left after high school, moved to California to study filmmaking. I haven't been back since, until two months ago. I take that back...I did visit twice before that briefly to scout locations. Why does any of this matter?"

"I'm just trying to get the full picture of what's going on," Sheriff Bryson said. "What's the name of the movie?"

Jennifer looked at him incredulously. "*The Turn of the Screw.* Again, what does that—"

"Oh yeah, I remember that book. But why film a movie in Forrestville, Indiana? It's not exactly Hollywood."

"Movies are made all over, Sheriff. We're saving a lot of money by working here, and there's less oversight from the studio. Creative freedom was a factor in the decision."

"Uh huh," he grunted. "What did Jordan have to do with all of this, besides letting you camp out here?"

"Jordan is one of the movie's producers. He's helping me achieve my vision for the film." Jennifer dropped her eyes back to the floor.

"Chef Jordan opened up his inn to our cast and crew, let us stay, made us feel welcome. He even set up a space for a few more of us in the loft next door, right over the event space he uses for weddings," Penelope said.

"That's where we were going to get married, but it's unavailable until you guys are finished here," Edie offered.

"We're in the middle of principal filming," Jennifer said. "There're a few sets over in the event space, and we're also using exteriors around the property."

"I've been hearing things around town about your project," Sheriff Bryson said. "Haven't been out to see for myself. What exactly does a producer do?" He glanced at the pair of EMTs as they wheeled Jordan's body, zipped inside a grayish-white body bag, from the walk-in.

Jennifer followed his gaze and the question hung in the air. The EMTs made their way with the stretcher out the kitchen door to the parking lot behind the inn.

Sheriff Bryson swung his gaze back to Jennifer, taking in her frozen expression. "You were saying?"

Without looking at him, she said, "Finance. Jordan trusted me when it came to the creative, didn't care to watch the dailies or have a say in the story or talent. He put up part of the money in exchange for a producer credit and a share of the profits after the movie is released."

"So he was a money man."

Jennifer shrugged in response, her eyes still on the kitchen door. "He was much more than that to me."

Sheriff Bryson sighed. "I'm sorry. Of course he was." He allowed a moment of silence to pass before asking, "How many folks did you say are here from out of town?"

When Jennifer didn't answer, lost in her own thoughts, Penelope responded, "Sixty-seven cast and crew."

"All staying here? How many rooms are upstairs?" Sheriff Bryson asked, looking at the ceiling.

"I'm not sure. I think six on each floor?" Penelope said.

"It's close quarters, but it's only temporary," Jennifer added. "The crew can sleep two or three to a room for a couple of months. It's not the hardest set I've run."

"Now, I know you were close, and this is a tough question, but can you think of any reason Chef Jordan might end his life?" the sheriff asked.

"Jordan didn't believe in suicide," Jennifer said quickly. She related a brief version of the story she'd told Penelope about their friend.

"People change, Ms. Carr," Sheriff Bryson said. "High-school boys and the men they become are hardly recognizable to each other sometimes."

"People don't change that much, Sheriff," Jennifer said.

"Okay, then. Thank you all for your help. I'll be in touch after I get Mr. Foster to the coroner's office over in Bloomington and notify his family."

He mumbled his goodbyes and pulled Edie aside.

"Poor Megan," Jennifer said, watching them walk to the back door. "This is awful for her, not to mention the kids. Jordan's whole family is going to be devastated."

Penelope thought about Jordan's wife and children, probably still asleep at this early hour, unaware that their lives had just been changed forever.

"We need to call an all-crew meeting this morning," Jennifer said, shifting into professional mode. "I want them to hear about Jordan from me."

"I'll be attending that," Edie said from the doorway. "We can't have you discussing any specifics. We haven't determined the cause of death."

"Suicide by hanging, most likely," the sheriff interjected. Penelope caught Edie's glance at him and her uncertain expression.

"I have to tell the crew something," Jennifer responded.

"They're going to want to know why we're not working today, and it's going to be obvious something's happened with you here."

"Of course," Edie said. "Generally informing the crew of Jordan's death is okay. But we're going to ask everyone to stay close until we figure things out. A forensic crew is on the way. I'll stay on the scene to greet them and answer any questions."

Jennifer sighed at Penelope.

"What time do you want everyone to meet?" Penelope asked.

"Seven. In the great room." Jennifer pulled her phone from her pocket to check the time. "An hour should be enough for everyone get dressed. Can you put on some coffee?" Jennifer looked around the kitchen, as if seeing everything for the first time.

"You'll have to stay out of here. Obviously," Edie said. "The kitchen is off limits."

"Probably not necessary. But to be abundantly cautious, that's the right thing," the sheriff said, straightening his hat. He gave Edie a tight smile then slipped out the back door.

"Can we still use Festa's kitchen across the way?" Penelope asked, watching him go.

Edie nodded slowly, thinking. "Sure. And the rest of the inn. It's just the kitchen we have to cordon off for now, to prevent contamination of any evidence, in the event the cause of death is determined to be a homicide. It's procedure."

"Evidence," Penelope murmured, her heartbeat speeding up. She thought about how she'd touched Jordan's arm, the doorknob to the walk-in, and almost every other object and surface in the kitchen they were standing in. And not just her—every member of her crew and countless other people coming in and out. "Do you think they'll shut down the movie?" Penelope thought about the crew upstairs, including Arlena, her best friend and the lead actress on the movie, all of whom had put over a month's work already.

Jennifer looked stricken, then recovered. "I hope not. I suppose we'll have to wait and see."

"If it turns out your friend was killed, that's the least of your worries," Edie said.

CHAPTER 3

Penelope stepped into her room upstairs and closed the door softly. She leaned against the door for a moment, then went over to the unmade bed, sitting down on the rumpled comforter and sliding her phone from her pocket.

She listened to a few rings as she stared at the early hour on the clock. Joey, her boyfriend back home in New Jersey, probably wouldn't be up yet, but she had an urgent need to hear his voice.

"Penny?" Joey's voice was thick with sleep, raspy and deep.

"I'm sorry I woke you," Penelope said quietly. The walls of the old inn were thin and she didn't want to disturb her slumbering neighbors.

"Is everything okay?" Joey asked, sounding more alert.

"No," Penelope admitted, then hastened to add, "Yes, I'm okay, but something happened. Something awful." Penelope told Joey about finding Chef Jordan, keeping her voice low and speaking in even tones.

"I'm so sorry, Penny," Joey said. She could hear he was up and moving around. She pictured him walking through the different rooms of his apartment, the dark sky outside his big living-room windows, the lights of the New York City skyline in the distance. "What can I do to help?"

"Hearing your voice is helping," Penelope said.

"Sure," Joey said. "I'd have my arms around you right now if I could."

"I know," Penelope said. "So...I don't want to hang up but I should go, I have to get some things together for the crew."

"Okay. Look, call me when you get a break later. I'm here for you whenever you want to talk about anything."

"Thanks," Penelope said. "Love you."

"I love you too," Joey said.

Penelope stepped out in the hall, her coat over her arm, and pulled the door closed, listening to the click of the lock. When she turned around she jumped when she saw the shadow of a figure near the staircase.

"Oh," Penelope whispered. "You startled me."

Marla Fenton, the inn's head housekeeper, stepped into the light and stood staring at her in the dimly lit hallway. She pulled off her knit hat and twisted it in her gloved hands. Her gray hair was short and wispy, static causing a few strands to stand on end. "Sorry. I just got in." She pulled open a narrow utility closet in the hallway and peered inside, then closed it again. "Seeing how much wood to bring up for the day."

The suites on either end of the floors had fireplaces, a cozy touch to the rooms that also provided much needed warmth on the coldest days. "Marla, have you heard about Jordan? You must have seen what's happening in the kitchen."

"Oh yes," Marla said, nodding quickly. "We can't go in there yet."

"Are you okay?" Penelope asked gently.

"I'm fine," Marla responded in a near whisper. "How are you?"

Penelope squinted at her, considering her response.

"Tragic thing," Marla said, pulling her hat back on. "He was a good man."

"Do you want to come in and sit down a minute?" Penelope asked, motioning to the door of her room. Marla's expression was so flat, almost stunned, and Penelope worried the older woman might be experiencing some kind of shock.

"No, lots to do, thanks," Marla said. She pulled her hat off again, causing more of her hair to stand on end.

"This has to be hard for you," Penelope stalled, concerned. "You've worked here for how long?"

"Many years now. I was here before all the fixing up. That's been my cabin out there twenty years at least," Marla said. "Not sure who will run things now, but I'll be staying. I'm going to get back downstairs and get started what work I can."

"Marla, I'm sure if you need to take a day off—" Penelope stammered.

Marla raised her hand in a placating gesture. "Thanks, but there's lots to do," she repeated. "Everything okay with your room?"

"Yes, thanks," Penelope responded.

Marla turned to go, her rubber-soled boots squeaking down the wooden stairs.

CHAPTER 4

Ava Barnes, general manager of Festa and the Forrestville Inn, entered the rear door of the restaurant's kitchen just as Penelope finished filling the two large coffee urns to bring back over to the inn for the cast meeting.

"Penelope," she said just above a whisper. Her face was still, but her eyes were still puffy from a recent cry. "Thanks for calling."

"I'm so sorry about Jordan," Penelope said, setting the coffeepot on the counter.

Ava pulled Penelope into a hug and sighed wetly into her long blonde ponytail. "Oh, Penelope, what are we going to do now?" She trembled and Penelope gave her a hard squeeze in return. After a moment, Ava pulled away. "I'm sorry you found him...that way."

Penelope gave a halfhearted shrug. "I can't imagine how you must be feeling." Penelope slid a stool from beneath the counter and edged it toward Ava, grabbing a coffee mug from the overhead shelf and holding it up, eyebrows raised. Ava perched on the edge of the stool and crossed her long denim-clad legs, nodding silently.

Penelope poured the coffee and handed it to her, then leaned against the stainless countertop across from her, arms crossed at her chest. "Was Jordan depressed?" she asked cautiously. She'd made a decision when she called Ava and told her about Jordan not to mention Edie's insistence that Jordan's death might not be a suicide. "You know him better than most people, being his business partner, managing all of this...why do you think he'd do this?"

Ava swept her gaze across the rubber mat on the floor, back

and forth slowly. "I don't know. He never shared with me that he was depressed."

"Was he in any kind of trouble? Financially, with the business?"

"No, everything is going really well. Ever since Jordan was named this year's Best Hoosier Chef, reservations are up and bookings at the inn are solid. People are coming from all over...Indianapolis, Chicago. Lots of guests planning to eat here and stay over. We've never been this busy." Ava's eyes flicked to the golden statue on the shelf next to the office door, Jordan's award, his name etched gold under a sculpture in the shape of Indiana.

"I hope our crew being here isn't causing you any issues," Penelope said. "Like not having rooms for people who want to come and stay." Penelope remembered what Edie had mentioned about her wedding earlier. "I know you've had to turn away some events."

"You're here in the slower winter season. It's what everyone decided." Ava waved her off and took a sip of coffee, then rubbed a smear of pale pink lipstick from the rim with her thumb. "Jordan had been asking Jennifer to come and make a movie here for years. They're dear friends, have been since they went to grade school together right up the road."

Penelope glanced at the kitchen service window and the photos of Chef Jordan thumb-tacked around it. In every one he was smiling, with different kitchen workers, servers, or patrons, his strawberry-blonde hair and boyish good looks radiating from the photos.

"Did Jordan have any other kinds of problems? Any enemies?" Penelope asked.

"No," Ava said. "Why do you ask?"

"I didn't say anything to you on the phone, but the police aren't entirely sure Jordan killed himself," Penelope said cautiously.

Ava placed her hand over her chest and leaned forward. "What are they saying happened?"

Penelope, alarmed she might have overstepped, backpedaled.

"Well, they don't really know. They said they have to investigate any unaccompanied death."

"Unaccompanied?" Ava asked.

"No, that wasn't it. Unattended."

"Oh," Ava said. "I don't understand."

"You know," Penelope said, "there wasn't anyone with him when he died, so they have to be sure of the cause of death before they can rule it a suicide."

"Could things get any worse? I suppose they always can," Ava considered.

"Suicide rates are higher in the culinary profession than many others. Being a chef brings a lot of pressure, long hours, time away from family. Especially when you get higher up on the ladder. Some cooks turn to alcohol or drugs to cope—"

"Jordan didn't do drugs," Ava interrupted, holding up a slender hand.

"Sorry," Penelope said. "I didn't mean to imply that."

Ava sighed and cradled her mug on her palm. "I know, I'm sorry. I just mean Jordan wasn't like that. He was focused on his, and our, success, and maintaining balance with his home life. I was around him all the time. I think I'd know if he was struggling with an addiction."

Penelope nodded. "Some people are good at hiding things like that."

"I guess. I suppose no one truly knows what's going on with another person completely," Ava said, more to herself than to Penelope. "It's possible he was under some kind of pressure he didn't share with me." She tucked a piece of her long black hair back into the messy bun on top of her head. "But enemies...I don't think so."

Penelope went to the service window to get a better look at the photos of Chef Jordan. "He always seemed happy when he was cooking, at least when I was in the kitchen with him." In several of the pictures he wore a chef coat, which he was in the habit of wearing without an undershirt. Penelope always wore at least a tank top under hers. The coarse fabric chafed her skin if she didn't, particularly on warmer days. His trademark silver chain hung around his neck, a knife and fork crossed in an X. Jordan had an athletic build and kept himself in shape by jogging most mornings, either through his neighborhood or along the forest trails in the woods behind Festa. He'd invited Penelope along a few mornings after she told him she liked to run also. Penelope quickly discovered that winter in Indiana was a different kind of cold than what she was used to back home in New Jersey. The icy air took her breath away. Her lungs felt like they were freezing a couple of times.

Penelope sensed Ava over her shoulder, looking at the photos from behind her. Without warning, the image of Jordan hanging from the rope sprang into Penelope's mind. She wasn't completely sure, but she couldn't remember if Jordan was wearing his necklace that morning. She supposed it could have broken from the weight of the rope around his neck. She made a mental note to mention it to Edie.

"Ava, if I can help with anything, please don't hesitate to ask," Penelope said, still facing the pictures.

"Thanks, Penelope," Ava almost whispered from behind her shoulder. "Jordan admired you, your energy, the way you ran your team. He was excited about the movie, all of it."

Penelope remained silent and stared at a recent photo of Jordan and Jennifer.

"I'll be in the office for a while, figuring out what needs to happen next," Ava said.

"Wait," Penelope said, turning around. "Jordan mentioned an important table coming in last night, someone he was getting ready for. Do you know who he was talking about?"

Ava put her hands on her hips and thought. "Oh, that. Yeah. I told him he was making a big deal out of nothing."

"What do you mean?"

"Festa got trashed by the local paper in a restaurant review when we first opened. Jordan's been trying to get them to come back in ever since, give us another chance. I told him nobody cares about some two-bit local newspaper in this little town, but for some reason it was important to him."

"Did the critic come in?" Penelope asked.

"As far as I know. I hope he enjoyed his dinner, not that it matters. The paper has a circulation of less than five thousand. Jordan's top chef in the state, and he's up-and-coming in the Midwest as an auteur."

"I know how it feels...you can get fifty positive reviews, but those one or two people you can't please can outweigh all the positive in your mind. If you let it. Jordan was a perfectionist. It must have been hard."

Ava shrugged, waving it off. "I told him to stop obsessing over it."

Penelope eyed her doubtfully but let it go. "I've got to get this coffee across the way for a cast meeting."

"Right," Ava said. "And I need to inform the restaurant staff. We're booked solid this weekend."

"I'm sure your guests will understand that you'll be closed for a while," Penelope said.

Ava rested her empty coffee cup on the stainless kitchen table and tapped her fingernails against the side while she thought. "We'll open back up on Saturday. We'll go dark tonight."

"You're only going to close for one night?" Penelope asked. "You don't think that's a bit soon?"

"We have to press on. Jordan would've wanted us to. We cut a lot of paychecks here, and the last thing he'd want is for the staff to suffer. I'll make the calls with our regrets and re-seat tonight's guests, but we'll be open for business tomorrow. Jordan would want that," Ava repeated.

Ava went inside the kitchen's office and closed the door.

Penelope shuffled out the front doors of Festa and into the courtyard, the handles of two stainless steel coffee urns in each gloved hand. The weight of them was almost too much and she breathed heavily with the effort. Halfway across, she set one down on the cobblestone street and took a break, shaking out her arms. She could easily carry one of them, but wanted to save time by bringing them both at once, a decision she began regretting almost immediately. She thought about leaving one and coming back for it, but the bitter air convinced her to press on. Although she knew the urns were thermal and the coffee wouldn't go cold, she didn't want to take a chance that it might.

She made it across the courtyard with effort to the inn's front doors and set them down again. A distant laugh caught her attention and she looked toward the forest that lined the edges of the restaurant and inn. The sun was just beginning to rise, and she could just make out three or four people approaching the inn, hikers coming out of the woods for breakfast, most likely.

Heaving open one of the heavy doors, she propped her hip against it and picked up the urns again.

"A little help?" a man's voice asked.

Penelope struggled to get her elbow inside the door without sloshing the coffee too much.

"Please," Penelope said. "I should have made two trips."

The hiker held the door for her and she eased inside, throwing a glance behind her as she entered. "Thanks, really appreciate it," she huffed.

The young man grinned at her, then gave a sly wink. "Always happy to help a beautiful lady."

Penelope laughed, caught off guard. "Um, thanks."

He was darkly handsome, and clearly much younger than Penelope. His two friends giggled into their gloves behind him as the door swung closed. Penelope continued inside, hefting the urns onto the bar in the inn's great room just inside. The fireplace was lit, Marla's first job of the morning, and she welcomed the warmth.

Penelope went back to the door to thank the hikers again for their help and offer them some coffee, but when she stepped outside, they were gone, headed down the hill toward the diner on Main Street, she assumed.

CHAPTER 5

Jennifer stood in uncomfortable silence in front of the stone fireplace in the inn's great room, her face pale and her expression flat after relaying the news of Jordan's death to the film crew. The only sounds were the metallic clicks from the antique cuckoo clock over the bar, a muffled cough, and the pop of a burning log. Penelope watched the different reactions from her place in front of the bar, her eyes skipping from face to face in the crowded space.

Edie stood in the doorway to the hall, her hands stuffed in the pockets of her jacket, her gaze roving among the faces in the room, lighting on one or two longer than others.

The film's young costume designer, Skylar, hugged herself and shivered despite the warmth from the fire. "What does this mean for us?" she asked nervously, her hands tucked tightly under her armpits.

Penelope caught Arlena's eye and watched her shake her head sadly.

Jennifer sighed. "We're taking today off and picking back up tomorrow, same schedule. Call time is nine in the morning. In the meantime, the police are requesting everyone stay on the grounds. Try and enjoy your unexpected day off." She glanced at Penelope.

"We've got coffee and some fruit here," Penelope announced. Francis, her sous chef, and the rest of her team had set out a few things for breakfast, mostly leftovers from the kitchen truck since the inn was off-limits.

"No hot breakfast today, huh?" Skylar mumbled sulkily.

"Sorry. Everything's in the kitchen and we were asked on short notice—" Penelope began.

"Listen," Jennifer interrupted, raising her voice for the room to hear as Skylar's cheeks reddened. "Jordan's my dear friend, and he was good to us. We will be respectful for his sake and for his family's sake."

Jennifer turned to go, brushing past Edie in the doorway and stomping up front staircase.

"Keep an eye on everything—we'll run out quick," Penelope murmured to Francis. His shoulders were stiff under his jacket and he appeared dazed. "Hey, you okay?" Francis looked away and she put a hand on his shoulder. "What's up?"

"I'm sorry, Boss," Francis said. "I'm having a hard time with it."

"You need a break?" Penelope said, stepping in front of him. His eyes were a darker green than usual and glassy like he was on the verge of tears.

"I'm all right," he said, clearing his throat. "It's just a shock, you know. Jordan was a good guy."

Penelope squeezed his shoulder. "Francis, how long have we worked together now? We're a team, through good and bad times. Anything you want to tell me, it's okay."

"I'm not over losing my dad, you know? I know it's been six months, and I shouldn't still be so...I'm not sure why, but the news about Jordan, it hit me harder than I expected," Francis said. He rubbed his short-cropped black hair with one hand, shiny healed scars from kitchen burns reflecting in the light.

"Listen, go out to the trucks and do a complete check of everything. We're going to need them up and running and a complete inventory done. We have to replace the items that we can't use from this kitchen too. Can you do that for me?"

"Yeah, sure," Francis said gratefully.

"Go on, get some air," Penelope said, giving him a smile.

Francis nodded and hurried away, grabbing his coat from a hook near the doorway before rattling through the front door.

Several of the crew stepped up to the bar, talking amongst themselves as they filled their coffee mugs. Penelope hovered nearby, picking up a few snippets of conversation as they passed by.

"This movie is a mess. I told you it would be. I was trying to get to the hardware store today too," one of the set carpenters mumbled to his coworker, throwing a glance toward Edie.

"You guys were planning on heading into town today?" Penelope asked.

"Town?" the taller one scoffed. "I wouldn't call a couple of old shops and a rundown diner a town. More like a wide spot in the road, am I right?" He thumped his buddy on the arm, causing a small wave of coffee to slosh onto his hand. "Sorry, man."

"Yeah," his companion said, annoyed. "They got one stoplight on Main Street, and half the time it's blinking."

"Have you been to Indianapolis yet?" Penelope asked, handing him a small pile of napkins.

"Yeah, but that's a three-hour drive." He dabbed at his sleeve. "It's not always worth the trip, especially if it starts snowing and you get stuck out on the highway coming back. It feels like it's always snowing here."

"There're the forest trails, if you want to get out for some air," Penelope said. "It's beautiful out there."

"That's an idea, even though I'm not very outdoorsy." He flicked his eyes at the frosted-over windows behind the bar. "It's tempting though, what with this cabin fever." He wadded up the damp napkins and handed them back to Penelope. "Maybe we'll luck out and it will get above freezing today."

Penelope watched him walk away and join his clumsy partner at a table. The coffee rush was over, so she took a seat at a nearby table and pulled out her phone, searching for the negative restaurant review Ava had mentioned earlier. Finding an article that looked promising, she clicked on the headline: *Festa Fails to Impress Despite the Hype*. Penelope's eyes skimmed down the piece, frowning as she read the review, apparently written by a secret diner on assignment from the local newspaper.

Forrestville's newest restaurant, Festa, is richly decorated but falls flat when it comes to flavor. Chef Jordan Foster, who attended culinary school in San Francisco and subsequently worked in high-end restaurants in Napa Valley, eventually returned to his hometown with a design on "elevating" simple dishes from the mundane dining experience we're all used to in Forrestville. Chef Jordan's food is fussy, overwrought, and unappealing. If I wanted to eat a piece of artwork, I'd head to the local museum and chow down on a painting. I'm sure that experience would be exactly the same, if not better. Festa? More like Fester. Make sure you stop for a burger on the way, as the portions are so small (and so expensive) you'll have to load up on several to feel full. I left feeling empty, both in my stomach and in my wallet.

"Ouch," Penelope said under her breath.

She scrolled back up to read the byline. Jacob Pears, senior editor. She tried to do the math in her head and figure out when Jordan would have been in California. They'd never talked about their culinary-school experiences, but she guessed he must have been there in his twenties, since his oldest twin children, Karen and Kyle, were now in their early twenties themselves. She wondered what he had done before opening Festa. She squinted at the date on the review piece and saw it was posted five years earlier. It was one of the first articles to appear in the search, so it probably still impacted the business, or Jordan's feelings at the very least. A bad review online trailed you around for eternity these days instead of being recycled with the next day's trash like in the pre-internet days.

It appeared not everyone was thrilled by Jordan's triumphant return to his hometown. Penelope felt a fresh wave of sadness as she reread the review. From all accounts Festa was successful, so surely Jordan had garnered some positive attention and fans since it was posted. Deciding there was no accounting for taste, Penelope closed the article and slipped the phone back in her pocket.

Arlena made her way to the bar, searching through the tea basket for her favorite brand of organic green. "Are you okay?"

"Yeah," Penelope said, standing up to join her. "Finding Chef Jordan like that was...I feel terrible for his family. And his staff." She reached into the basket and plucked out a tea bag and handed it to Arlena.

"Thanks," Arlena said. "What is she still doing here?" she asked, tilting her head in Edie's direction as she made her tea.

"Keeping the kitchen off limits," Penelope whispered. "There's a possibility it wasn't a suicide."

"What?" Arlena said loudly.

"Shh," Penelope said, glancing around, thankful they hadn't caught anyone's attention. "It's standard procedure, they say. I don't think there's anything to worry about."

Arlena sighed, calming down. "Look at them," she said, throwing a glance at the table where her fellow actors were huddled together. "When Jennifer called this morning, she said she'd been in touch with the executive producer. According to her, we're staying put. Jennifer already has too many reels shot to have to redo all the scenes. If we move now, the exteriors and sets won't match up. The EP told Jennifer she either had to stay and finish filming or they'd pull the plug."

"Really?" Penelope said. "They'd rather waste the whole project than reshoot some of the scenes?"

Arlena set her mouth in a line. "Yep. I don't know how to feel. Is it right to carry on, business as usual, on a man's property twenty-four hours after his death?" She pulled her thick sweater tighter over her lean shoulders and watched her tea steep on the bar. "I bet if we had a male director they'd be more flexible, more willing to fund the picture if we moved somewhere else."

"I hadn't thought of that. You really think that's the issue?" Penelope asked.

"Don't kid yourself. It was an uphill battle to get the studio to green light this movie. This is Jennifer's first major project."

"I had no idea," Penelope said. She swiped a few sugar crystals from the bar into her palm. "I thought the movie had been in development a long time. I remember reading about it in one of your trade magazines back home."

"Yes, the movie was planned. This reboot of *The Turn of the Screw* has been making the rounds for a couple of years now, always attached to male directors. It's a perfect classic gothic ghostly horror story, all the rage right now. But it kept falling through, didn't get on any schedule, and then the interested directors had moved on to other projects. Jennifer had to fight for the job, even though most of her smaller films have performed. She's got a cult following, but you better believe if this movie doesn't do well, her chances of working at a major studio again will be diminished."

Penelope looked at her doubtfully.

"Pen, Jennifer has to work twice as hard to get half as much respect as any male director. It's despicable the way women are treated in this business." Arlena picked up the tab of her tea bag and began dunking it quickly. "I'm going to do something about it. I'll set up a production company for women writers and directors."

"That's not a bad idea," Penelope said, picturing Arlena behind a big desk, fielding offers and reading scripts. "How did your young costars take the news about Jordan?" Penelope glanced at the children sitting at the actors' table, a young girl and boy, aged eight and ten. Their mother sat between them, fussing with the collar on the little girl's shirt.

"Dakota and Jackson are okay," Arlena said. "Jennifer didn't go into details with them. She let their mother tell them." She rolled her eyes in the direction of the hovering woman.

Penelope hid a small smile behind her hand. "Still getting tripped up by the famous stage mom?"

"Don't get me started," Arlena said. "'Dakota can't play off you unless you look her in the eyes.' 'Jackson is following your cues—be sure you don't ad lib any lines at the end of dialogue.'" Arlena mimicked the woman's voice, pulling her face into an exaggerated frown.

"Stop," Penelope whispered, biting her cheek to keep from laughing.

"They say never work with children or animals. The kids are fine scene partners, but Sybil...I don't know, it feels like she's living through them, like they're supposed to pick up where her career left off."

Penelope had vaguely recognized Sybil Wilde, Dakota and Jackson's mother, when they all arrived on set, but she couldn't place where she knew her from. She'd asked Arlena, who reminded her Sybil had starred in a popular daytime soap, one that Penelope had never watched. After a contract dispute with the show, she'd left and had two children on her own via surrogate with eggs she had frozen many years before and an anonymous sperm donor at one of the most expensive fertility clinics in New York. Sybil had one short-lived marriage well in her past and had become a mother for the first time in her mid-forties. Now she was her children's agent and manager, not to mention their on-set tutor, and in some ways their personal assistant.

"She's too close to them all the time," Arlena said, cutting her eyes at Sybil. "I'm supposed to be playing their governess, their main caretaker. I don't how they're going to give convincing performances as orphaned and abandoned children with their mom fetching them pomegranate smoothies every five minutes."

Penelope stifled another laugh, then felt guilty about the smoothies, since it was her team making them to order for the kids, following Sybil's strict dietary instructions. "They seem like they're doing a good job on the set though."

Arlena relented as she looked at Jackson and Dakota. "They're sweet kids, really. Which is surprising. They ought to be spoiled rotten. I'm just waiting for Jackson to pull a diva move, flip out on everyone." Arlena allowed a small smile, then cleared her throat and became serious again.

Jackson and Dakota both had white blonde hair and slender faces. They looked very ghostlike, perfect for the roles of two haunted children. "I hope they're not too upset. I can make them something special for lunch if you think that would take their mind off things."

Arlena shrugged. "That sounds like a good idea to me, but run it by their mom-ager first."

"Of course," Penelope said.

Arlena picked up her mug. "I'm going upstairs to call Sam. Stop by later if you have time." Arlena had been dating Sam Cavanaugh, the A-list action-movie star, for over a year. She was making her way up the acting ranks herself, and together they were quite the power couple in Hollywood.

Penelope took a few minutes to refresh the coffee station, glancing at the different tables around the room to judge how much longer the crew might be lingering. She heard the front door open with a *whoosh* and watched Marla approach the bar, her body rigid under her oversized wool sweater. She ducked away quickly, heading toward the basement stairs off the main hallway.

"Marla, are you okay?" Penelope asked, noting the dazed look on the older woman's face.

"No," she managed, darting glances at the crew lingering around the tables. She appeared disoriented, like the room was unfamiliar, as opposed to the inn she'd cared for on a daily basis for many years.

"Why don't you sit for a minute," Penelope said, pointing to a nearby chair.

Marla shook her head quickly, looking a bit unsure on her feet. "I have things to tend to." She wandered through to the hall and disappeared behind the staircase.

Penelope watched her go, concerned for the older woman's health. The other morning she'd watched Marla through the kitchen windows stacking firewood on her shoulder and trekking up the icy backyard. Penelope had been impressed with her strength and stamina, but there were also times she appeared frail, her cheeks sunken.

Skylar stalked up to the bar a few minutes later, hungrily grabbing at the fruit bowl's serving spoon.

"Are you cold?" Penelope asked, eyeing her jacket and then the lit fireplace.

"Forrestville, Indiana is the coldest place on earth," Skylar declared through clenched teeth.

"There might be a few places on earth colder than here," Penelope said, teasing.

"None I've ever been to," Skylar said flatly.

"Well, being from southern California I guess it feels colder to you than some of us," Penelope said.

The girl snorted a quick laugh. Red spiral curls escaped the knit hat she had pulled down over her ears. "I was so happy to get my first job on a real movie. Little did I know I'd be sewing period costumes in Boring-ville, which by the way is also frozen."

"It's Forrestville. And a job's a job, right?" Penelope said, keeping her tone light. "You'll get a screen credit on a major motion picture, and different projects will open up to you."

"That's the plan," Skylar said. "I guess I'm paying my dues." She chewed on a piece of pale cantaloupe and Penelope winced at the weak-colored fruit. She was having a hard time working up sympathy for Skylar, who had a job and a strong career path many people would kill for. Penelope didn't think staying in a quaint rustic inn for a few months with everything being taken care of for you qualified as paying dues. But then again, everyone had different ideas about working hard.

Their fellow crew members sat at the tables, loosely broken into their respective departments. The sound technicians sat together, the hair and makeup team huddled in the corner near the fireplace. She thought about what her team would do for the immediate future, deciding they'd go back to cooking on the catering trucks, which were parked in the lot behind the inn. She assumed the inn's kitchen would be closed for a while. She wasn't looking forward to going back inside the walk-in anytime soon anyway.

The great room and bar slowly emptied out, some of the crew heading back upstairs, some venturing outside into the cold.

"How much longer are we going to be here? Have you heard any updates?" Skylar asked after a few minutes. Penelope had forgotten she was standing there, having gotten lost in her own thoughts.

"I don't think we're halfway finished yet, from what I've heard in the department meetings. I'd say we're here at least another six weeks."

Skylar rolled her eyes so dramatically Penelope worried they wouldn't come back down from her eyelids. "Ugh." She stalked off, almost tripping on the area rug in the center of the room when her thick-soled snow boots caught the edge of it.

Penelope sighed and watched her go.

CHAPTER 6

After the meeting broke up and she and her team cleared up from breakfast, Penelope retrieved her messenger bag from her room upstairs and went across the courtyard to check on Ava. When she entered Festa's kitchen, unlocking the rear door of the restaurant with her key, she could hear Ava's muffled voice through the office door.

Penelope took in all the gleaming silver prep tables and appliances. It was much larger than the inn's kitchen, where they only offered light fare and continental breakfasts during the day. Guests of the inn dined across the courtyard at Festa, and all of the events were catered from this big state-of-the-art kitchen. A couple of times Penelope and her team had used the kitchen to cater for the film crew when they had a group of extras on the set and more mouths to feed than usual.

Knives and a variety of utensils lined the wall, suspended against the tiles by a magnetic strip, making them easy to grab from the prep stations. The crisp, acrid smell of lemon cleaner clashed with the earthier aroma of food, the memory of the previous night's dishes still lingering in the air.

Penelope pulled her iPad from her messenger bag and scrolled through a few emails. She was forwarding an invoice to accounts payable in the production office just as the back door to the kitchen swung open.

Denis Billings walked in, his arms hugging a cardboard box with a swan logo on the side, its wings arching up to enclose an ornate W. Muffled clinks came from inside the box as wine bottles shifted together. He said a quick hello and set the box on the table against the back wall, rubbing his hands together and pulling the kitchen door closed.

"Hi, Denis," Penelope said. "This isn't your usual day, is it?"

Denis's round face broke into a crooked grin. "You're right, it's not. I'm going to be a few towns over all day and wanted to drop these samples off for Chef Jordan. Ava said he's looking to switch up the wine list, and I'm hoping he likes a couple of these." His light blue eyes were hooded by thick orange eyebrows that made him appear constantly concerned, which didn't fit with his lighthearted personality at all.

"Yeah, she's here, but...Denis, something's happened," Penelope said gently. She watched his face morph from its usual jovial expression to sadness as she broke the news about Jordan's death.

He steadied himself against the counter, looking as if the wind had been knocked out of him. "How can this have happened?"

"I'm sorry, Denis. I know you liked working with Chef Jordan," Penelope said. "And he always spoke highly of you. I think you were his favorite wine rep."

Denis nodded absently. "I just saw him."

"I know. I was here when you brought over that nice cabernet I tried on Tuesday," Penelope said, nodding.

"No. Last night. I stopped in for a drink on my way home," Denis said.

"You saw him in the dining room?" Penelope asked.

Denis shook his head. "No, I met a friend of mine at the bar. I needed a smoke, so I stepped around back. Chef Jordan was too nice to say anything, but I know he didn't like people smoking right outside the front door. I always come around behind the kitchen, at all my customer's places. I saw him back there." Denis nodded at the kitchen door. "Talking with someone. At first I thought they were joking around, but after a minute I could tell they were arguing about something."

"Who was it?"

"Not sure. Little guy, bald, glasses. Old."

Penelope eyed Denis, who was in his early twenties.

"Old?" Penelope asked. "Like elderly?"

"No, like older than Chef Jordan. Not grandpa old. Well, maybe."

Penelope put aside the discussion of age for a moment. "Did you hear what they were arguing about?"

"Kind of. Something the man had for dinner, I guess. Honestly, I'd told Chef Jordan that I quit smoking, so I didn't want him to see me sneaking one. I took off before he noticed me." Denis's expression was one of defeat as he hitched up his belt, tight across his soft middle. "He was always on me to clean up my diet, start running."

"He was very fond of you," Penelope said.

"Yeah, once in a while he'd take me out hunting, or we'd run across each other up in the woods during deer season."

"I didn't know you hunted."

"I don't really," Denis said. "I just go out a few times a season with the guys. It's a tradition, me and the buddies I grew up with. We used to get the first day of hunting season off school, and our dads would take us out."

"I've never been myself," Penelope said. "I've never shot anything, matter of fact."

"Some girls do around here," Denis said absently. "Sorry, women," he amended, his cheeks reddening. He pressed a meaty fist to his mouth, suppressing a cough.

The office door opened and Ava appeared, her eyes wet and freshly rimmed with red. "So you've heard," she said when she saw Denis.

Denis nodded, clearly uncomfortable. "I'm sorry. I didn't mean to intrude."

"Denis, we're all family here," Ava said. "We've all lost him."

Denis mumbled a string of condolences and headed for the door, pausing at the last minute and turning back to them. "What does this mean? For the rest of us?"

"Don't worry, Denis. I'll be in touch. We'll get everything sorted out," Ava said.

He nodded goodbye and clumsily pushed his way through the door without another word.

"That's how it's been all morning," Ava said. "The whole town will be in shock by lunch." The phone in the office rang and Ava strode back, closing the door behind her.

Penelope glanced at the cardboard box on the back counter and went to the door, hoping to catch Denis before he drove away, but she was too late. The lot was empty except for Ava's SUV. Thinking she might want the wine samples after all, Penelope carried the box into the dining room and set it on the floor behind the bar, nudging it with her toe next to a case of fruit juices. She took the marker from next to the register and wrote *Samples, Not Inventory* in big letters on the flap.

When she went to tuck the flap back down, an unsealed envelope that was tucked down between the bottles caught her eye. Assuming it was an invoice, she pulled it out and opened the flap. The only thing inside was a personal check, signed by Denis, made out to "Herring – Steele" in the amount of $425. She looked once more to confirm there was no accompanying paperwork.

"Great," Penelope said. She reminded herself to find Denis's phone number and call him to let him know he'd gotten his boxes mixed up or had dropped his utility-bill payment inside of his sample case by mistake. She tucked the envelope in the interior pocket of her chef coat, then folded the box's flaps closed and eased it under the bar with the toe of her boot.

Back in the kitchen, Penelope sipped her coffee and pulled up the *Forrestville Gazette*'s website on her iPad to see if there was any news about Jordan's death from the local paper. The feature story was about an upcoming farm-equipment expo, which was followed by a report on the current cold snap and a potential blizzard the following week. She scrolled down, finding no mention of the morning's events. Penelope got the impression only a couple of people worked at the tabloid that came out once a week. Their office on Main Street was often dark behind the plate-glass window, the peeling gold letters on the glass and the vintage paper vending machines out front on the sidewalk looking neglected.

Ava emerged from the office and leaned against the doorframe, her hands tucked in her front pockets. "Megan just called. She's asked us to come to the house."

"Us?" Penelope asked, wondering why Jordan's wife would want her to join Ava for a visit. "Why both of us?"

"She wants to ask you a favor."

CHAPTER 7

When Ava and Penelope reached the Fosters' winding driveway, a woman in a bright red coat stood at the edge of the road in front of a collection of mailboxes. She had a newspaper tucked under her arm and watched as Ava slowed down to make the turn. The woman raised her arm in greeting, squinting at them as they passed. Penelope waved back, then watched the woman decrease in size in the side-view mirror as they drove up toward the house.

Jordan and Megan Foster's home was a well-maintained white clapboard house with a wide front porch anchored by round pillars. The Foster family lived a few miles from the center of town on a winding two-lane road. Ava eased her SUV up the newly paved driveway that led to a parking area and a detached garage behind the house. A basketball hoop was centered between the middle two garage doors, the red and white net swaying slightly in the breeze. A few lawn chairs lined the asphalt next to the garage, the spectator seats to the family basketball area. An orange tabby cat swished its tail at Penelope from the narrow path leading from the garage to the rear kitchen door.

"Hey, kitty," Penelope said as she closed the truck door. She took a step closer and the cat darted away, slipping through a small hole covered by a flap at the base of the garage door. Through the kitchen door's window, Penelope could see Megan at the counter talking to someone else she couldn't see, her expression pained, her arms folded tightly across her chest.

"Let's go around to the front door," Ava said, pausing her

stride after noticing Megan also. "I normally just let myself in through the kitchen, but today—"

"Feels different," Penelope said, nodding. "Of course." She followed Ava along the slate path to the front door, counting the alternating red and yellow mums in matching pots as they went. There were exactly six on each side, all completely uniform and trimmed to the same size.

A woman with silver-gray hair wearing dark jeans and a sweater greeted them at the front door and took their coats.

"Thanks, Cynthia," Ava said as she slipped off her boots and placed them near the others lined up in the foyer. Penelope did the same, glad she'd worn presentable socks that day. "How are you holding up?"

Cynthia shook her head slightly. "It's a terrible time for the family. The kids especially. Come inside. I'll let Megan know you're here." She motioned them forward, their coats hanging over her arm.

The Fosters' home was warm and inviting, traditionally decorated and very neat. The walls were painted in bold colors and sleek furniture adorned the rooms, all in keeping with the traditional style of the home.

Megan greeted them in the foyer and offered a few awkward pleasantries before leading Penelope and Ava to the airy sitting room at the rear of the house. As they made their way through the formal living room, Megan moved slowly and brushed her dusky pink gelled fingernails lightly across the tabletops and backs of chairs as she passed. She wasn't leaning on things for support; it was more like she was feeling the edges of her things to make sure they were still there.

She sank carefully down into a brocade wingback chair and waved her guests to a matching couch opposite her. The room was richly colored in maroon and teal, a theme picked up in the furniture, artwork, and ornate wallpaper. Ava and Penelope settled onto the couch and waited for Megan to begin, allowing a few moments of silence to pass as she gathered her thoughts. Penelope stared at the vase of flowers on the table between them. They gave off a cloying, slightly unpleasant scent, an earthy whiff of wet rot just beneath the floral aroma.

"Thank you both for coming," Megan finally began. Her voice was shaky and her expression confused, as if she couldn't remember why Penelope and Ava were visiting. She went silent again, her eyes dropping to the flower arrangement.

"I'm so sorry for your loss," Penelope said quietly, smoothing her palms across her thighs. She knew that was the correct thing to say in situations like these, but she often wondered if it was enough. It didn't feel like it was, but maybe that was the point, to not assume to know how the other person was feeling.

"Thank you, Penelope," Megan said, coming back to full attention. "That really means a lot."

Penelope smiled and lightly bit the inside of her cheek. She was feeling emotional, being in the house where Jordan lived and raised his family. She didn't trust herself not to tear up in front of Megan.

"I wanted to ask you, and thank you in person, for helping out at the restaurant until we can figure out what is happening."

"We have to make sure Festa, and everything we've created, continues," Ava added immediately after Megan finished speaking.

Megan smiled at Ava gratefully. "Yes, that's important. We employ so many people in town, young people, some of them the children of our lifelong friends. Jordan wouldn't want to let anyone down. I'm so grateful to you, Penelope, for your help with this."

Penelope paused a moment before speaking. "I'm sorry, but I'm not sure what you're asking." She had the odd feeling that she had been part of a conversation she wasn't aware of yet.

Megan's face creased with fresh sadness. She pulled a tissue from a box on the table and looked down at her lap, twisting it into a thin rope as she spoke. "I know it's a lot to ask, Penelope, but we'd love for you to fill in as head chef until we find someone...I know it's a lot to ask, what with your responsibilities on the set."

Penelope glanced at Ava beside her on the couch, taking in her hopeful expression. She looked back at Megan, who plainly wore her grief on her stunned puffy face.

"It would only be temporary, until we can find someone to run the kitchen," Megan said. "We'd love your help with that too. I wouldn't even know where to begin."

Penelope thought for a moment, considering what they'd asked.

"I suppose I can call my culinary school for a recommendation. They maintain a database of chefs and what area of the world they're working in. It's sort of a job-placement service. I can see if anyone is available to audition."

Megan's round shoulders sloped forward. "That's a good start. You and Ava can test the candidates out, have them cook a night or two. See what happens." Megan's hair moved with her head as she nodded. It was cut in a blunt wedge with chunky blonde highlights, teased on top with two symmetrical points coming to rest just above her jawline, which was just beginning to soften with age.

"Sure," Penelope said. "You can come and meet them too, taste the food."

Megan shook her head. "That's not necessary. I've always left the restaurant decisions to Jordan and Ava. That's their department. Mine is the kids and our home."

"Oh," Penelope said, realizing she had never seen Megan at Festa. She stopped by sometimes to say hello if she was dropping off one of the kids after school, or if she had a book or garden club meeting in town, but Penelope had never seen Megan dine at the restaurant during the six weeks they'd been filming. Karen, their oldest daughter, was the family member Penelope knew the best. She'd spent many afternoons with her dad in the kitchen before she and her twin brother, Kyle, headed back to college when winter break was over.

"And you won't mind filling in for a short time until we find someone new," Megan said. It was more of a statement than a question.

"Don't you think one of the cooks you already have working in the kitchen would be a better choice?" Penelope asked Ava. "I'm sure one of the assistant chefs could take the lead."

Ava shook her head. "None of them are classically trained. They're just townies, kids most of them. Definitely not head chef material. Look, of course they can cook like they always have, day to day. We're just asking you to oversee, make sure the standards don't lag during the transition. We can't lose our reputation or customers." Ava glanced at Megan.

Penelope took a moment to consider. "I'd like to help," Penelope said reluctantly. "I'll help you look for a replacement, and work with whoever you choose from the current kitchen staff, make sure he's up to the job in the meantime."

Ava sighed.

"Thank you, that's a relief."

"I'll have to run this by Jennifer, make sure she's okay with it." Penelope's eyes came to rest on the framed picture on the end table next to Megan's chair. It was her and Jordan surrounded by their kids in one of those professionally taken photos meant to look like a candid shot. The six of them wore matching red and white ski sweaters and were staged in front of a backdrop printed with a forest scene, all laughing at something off to the right of the photographer.

"Jennifer will be fine with it," Megan said without hesitation. "She's a dear friend of the family and only wants what's best for us."

"Okay," Penelope said, knowing the whole time she would get full approval from Jennifer before doing anything. Penelope and Red Carpet Catering were under contract with the studio, and that meant Jennifer was her boss. She wouldn't do anything to put her team's employment or her own reputation in jeopardy.

"Now that that's settled, I have to arrange a funeral," Megan said. The turn in conversation brought unexpected tears from Megan and an uneasy silence from Penelope and Ava. "Sorry." Megan sighed wetly. "The kids are devastated. None of us knows what to do." She gazed at Ava, who looked down at her socks.

Muffled footsteps down the front stairs and conversation from the kitchen broke the silence. Penelope craned her neck toward the sounds.

"Karen's here," Megan said. "I called her and Kyle before dawn, right after I heard. I'm glad I caught them at the apartment before classes started."

"How long is the drive to IU?" Penelope asked.

"Bloomington is two hours away," Ava said.

"My younger two are in high school, sophomore and junior year," Megan said, looking at the photograph. "They wanted to go to school today, even though I told them they should stay home."

The two younger kids in the picture had the same toothy grins as their dad. Karen and Kyle had the same closed-lipped subdued smile as their mother.

"They wanted to be with their friends," Megan said, her voice breaking at the end. "I don't know if that was the right thing. I told them to come home if it got to be too much." Megan wiped a smudge of eyeliner from her cheek with her tissue and sighed.

"Mom? I'm sorry, I didn't mean to upset you before."

Penelope realized Karen was the other person she couldn't see in the kitchen having the heated discussion with Megan.

"Oh, honey," Megan said, standing up from her chair and taking a few awkward steps toward her. "I love you." They hugged each other tightly, Karen's eyes pinched closed, her cheeks splotched red from crying.

Penelope looked away, feeling like she and Ava were intruding on an incredibly personal family moment. Megan led her daughter out of the room toward the kitchen and Penelope sighed, her shoulders relaxing slightly.

"Should we go? Let them deal with—"

"I'm sorry," Megan interrupted, reappearing in the doorway. "I just realized I haven't offered you anything. Would you like some tea?"

Penelope and Ava shook their heads in unison, but Megan insisted.

"Please, don't go. Come in the kitchen."

They stood up reluctantly and followed Megan through the formal dining room into the kitchen, the swinging door separating the two closing quietly behind them.

Penelope put her hands in her pockets and stood near the kitchen door, eyeing the updated appliances and blonde-wood cabinets while Megan busied herself with the kettle. She set it on the stovetop and blue flames licked up the sides.

"Is Karen okay?" Penelope asked.

"No," Megan said without hesitation. "She went upstairs to freshen up. Tea always helps us feel better." She busied herself by wiping the island counter with a towel and placing a collection of mugs from the overhead cabinet on the marble. She then laid out a small wooden box filled with a variety of tea bags.

A floor-to-ceiling built-in wine rack sat at an angle next to the pantry, most of the slots filled with differently shaped bottles. Penelope thought about Jordan in the kitchen, swirling a wineglass and asking her to join him in tastings with the different wine reps. Penelope sometimes bought wine for the set for special dinners and liked hearing about the different brands. Jordan said it was an art every chef must master, pairing the perfect glass to a particular dish, something he learned a lot about during his time in Napa.

"Do you need help with the arrangements, Megan?" Ava asked. "I can make some calls for you."

Penelope thought she saw a flash of irritation cross Megan's face before her expression returned to a mask of sadness. "Thanks, but I can manage. What else can I do? I have to stay strong for the children."

"Of course," Ava said, her cheeks reddening. "I just meant I can help, if you want."

"No one can help me through this. My husband just took his own life. I mean, what was he thinking? Was his life so bad? He never said it was to me. I thought we were a happy successful family. Now look at us." Megan choked back a sob and gestured around the kitchen. "I'm left here to pick up the pieces, explain this to everyone in town, at church. How am I supposed to face them?"

Penelope kept her eyes on the marble countertop, thinking whatever she might say would be the wrong thing.

"It's plain selfish of him to do this. It goes against all he believed too, everything we've talked about, taught our kids," Megan said, lightly touching the side of the kettle and pulling her finger back quickly from the heat. "I'm sorry, this is just so overwhelming. The sadness, it feels like a hole right through me." Megan poured boiling water into mugs and slid two of them across to her guests.

"Please don't apologize," Penelope said quietly. She picked up a jasmine tea bag and dunked it in the water.

"Thanks for your understanding, Penelope," Megan said, flashing a glance at Ava, who was busy making her own cup of tea. "This is going to sound selfish of me, but a scandal like this...this kind of thing doesn't happen in Forrestville."

"What do you mean?" Penelope asked. She was tempted to press Megan, but hesitant since she was clearly distraught.

"I can't think of anything like this, at least with anyone of Jordan's stature and reputation. Except for Helmsley," Megan said with a look of disgust. "He had a heart attack, right there at his desk. They found filthy pictures on his computer that he was looking at right before he died." Megan drew an X with her thumb across her heart and pressed her lips together in disapproval. "That's the only other scandal I remember in our lifetime."

"They weren't just filthy, they were illegal, from what I heard," Ava added.

"What's happened to Jordan...his situation is hardly comparable to something like that," Penelope said carefully.

Megan's lips stayed rigid, but her eyes softened a bit. "Thank you. That's nice of you to say."

They all remained in uncomfortable silence until Penelope asked, "May I use your restroom?"

Megan waved a hand toward the hallway and went to refill the kettle. "Use the one upstairs. They haven't finished putting in the new floor in the powder room down here yet."

Penelope excused herself and slipped away, relieved to take a break from the tension. In the upstairs bathroom, she looked at herself in the mirror over the double sink. Even though she felt haggard from the day's events, her skin still looked healthy, her cheeks glowed, and her blue eyes were clear. She closed the lid of the toilet and sat down, putting her head in her hands and closing her eyes, breathing in the strong aroma of potpourri from a clay bowl on the tank behind her.

Stepping into the hallway a few minutes later, she listened for a moment to Ava and Megan's mumbled conversation downstairs, discussing the funeral from what she could tell. She tugged down the sleeves of her sweater and craned her neck to look into the doorway of the bedroom across the hall. It was one of the boys' rooms, decorated in shades of blue with framed posters of various sports stars and musicians on the walls. The bedspread was tucked tightly at the corners and a pile of books had been stacked in order of size on the desk. There were fresh lines from vacuum cleaner wheels along the rug, backing out of the room and into the hallway. Penelope looked at the carpet under her feet and saw she stood on two of them, the tracks leading in even lines back to the stairs.

The neighboring bedroom door was closed, Karen's muffled crying coming from the other side. Penelope took a step closer and raised her fist, hesitating before knocking on the door. At the last minute, she decided to step away and give Karen her privacy. Just as she turned to go, Karen opened the door.

"Sorry, Karen," Penelope said, startled. "I didn't mean to intrude. It's just your mom is making tea and I wanted to see if you'd like some."

Karen put a tissue to her nose and smiled weakly. "Mom always makes tea when anyone is upset. Or cocktails, depending on the time of day."

Penelope returned her smile. "That's what people do, offer comfort with food and drink."

"I'm not ready to come back down yet. Maybe in a while." Over Karen's shoulder, Penelope saw Cynthia, the woman who had met them at the door when they arrived, sitting on the bed, her hands folded in her lap, a tragic look on her face.

"Sure," Penelope said. "There's no rush."

Karen came forward and threw her arms around Penelope's shoulders, hugging her tightly. "Thank you."

Surprised, Penelope hugged her back, rocking gently and letting her cry. She looked at Cynthia, who returned a sad smile. Penelope had only met Karen a few times before in Festa's kitchen, but knew her well enough to know she was a hard worker and a good student. Jordan was proud of all his kids, but he said Karen was the one most like him. Jordan had named dishes on his menu after each of his children, and Karen's entry was a golden root-vegetable bisque, one of the most popular dishes they served.

Karen gathered herself and pulled away from Penelope, then went into the bathroom, closing the door behind her.

"I didn't mean to interrupt," Penelope said quietly to Cynthia, still perched on the edge of the bed.

"You didn't," Cynthia said. "The poor girl is in shock."

"I'm sorry, but you introduced Megan as Mrs. Foster downstairs. Aren't you family?"

Cynthia took a deep breath. "I suppose I am in some ways, but I'm old fashioned. It doesn't feel right to call my employer by her first name. I'm the nanny. I came to live here when the twins were born, and then the other two babies came along soon after. Now I mostly look after the house, but I still help with the children, even though they're almost all grown now."

"It's good you're here to help the family through this," Penelope said.

Cynthia nodded and swiped invisible dust from the nightstand next to Karen's bed.

"I should get back downstairs," Penelope said. "Nice meeting you."

Cynthia looked around the tidy bedroom and didn't respond.

Penelope slid her hand along the polished wood banister as she descended the stairs. The trill of a phone echoed on both levels and Penelope paused, listening to it ring twice more before hearing Megan pick it up. Penelope continued her descent, her socks padding lightly on the carpet.

When Penelope entered the kitchen, Megan stood behind the counter, a look of disbelief on her face. Ava stared at her, her eyes wide and questioning.

"Okay, yes, I understand," Megan said, the color draining from her already pale face. Her arm went limp and her hand fell to her thigh, her fist tight around the cordless phone.

"What is it?" Ava asked urgently.

"That was the sheriff," Megan said. "They're saying Jordan was murdered."

The phone slipped from her hand and clattered against the kitchen floor.

CHAPTER 8

Ava dropped Penelope back at the inn a short while later, neither of them saying much during the drive back through Forrestville's small strip of downtown shops. Penelope felt like someone had punched her in the stomach when she heard that Jordan was murdered. When she got out of the truck, Ava said she had things to take care of then sped away, peeling down the cobblestones back onto the main road.

Jennifer's assistant director was sitting in the great room at one of the tables with his laptop open, his usual anxious expression amplified by ten. Penelope was grateful to be back at her temporary home, but he reminded her that Jordan's death had made an impact on all of them.

"Jennifer around?" Penelope asked him as she pulled off her coat.

He nodded tightly, a wave of blond hair brushing across his forehead. "She's in the suite, been holding meetings with the different department heads all morning. She'll get to you soon, I'm sure." He typed away on his keyboard, his hands lightly tanned, although faded from his weeks away from the California sun.

Penelope thought about what she would say to Jennifer. When Megan recovered and told them what Sheriff Bryson had said on the phone, she and Ava learned the coroner ruled Jordan's death as suspicious, and that it could not be conclusively ruled a suicide. They'd be investigating his death more thoroughly. She made her way to the top floor and to the end of the hallway. The walls were thin at the old inn, and she could hear murmured conversations behind many of the doors.

Jennifer's suite consisted of two bedrooms with a living room between that had been converted into the movie's production office. The antique furniture that normally decorated the room had been stored in the basement, a glass-topped desk with visitor chairs and an oblong meeting table taking its place. Penelope could smell the smoky fireplace as she got closer. She rapped her knuckles lightly on the doorframe before entering. Jennifer sat behind the desk facing the door, staring intently at her laptop. A few members of the writing team were huddled at one end of the meeting table, the tapping of keyboards the only sound in the room besides the crackling logs. Jennifer's eyes jerked up from the screen when she realized Penelope was approaching her desk.

"Penelope," Jennifer said. "Can you come up with something simple for the crew to eat? Maybe some soup or chili so they don't starve to death?"

"Of course. We'll cook off the trucks until things are—" Jordan's body being taken out on a stretcher in the kitchen flashed through her mind.

"Good," Jennifer interrupted her thoughts. "I've been reminded by the union reps that even though we technically didn't work today, they need a full day's notice per their contracts to not have meals served."

Penelope nodded. "I know that's usually in there, but it's not always enforced. Especially in unforeseen situations. Like this one."

Jennifer waved her hand in the air. "Whatever. Just do what you can so we're in compliance."

Penelope cleared her throat. "Ava and I just got back from visiting Megan Foster."

"I know," Jennifer said. "I can't believe what's happening. Someone might have murdered Jordan? Who?"

"I have no idea," Penelope said. "It's a suspicious death."

"They can't think it was one of us," Jennifer said. "Who would have a reason to kill Jordan?"

Penelope shrugged and Jennifer stared back at her computer screen. "They're going to investigate all of us. This could really be the end. Officer Collins is downstairs, guarding the kitchen like we're a bunch of maniacs on a murderous rampage."

"Edie's still here?"

"Yeah. And a team will be joining her soon. It's a crime scene."

"She thought it might be, which I guess is why she never left today," Penelope said. "They'll find out who did it."

Jennifer looked at her doubtfully. "She's pretty green, from what I've seen of her. And that sheriff, he seems like he doesn't want anything to do with it."

Penelope shook her head. "I think she's new on the job, but Edie seems to be on the ball."

"You have more confidence than I do," Jennifer said. "This is a tragedy, and a mess on top of it."

Penelope decided to postpone the conversation about helping out at Festa, feeling it wasn't the right time to throw Jennifer yet another curveball.

"I gather from my conversation with Megan I'm supposed to share you with Ava now," Jennifer said.

Penelope couldn't tell if she was perturbed by the request or not, so she stayed silent and waited for Jennifer to continue. "I know Megan. She'll find a way. Megan wants to keep things going here for the sake of the community, and the people who work here. And also to carry on Jordan's legacy. So, yes, you have my permission. I don't have much choice."

"Yes, you do," Penelope said.

Jennifer sighed heavily and closed her computer. She leaned back in her chair and thought for a minute. "I understand where Megan is coming from. I can't say no to her, especially with all she's dealing with. Just don't exhaust yourself. The last thing I need is for you to complain to the studio about being overworked or have you doing anything to violate your contract."

"I won't. And it's only for a short time. Francis and the rest of my team are fully capable of running services on the set." Penelope was still trying to gauge how Jennifer was feeling, with no luck. Everything was off kilter with everyone.

Jennifer raised her palms in the air in a "who knows" gesture. "It's okay by me, then."

"I'll work fast to find a replacement," Penelope said.

"It won't be that easy to replace Jordan," Jennifer said, brushing at something on her cheek.

"I didn't mean literally replace him..."

Jennifer waved her off. "I know what you meant. But things are different here. Professional chefs aren't falling off the trees, if you hadn't noticed."

Penelope nodded. "True. Jordan was here though. There has to be someone."

"Doubtful. But good luck with that. I'm beginning to think coming back to Forrestville was a terrible decision. Like this is our fault somehow. Like I had a hand in Jordan's death."

Jennifer opened her laptop again and started typing.

Penelope backed away, dismissed.

CHAPTER 9

Penelope walked across the cobblestone courtyard to Festa, catching a glimpse of a few people in winter coats, huddled in a loose circle in the parking lot behind the inn. The inn's jeep was in its normal place, in the last spot near the uphill walkway, the chips in the paint on the dark green grill shining silver in the fading afternoon light. Soup and chili would be perfect for dinner, and easy to pull off in the kitchen truck with things they already had on hand.

Penelope tugged one of Festa's front-door handles and felt the double doors rattle against the deadbolt. She jangled the keyring from her pocket and picked out the bright orange one Jordan had made for her. She stepped into the foyer and pulled the door closed, locking it behind her.

The silence of the restaurant washed over her, the normally bustling dining room eerily quiet. Penelope moved through the dark-paneled room, glancing at the tables as she went, tugging on the tablecloths here and there, adjusting napkin-wrapped silverware on the plates, and making other minor adjustments to set the room perfectly. She eyed a half-full salt grinder on one of the tables and snatched it up, making a mental note to mention to the wait staff everything should be completely refreshed before they left for the day.

Penelope rolled the salt shaker between her hands, the clear plastic rubbing against her palms. She remembered Jordan's infectious excitement when he got to work, always interested to hear how their day had gone. Penelope and her crew could have easily worked the entire movie from their trucks; they'd worked that way countless times before. But the inn's kitchen allowed them more space and cut down on a lot of the back and forth with ingredients and dirty dishes. Jordan was generous to share his space with them.

Penelope thought back to an afternoon two weeks earlier, Jordan hurrying through the back door with a large parcel wrapped in twine and brown paper over his shoulder. He set it down on the counter and waved her over.

"You ever serve venison back home in New Jersey?" Jordan's blue eyes twinkled as he spoke.

"Nope. I've never made it." Penelope eyed the bulky parcel. "It's not a popular dish back home."

Jordan slipped off his sheepskin coat and hung it near the office door, returning quickly to the table and placing his hands reverently on the brown paper. "Then you're in for a treat," he said, excitement speeding his words. He grabbed a pair of shears from the metallic strip that lined the wall of the kitchen and snipped through the twine. The paper fell open, revealing a dressed side of deer.

"Wow," Penelope said. "Where did you get this?"

"I shot him myself, yesterday morning." Jordan eyed his prize proudly. "Local venison stew is tonight's special. And I'm making sausage for weekend brunch from this guy too. There will be enough for your crew."

Penelope nodded uncertainly. "I'm not sure how it will go over. I guess some will appreciate it."

"I guarantee they'll love it. You'll see," Jordan said, pulling the paper from beneath the slab. "Jennifer likes it, I know that for sure."

Penelope laughed. Jordan's confidence was beginning to sway her. "I'm having a hard time picturing Jennifer eating sausage, unless it's tofu. I've only ever seen her eat granola and organic yogurt for breakfast. Maybe turkey bacon, but venison?" Penelope shook her head.

"Jennifer's an LA lady now, I know. But she hasn't completely changed. You know you can take the girl out of Indiana, but..."

"Yeah, I've heard the saying." Penelope waved Francis and the other chefs over to watch Jordan break down the side of deer. He butchered the meat with a practiced hand, removing muscle and tendons and carving out perfect lean portions. He made it look simple and seemed to enjoy the role of instructor, pausing to explain what he was doing as he worked. Penelope took quick glances at her team while they watched intently, four young chefs from New Jersey, only one of whom had gone to culinary school.

Wiping a stray tear from her cheek, Penelope pulled herself back to the present, sitting at the end of the mahogany bar in Festa's dining room. She placed the half-empty salt grinder down on the wood and stared at the crystals, which soon became blurry as more tears slid down her cheeks. She dropped her head into her hands and gave in to her emotions, crying for Jordan, for his family, and for his tragic loss of life.

Penelope's phone buzzed in her back pocket and she considered not answering it, removing herself from everyone and everything. She swiped her face with her sleeve and pulled the phone up to read the screen, smiling weakly when she saw the name there: *Joey.*

"Hi," Penelope said after clearing her throat.

"There's my girl." Joey was walking outside, the familiar sounds of traffic and mingled conversations in the background instantly bringing her home. "It's not a bad time, is it?"

"It's never a bad time to talk to you," Penelope said, unzipping her jacket. She slid it from her shoulders and stood up, folding it over her arm. She snatched the salt grinder from the bar and walked to the kitchen.

"Are you okay?" Joey asked.

"Yeah, no. It's nothing," Penelope said unconvincingly.

"Nice try," Joey said. "You found a dead body today. It's okay to be upset."

Penelope sighed and entered the kitchen, thinking about what to say. She placed the salt shaker on the kitchen counter and went to the office, crooking the phone under her chin and patting her pockets to find the keys. They fell to the floor and she scooped them up, unlocking the office with the red one. "You're right. It's been a bad day," Penelope began. "And I feel all on my own. The police are saying that Jordan's death is suspicious. He might have been murdered, Joey. They're investigating."

"Suspicious. That means they can't rule it a suicide yet. They must have found something on the body to indicate foul play."

"Like what?" Penelope asked.

Joey blew out a sigh. "Could be a lot of things. Something doesn't line up for them. Signs of a struggle beforehand, fingernail scrapings, bruises..."

"But those things could be there without it being murder, right?" Penelope asked. "How do they know?"

"The coroner can tell things," Joey said. "If someone killed him, Penny...you were there right after, maybe. You have to be careful."

"I'm always careful," Penelope said. She wondered if she was safe then, being locked in a deserted restaurant alone. "Joey, if someone killed Jordan and tried to make it to look like a suicide...that sounds personal."

"About as personal as you can get," Joey agreed.

"I wish you were here. I'm not totally alone—Arlena's here— but this place feels so cut off from everything."

"I know," Joey said. "Listen, I was going to wait until you got back, but I think we should talk."

Penelope fell silent and her stomach dropped.

"Talk? No, Joey. No one ever says anything good after they say they want to talk."

Joey laughed under his breath. "No, I don't mean that kind of talk. A good talk."

"Oh," Penelope said, still uncertain. "Okay."

"I'm just saying, I don't like being away from you, Penny Blue. I want to be with you every day. I want to talk about how we can make that happen. Especially if we want to take our relationship to different levels."

A flutter slipped across Penelope's chest. "Levels?"

"Yeah, levels," Joey said. "We'll talk about the levels later. Point is, we should be together. I don't want you going off for months at a time where I can't be with you."

Penelope sighed. "It's part of the job, Joey. I have to go where the work is."

"There's plenty of work in New York. You know there is."

"True," Penelope relented. "Look, I'm supposed to be getting things together for dinner. Will you be around later? Maybe I can call you before bed."

"Sure. But text before you call. I'm heading out now with friends. Don't want to have to yell at you over a crowded bar."

A wave of disappointment washed over her. "Okay, have fun. I wish I was going with you."

Joey's voice turned serious. "Penny, I know it's hard when we don't know why things happen, like what you're all going through out there now." He fell silent as a bus rolled by on the other end of the line. "But everything will be okay. I promise. Just be careful."

"I will. And I hope so," Penelope said. "I really do."

"Look, I just got to the restaurant. I should let you go," Joey said. "You still up for a visit?"

"Joey, I'm dying to see you. Six weeks is a long time to be apart."

"Okay, done. Are you still going to throw a birthday party for Arlena?"

Penelope's stomach dropped. "I'd like to, but now with everything going on, we may have to scale it back." She shook her head. "It's kind of depressing now. I'm not sure a big birthday bash would be appropriate. Maybe in a few days things will feel different. I'll have to play it by ear." Penelope sat down heavily in the rolling chair behind the desk and shook the mouse, bringing the screen to life on the desktop monitor. The phone next to it began to ring, and Penelope glanced at it, unsure whether to answer.

"You know best. If you think it's bad timing, I'm sure Arlena would understand," Joey said.

"It's a surprise. She's not expecting a party. At least I don't think she's guessed. Sam's flying in from where he's filming in Oregon, said they rescheduled his shoot so he could get a few days off to visit Arlena for her birthday. What a mess," Penelope said, deflating. The phone on the desk stopped ringing abruptly and immediately started ringing again, the sound cutting like a knife through the still office air. "Obviously a lot is happening now," she said, gazing at the phone.

"You have to get that?" Joey asked.

Penelope bit her bottom lip and closed her eyes. "I don't want to, but I probably should." Penelope put off telling Joey about helping at Festa, knowing he'd be concerned she was overdoing it. For the first time since Ava and Megan had asked, she regretted agreeing to it.

"Go ahead and get it," Joey said, his tone lightening. "I can't wait to see you, Penny Blue."

Penelope's chest warmed and tears pricked her eyes again. She squeezed them closed and willed her voice to remain clear. "Can't wait."

Penelope ended the call and put the desk phone to her ear, hearing the dull metallic thrum of a dial tone. She set the receiver down. The message light blinked red on the handset. Not knowing how to retrieve messages, and figuring they were probably for Ava anyway, she turned her attention to the computer. She typed in the password Ava had given her. FAILED LOGIN blinked back at her from the screen. Her head was swimming and she was overwhelmed, but she was almost certain she'd typed it correctly.

She tried again, and even though she was convinced she typed the same exact password, the screen went black for a moment and then came to life, three silhouetted avatars staring back at her in the same spots as always, one with her name, one with Jordan's, and one with Ava's. She hovered the arrow over hers, then slid it over and clicked on Jordan's. A screen opened up with various folders labeled *Recipes, Menus, Wine lists,* and *Guests.* The last one was designated as *Personal* and Penelope hesitated, then double clicked it.

A list of documents filled the screen, some appearing to be letters to or from customers, a couple of news articles, and other correspondence. Penelope clicked the menu to arrange them in time sequence, with the latest document appearing first on the list.

"Last night," Penelope murmured as she opened the file. "'Dear Jacob,'" she whispered as she read, "'as previously stated, I intend to take legal action against you if you continue to slander my business and my good name, and damage my reputation with your putrid lies. Your jealousy is clear, but you can't continue to misuse your position to malign my character or skill any longer.'" The letter ended and Penelope sat back in the chair, crossing her arms at her chest. "Jacob." She tried to remember where she'd seen the name. When it came to her she sat up straight and searched for the review she'd read, pulling it up on the screen. "Jacob Pears," Penelope said in a clear voice to the empty room. "He was the important guest last night."

The desk phone began to ring again and Penelope snatched it up. "Festa, can I help you?" She spoke in a sharper tone than usual. Her iPhone vibrated on the desk, Ava's name appearing on the screen.

Someone started pounding on the back door of the kitchen. Penelope stood up from her chair, causing it to roll away from her and bump into the office wall. She craned her neck to peer out, but couldn't see the back door from where she stood.

"Who am I speaking to?" An abrupt male voice urged from the other end of the line.

"Penelope Sutherland. Who is this?" Penelope asked, distracted by more pounding from the kitchen. Her phone vibrated again, Ava's name flashing insistently.

"This is Sheriff Bryson. Open the kitchen door, please," he said sharply before hanging up on her. Penelope logged off on the computer and snatched up her iPhone. "Ava?"

"I'm on my way back," Ava shouted. "Can you go across and let the police into Festa? They'll be there soon."

"Yeah, I'm already here, was going to put a new order in for tomorrow," Penelope said, her heartbeat skipping as she walked toward the door.

"Okay, they're going to..." Ava's voice crackled and the connection went dead just as Penelope slid the deadbolt aside and swung open the door. Two police officers dressed in brown uniforms stood behind Sheriff Bryson, their wide-brimmed hats casting shadows over their faces. A young woman in a baseball cap stood off to the right, a leather bag slung over her shoulder.

"Miss Sutherland," Sheriff Bryson said. He stepped into the kitchen, his team right behind him. The cold followed them in, clinging to their leather bomber jackets.

"Ava said you were on the way. How can I help, Sheriff?" Penelope asked as she closed the door. Sheriff Bryson pointed out different areas of the kitchen to his officers and they dispersed.

"I'm going to have to ask you to step outside," Sheriff Bryson said.

CHAPTER 10

Penelope rocked her boots on the pavement of the loading area behind the kitchen, taking regular glances at the door, hoping someone would come out and tell her what was happening. Ava's SUV bounced up the hill toward the restaurant, her headlights flickering as she sped over the cobblestones. The sky was darkening, a sheet of slate gray clouds further dimming the fading light. Ava's SUV jerked to a stop and she hopped out, hurrying over to Penelope.

"What are they doing in there?" Ava said breathlessly.

Penelope's teeth chattered from the cold as she shrugged. "They just came in, asked me to wait outside. I guess they're looking for evidence."

Ava's eyes flashed and grew wide. "Evidence of what? He wouldn't tell me anything on the phone. This can't be happening. They've made a mistake."

Penelope's mind skipped back to finding Jordan's body. She tried to see the scene in a different light, grasp onto something out of the ordinary. Something nipped at the edge of her mind, but she couldn't focus in on it.

"I wonder what they're trying to find." Ava said, hugging herself.

Penelope shook her head. "I'm freezing. I'm going to head back to the inn—"

The door swung open and a deputy waved them over.

"Sheriff, what is happening?" Ava asked after they'd stepped inside the warm kitchen.

Sherriff Bryson handed her an envelope with several sheets of paper inside. "We're getting our ducks in a row, making sure we have all the necessary information to create a full picture of what happened to Jordan."

"Well, I can help with whatever you need, of course," Ava said, glancing at the paperwork.

"Do you have a security system on the property?" the sheriff asked.

"Sorry, we don't," Ava said. "I thought about putting one in, but Jordan always said his town was safe."

Sheriff Bryson grimaced. "Normally, that's true. Look, we don't think Jordan died alone. It's looking more and more like it wasn't a suicide, I hate to say. Jordan had bruises, several of them, that maybe someone gave him, helping his death along."

"Bruises?" Penelope asked. "Where?"

Sheriff Bryson's face flushed and he kept silent.

"Where was he bruised?" Penelope persisted.

The sheriff considered another minute then said, "Bruises inconsistent with self-inflicted hanging. That's all I can really say."

"Sheriff, what you're saying...look, everyone loved Jordan," Ava said. "He didn't have enemies."

"Everyone has enemies," the sheriff said.

Ava stared at him, looking like she was trying to work out a complicated math problem in her head.

"Jordan was active," Penelope offered. "He ran the forest trails, he hunted, dressed deer out in the woods." She pulled up the sleeve of her sweater, revealing a bruise on her forearm. "I got this from dropping a pan on myself the other day."

"Not the same kind of bruising. Look, we know what we're doing. I know the fact that someone might have had a problem with Chef Jordan is shocking, but that might just be the case."

Penelope watched the woman in the baseball hat behind the desk, staring at the computer monitor. Her stomach dropped when she remembered the note she'd found. Maybe Jordan did have enemies after all.

"The lab is going to gather your fingerprints, everyone who works here, members of the film crew," Sheriff Bryson announced.

"You're talking about a lot of people," Ava said. "We have delivery drivers in and out of both places, not to mention sales reps, farmers, customers, friends. You might as well fingerprint everyone in Forestville."

Sheriff Bryson nodded. "If that's what it takes to solve a homicide, that's what I'll do."

"Homicide?" Ava echoed hoarsely. She put a hand on her forehead and turned away from the sheriff.

"I'll make a list of the crew," Penelope said quietly. "And help with the one for the inn and Festa. Whatever we can do to help."

"That's a start. And we'll need a formal statement from both of you too. I need official details about what you saw this morning, things of that nature." He squinted up at the halogen lights, thinking.

"That's going to take forever," Ava said weakly.

"We'll move as quickly as we can. No one wants this to be resolved more than I do," Sheriff Bryson said.

"I know. I'm only thinking of all the arrangements that have to be made here—the staff, and Jordan's funeral."

"I'm not saying it will be easy, but we can't let a killer walk free."

CHAPTER 11

Penelope made her way back over to the inn while Ava stayed behind to give a statement to Sheriff Bryson. Penelope agreed to gather her staff and meet him a half hour later downstairs in the great room. Fighting the instinct to rush across the courtyard, she breathed in the cold air and slowed her pace to clear her head. She felt numb, her legs rubbery as she thought about what the sheriff had said about bruises on Jordan's body. Penelope had picked up her fair share of bruises working over the years, and sometimes she couldn't figure out how they ended up where they did. She hoped the sheriff was being overly cautious and they would turn out to be incidental.

Penelope paused as she reached for the handle on the heavy wooden door, the fleeting thought about that morning when she'd found Jordan landing with a thud in her mind.

"Why did he take off his boots?" Penelope whispered to herself. Her mind skittered back to the scene, Jordan's blue toes twisting just above the metal floor of the refrigerator. She hadn't noticed his boots in the kitchen. Even though the inn had been remodeled, the floors in winter were still cold. Why would he be barefoot? She made a note to check the office at the inn. Maybe he'd slipped his boots off in there before heading into the kitchen. But still, a commercial kitchen floor, even a clean one like the one at the inn, wouldn't be a place any trained chef would walk around barefoot.

The dry heat from the fireplace warmed Penelope instantly. A few members of the crew were filling crystal tumblers from a bottle of scotch on the bar and speaking in low voices. The windows on either side of the bar were edged in frost, the sky almost completely dark behind them. Penelope slipped past unnoticed and headed upstairs.

Penelope rapped her knuckles on the door to Jennifer's suite. Normally it was open, but now it was locked, and there was no answer. Penelope turned and went to the opposite end of the hall to Arlena's suite, knocking once and entering when she heard Arlena call "come in" softly.

"There you are," Arlena said when she saw Penelope. She stood on a raised platform in front of a tri-fold set of full-length mirrors. She had on her primary costume, the one she wore in most of her scenes: a long black dress with a squared collar. She looked every inch the unreliable frail governess from the story, at least what Penelope remembered from when she read *The Turn of the Screw* back in school. Skylar was perched on a low stool in front of Arlena, holding a section of the skirt in her hand. She glanced over her shoulder at Penelope, brightly colored pins pinched between her lips, before sticking one in the hem of the dress.

"Is this a bad time?" Penelope asked.

Arlena shook her head and waved Penelope over. "It's never a bad time to see you. I've lost some weight since we've been here. They need to bring in the dress again." Arlena had gained fifteen pounds a few months earlier as part of a push to land a role in a movie. She didn't get the part, and had been losing the extra weight ever since. "Jennifer is going to flip out if I have a ten-pound weight variance during filming. It will be too obvious, I think."

"Keep coming to dinner. I can make you some extra shakes too," Penelope said. She suddenly felt exhausted and looked for a place to sit down.

Arlena's assistant, Sarah, emerged from the adjoining bedroom and shuffled through a few script pages. Her thick slouchy sweater pulled down her narrow shoulders and left bright pink balls of fuzz on her leggings. "I've marked all of tomorrow's dialogue changes," the young girl said, tucking a red pen behind her ear. Her black hair was styled in a pixie cut and dyed purple at the fringes, the same color as the frames of her glasses.

"What's wrong?" Arlena asked, her expression becoming concerned as she looked closer at Penelope. Skylar and Sarah stopped what they were doing and turned their attention to her also.

"The police are at the restaurant," Penelope began.

"Who, the sheriff again?" Arlena asked. Skylar pulled the pins from her lips and stood up from her stool. The three of them waited silently for Penelope to continue.

"They're saying Jordan's death might not have been a suicide. That maybe he was murdered." Penelope plopped onto the nearest chair.

Arlena stepped down from the platform and went to Penelope, draping an arm over her shoulders. "So there's a maniac on the loose in this little farm town?" Arlena asked with disbelief. "Who killed Jordan?"

Penelope shrugged. "They don't know. It's an open investigation now."

"He was killed here?" Sarah asked in disbelief. She put her hand over her mouth immediately afterwards and mumbled "Sorry" through her fingers.

"It's not safe," Skylar said, sounding more excited than scared. "They're definitely going to shut the movie down now."

Arlena looked at them and said, "Would you two stop? Go on, give us a minute."

Skylar and Sarah got up and went into the adjoining bedroom reluctantly, appearing anxious to hear what was happening. They left the door partially open and began a hushed conversation.

Arlena hugged Penelope closer to her side on the settee. "They're right, you know. I love Jennifer, but I've never worked with a director who had so many day-to-day changes. Scenes, dialogue, schedule changes...she's rewriting every day. Some of the crew members are disgruntled—the accommodations here aren't working for everyone. Now a murder?"

"I know. I've heard grumblings around the set too. I've never been on a project that felt so...depressed."

Someone knocked on the door, a persistent series of raps. "Who is it?" Arlena asked, sighing.

Whoever it was knocked again, a playful series of beats that reminded Penelope of a childhood rhyme.

"Who's there?" Arlena asked again, becoming impatient with the unannounced visitor.

There was no response, just the continued rhythm on the door. Arlena pushed herself up from the settee and took a few long strides, then yanked it open. She looked like she was about to give the person on the other side a strong opinion about their interruption, but then Penelope saw Arlena's face move from irritation to delight in a matter of seconds.

"Daddy!" Arlena cried, reaching up to throw her arms around Randall Madison's neck.

CHAPTER 12

Randall Madison always liked to make an entrance. This wasn't the first time Arlena's father had shown up on her doorstep unannounced, much to Arlena's delight. Randall lived his life on the road, never staying in one place too long, moving from one movie set to another. He'd been doing it his entire career, for over forty years. Arlena was one of Randall's many children—Penelope was never quite sure of the exact number—who had resulted from various relationships and marriages during that career. But even though Randall had a lot of kids, and he said they were all unique in their own way, Penelope knew he had a special place in his heart for Arlena.

"Daddy, what are you doing here?" Arlena asked, hugging him tighter. They stood in the doorway, Randall filling the space with his wide shoulders.

"I can't believe we found you out here in the middle of nowhere," said another voice from the hallway.

Arlena broke off the hug and pulled her father inside the room by his hand. "Max is here too?" Max Madison, Arlena's half-brother, strode into the room and crushed her to his chest.

Arlena hugged him back, the stunned expression remaining on her face. Randall caught Penelope's eye and gave her a knowing wink, which caused her cheeks to redden. Arlena took a step back to look at them and almost tripped over her skirt, her feet getting caught in the too-long hem brushing the floor. "Seriously, what are you guys doing here?"

"You think I'd miss your birthday?" Randall asked. "My little girl only turns thirty once. There's no way I'd miss that."

"Shh," Arlena said, throwing a glance at the bedroom door. "I'm trying to stay in my twenties a little longer, Daddy."

"You can't hide your age these days. Everything is on the internet. Not that you need to," Max added hastily, ducking from Arlena's scolding look. He dropped his duffle bag on the floor. "Good to see you too, Penelope."

Penelope gave him a quick smile. "Hi, Mr. Madison," she added shyly.

"How many times is it going to take, Penelope?" Randall asked. "If you can't remember to call me Randall, just call me Dad."

Penelope blushed when she smelled the sweet cherry cigar smoke on his heavy leather jacket as he stepped toward her. She had grown to love the Madison family over the past couple of years and considered them an extension of her own family. Not having siblings of her own, Arlena had become like a sister to her, and the thought of Randall as a surrogate father warmed her heart and brought an unexpected prick of tears behind her eyes. She wondered for a moment why she was so prone to crying lately, then gave herself a pass when she thought about the day she'd had so far.

Penelope cleared her throat. "Okay, Pops," she said jokingly.

"Atta girl." Randall brushed a strand of hair from her cheek with his thumb.

"Will someone tell me what's going on?" Arlena asked again.

"We're on a road trip. Heading west." Max slipped off his ski jacket and draped it across the back of a chair. "We thought we'd stop and visit a few days."

"A trip, since when?" Arlena asked. "Aren't you working?" Max's job was starring as one of the featured regulars on a reality show that followed the exploits of the children of the rich and famous. He lived in lower Manhattan in the same apartment building where they filmed the show.

Randall paced carefully around the room, his motorcycle boots squeaking dully on the hardwood floor. He eyed the antique furniture, all of which appeared too fragile for him to use. He looked like a bear wandering around inside a dollhouse.

"We just filmed the last episode of the season. I have a couple of months off. I'm going out to LA to audition for a few parts," Max said. "*Film* roles. And not just bit parts either."

"So you thought you'd drive all the way from New York to Los Angeles?" Arlena asked, laughing with surprise.

"Why not?" Randall asked. "You can't see the countryside from the window of an airplane. Both of you should slow down, set aside more time to appreciate the people and things around you. Life goes by quickly."

Randall's adult children gaped at him after the unexpected life lesson from their free-spirited father.

"Besides, I don't start work on my next movie for a month," Randall continued. "Me and the kid will get some quality time together, see the sights, wander around a while."

"We *are* going to California though, right, Dad?" Max straightened his spine in alarm.

"Sure, kid." Randall chuckled. "I'll get you there eventually."

"I don't think there are any empty rooms here to stay," Penelope said. "There's a hotel the next town over, about twenty minutes north on the highway."

"We're going to camp in the woods." Randall squinted out the frosted window pane at the forest behind the restaurant.

"Camp?" Arlena said. "Daddy, it's freezing outside."

"Exactly," Randall said, turning back around to face them and rubbing his hands together. "My next movie takes place on Mount Kosciuszko. It's about the guys who discovered it, trekked to the summit. I have to prepare. Me and Max are going to find out what it's like to set up camp in the snow, the unforgiving tundra."

Max's face fell. "When you said camping, I thought you meant somewhere on the beach. You know, cooking over a fire, frosty drinks. In California."

Randall smiled, amused.

"You don't have to do this with me, but I hope you decide it's worth it."

Max started answering before he could finish. "I want to do it with you, Dad. But...you have a heater for the tent, right?"

Randall shook his head and grinned. "Of course I do. I won't let you freeze to death. You do need some toughening up though. You're too used to Thai takeout at three in the morning in the city."

"You're close enough to the inn you can come inside and warm up when you need to," Arlena said. "And take showers. There's plenty of room in here, a spare bed and a rollaway. I'm not sharing with anyone." She glanced at the closed door next to the fireplace.

The phone on the desk rang once before it was answered by one of the girls in the next room with a muffled "hello."

"Thanks, sweetie. You know, those guys on Kosciuszko didn't have an inn to warm up in," Randall said, rubbing the dark stubble on his chin. "We might have to stick it out to maintain the authenticity of my research."

Max dropped his head in his hands and said in a serious voice, "Dad, there's no mountain here either. And we're in the middle of the United States. Let's take showers and fall back on your acting skills."

Sarah poked her head through the bedroom door. "Excuse me, Miss Madison?"

"Yes?" Arlena said, suppressing a grin at her brother's discomfort.

"The police are looking for Penelope." Sarah's voice tended to lilt up at the end of sentences, but it was more pronounced when she was nervous. Her eyes widened behind her glasses when she saw Max sitting in the chair, gazing at her with his long arm draped lazily over the back.

Penelope's phone buzzed in her back pocket. She pulled it out and read the message from Jennifer. The letters shouted in all caps: "NEED YOUR TEAM IN GREAT ROOM NOW." She turned the phone over and rubbed the fingerprint smudges onto her jeans.

"I'm being summoned," Penelope said.

"What have you been up to?" Max asked. "Got caught cow tipping?"

Arlena set her mouth in a line and looked at Penelope.

"The police are investigating a suspicious death that happened this morning," Penelope said, the words drying her mouth. "The owner of this inn might have been murdered."

CHAPTER 13

After the tech held her fingers against the small screen on the bar and she watched a sketch of her fingerprints fill the tiny monitor, Sheriff Bryson ushered Penelope into the inn's cramped office under the main staircase. He looked out of place behind the vintage metal secretary desk, which had been built many years earlier and designed for a much smaller person. He looked more like a teacher from the 1950s than a modern-day police officer. A coffee cup sat at the edge of the desk, *Indiana* baked into the side, painted in a child's handwriting. It held a collection of pens, and Penelope counted them while the sheriff shuffled a few papers inside a brown folder on the desk.

"Penelope Sutherland," he muttered under his breath, choosing one of the sheets and jotting her name at the top.

This was the first time Penelope had seen Sheriff Bryson out of his bulky leather jacket. His brown uniform shirt was freshly pressed, the seams perfectly lined down his sleeves, and his collar crisp. His hair wasn't fully gray, just his sideburns, the rest sandy brown, and his face was smooth from a recent shave. He was orderly perfection personified.

"Tell me again everything you remember about this morning," Sheriff Bryson began, bouncing the ball of his pen on the form.

Penelope recounted entering the refrigerator, bumping into Jordan's dangling legs, and stumbling back out. "That's it. Then you were here."

He nodded at her, watching her mouth as she spoke. "And you spoke to Mrs. Foster this morning. Afterwards, I mean."

Penelope nodded and watched him jot something down.

"What did you talk about?" Sheriff Bryson asked.

"Restaurant business. She and Ava want to find a new chef quickly," Penelope said.

The sheriff smiled tightly and bent his head toward the desk, scribbling.

"Did she seem upset to you?" he asked, brushing his lip and watching her intently.

Penelope paused, deciding to tread carefully into the rest of the conversation. "Of course. In shock, really. I think we all are. Why do you ask?"

Sheriff Bryson leaned back in his chair. "I'm trying to find out what happened to her husband is all. Just gathering information."

Penelope sat up straighter. "Where were Jordan's boots? He always wore his hiking boots in the kitchen. Zamberlans. He was barefoot when he died."

He folded his hands and gazed at her. "Yet to be located," he said matter-of-factly. "Those are pretty fancy shoes for cooking."

"He said they saved his feet, and his back, from the hours standing in the kitchen. Those floors are hard. I don't think he'd walk barefoot through his own kitchen. It's a health-code violation."

"What makes you think he'd be wearing them near the time he died? He wasn't working in the middle of the night, when we've determined it happened."

"But he was wearing his chef coat and pants. It makes sense he'd also be wearing his work boots," Penelope said.

"Do you remember if he was wearing the same clothes from earlier in the day?" he asked.

"I think so, but I can't be completely sure. His uniforms were all similar."

Sheriff Bryson mumbled something in response, his expression a mask of disdain, or possibly defeat.

"Can I ask you about the bruises you mentioned?"

He eyed her for a moment, considering. "I shouldn't have

shared that with you." He crossed his arms at his chest and leaned back in the chair.

"But you must think Jordan was murdered or you wouldn't be going through all of this," Penelope said.

"I do. Terrible thing, and I hate to admit it, but yes," Sheriff Bryson said.

"I get the impression that doesn't happen around here too often," Penelope said, prodding.

"Forrestville is a nice place to live. There's nothing wrong with that."

"Sorry," Penelope said. "I really just want to help."

"Then let's get back to the point. Did Jordan do a lot of drinking at the restaurant?" His tone softened a tad but maintained its authoritative sharpness.

"Yes, but I wouldn't characterize his drinking as excessive," Penelope said. "He drank wine on occasion in the kitchen while he was cooking, and sometimes at the bar with his favorite customers. But he always stayed focused while working."

"Okay. Did he seem particularly close with any of his employees?"

Penelope paused a moment to think. "I'd say he was close to most of the staff. He always said they were his extended family. I heard him mention more than once that the young people he hired were all known to him through their parents in town. He was very protective of everyone working on the floor and in the back of the house."

"Did he seem particularly close to anyone from the movie crew?"

"I guess. He said he really liked working with all of us. Jennifer, obviously."

"And the other chefs?"

"Jordan was friendly with everyone, Sheriff Bryson," Penelope said, feeling a bit hopeless.

Sheriff Bryson sighed. "From what you're telling me, and from what I've heard around town, Jordan Foster was the perfect man.

Happy family, successful business, well-liked by everyone, generous, a regular guy with lots of friends..."

Penelope nodded in agreement. "That's what I think of him too. Granted I've only known him a little over a month, but I wouldn't disagree."

"And yet, someone may have killed him. A man with no clear enemies ends up hanging in his own freezer. I think he came across the wrong out-of-towner, someone who thinks they're smart enough to throw us off track, make it look like a suicide."

"What makes you think it wasn't?" Penelope asked.

Sheriff Bryson ran his finger along the edge of the pile of papers on the desk and dropped his voice a level. "Certain facts have come to light."

"So he was definitely murdered." Penelope lowered her voice too.

"Yes." His mood shifted abruptly and he straightened up in his chair. "That's all the questions I have for now, Miss Sutherland. If you wouldn't mind, please send in the next person..." He eyed a short list of names on his pad. "Francis Moretti."

"Sure. He's my sous chef," Penelope said, standing up. She glanced at the list, noticing it was less than ten names long, far from the entire film crew. She didn't see any of the actors' names, but every one of her chefs was listed. "You're not questioning everyone from the movie?"

Sheriff Bryson scooted a piece of paper over the names. "That's not your concern."

Penelope stifled a nervous laugh and straightened the hem of her sweater at her waist. Seeing her name at the top of Sheriff Bryson's list had unnerved her. When she'd come into the office, she felt like she was there to help. Now she felt like she was on the top of a short list of suspects.

"Don't you normally take witness statements at the police station?" she asked.

He shot her an irritated glance.

"Not that I need to explain, but it doesn't make sense to shuttle people back and forth to the department when everyone I'd like to talk to is right here."

Penelope thought about the small police station next to the diner on Main Street. "I didn't mean to imply you weren't doing things correctly."

"Well, I'm sure they do things differently in New York. We'll try to keep up, not trip over ourselves."

Penelope stared at him from across the desk. "New Jersey."

Sheriff Bryson sighed, and some of the color drained from his cheeks. "Please send in Mr. Moretti. Thank you for your statement."

Penelope stepped through the office door and closed it behind her, giving Francis a warning glance. She pulled him by the elbow away from the door and lowered her voice. "You feeling better?"

"Yeah, I'm okay," Francis said. "What's he asking about in there?"

"I don't know. Questions about Jordan. Just answer the best you can. Don't guess anything, and only say things that you know are true."

"Yeah, of course." Francis slipped inside and closed the office door behind him.

Penelope walked to the end of the hallway and peered into the kitchen, craning her neck in the entryway. Officer Collins was talking with the female technician Penelope had seen at Festa. Both of them had on latex gloves and were looking at a diagram of the kitchen in Edie's hands. The doorway was sectioned off with yellow tape, and many of the counters, doorknobs, and handles had a fine mist of black dust on them.

Edie glanced up and saw Penelope in the doorway. "Help you?"

Penelope stuck her hands in her back pockets. "No, I was just checking in. Just finished giving another statement to the sheriff."

Edie said something to the tech, who nodded and went inside the walk-in, before approaching the doorway. "You can't come in here."

"I know," Penelope said quickly. "I wanted to see..."

"You're curious what we're doing in here," Edie said, not unkindly.

"A little," Penelope said. "Have you found anything?"

Edie set her lips in a line and looked at a spot on the wall next to Penelope's head. "I can't tell you that."

"Sorry," Penelope said, turning to go, then pausing. "Hey, I forgot to mention." She pointed at the walk-in. "I never saw Jordan without his necklace, even when he was running. It was silver, made out of a real knife from Jordan's first restaurant. He had it melted down and soldered together like this." She crossed her fingers together to make an X.

Edie turned on her heel and went to the kitchen counter, then picked up a manila envelope marked with a black grid covered in scribbled handwriting. Pulling out a small plastic bag, she held it up for Penelope to see. "This the one?"

"Yes!" Penelope said. "Was it on the floor in the freezer? I didn't remember seeing it when I found him, but with the rope around his neck..."

"Funny you ask," Edie said, her expression neutral. "It was found outside in the parking lot. One of the techs found it wedged under the front tire of your truck. That is your truck, right? The one with Red Carpet Catering painted on the side?"

Penelope's knees weakened slightly. "That's weird," she said.

"We thought so," Edie said. The woman emerged from the walk-in, her eyes boring into Penelope from beneath her baseball hat. "It's also weird that we found a partial print on it, and it wasn't Jordan's."

Penelope's mind reeled, spinning back over the past weeks, trying to remember if she ever had occasion to touch Jordan's necklace. She couldn't think of anything, although it was possible she had. She'd hugged him a few times. Had she touched it while admiring it or by accident?

"The print is a match to one of your employees, Francis Moretti."

"No, it's not," Penelope said instinctively. "That's a mistake."

"There's no mistake," Edie said, her expression remaining neutral. "His prints were already on record in the system."

"Excuse me," Penelope said. She hurried back down the hall to the office and knocked on the door rapidly, then opened it. Sheriff Bryson stared at her from behind the desk as Francis swiveled around in his chair. "Don't say anything else, Francis."

"Ms. Sutherland, excuse us please," the sheriff began.

"No, come out with me," she urged. "They think we're responsible for what happened to Jordan."

"Close the door," Sheriff Bryson ordered. When Penelope hesitated he repeated himself, in a much louder voice. She reluctantly pulled the door closed and stood next to Francis, grasping his shoulder.

"What are you doing?" Sheriff Bryson asked.

"If you're zeroing in on me or a member of my team, trying to say one of us killed Jordan, we have rights," Penelope said. "You can't question him without a lawyer."

"Yes, I can, if he doesn't ask for one," Sheriff Bryson said.

"I saw your list," Penelope said. "It's only my team and some of the restaurant staff," Penelope said. Francis's shoulder shrank beneath her grip.

"You're the ones who had the most contact with the deceased," Sheriff Bryson said. "It's natural we'd start with you."

A thought suddenly came to her. "Jordan had an argument last night. One of the sales reps, Denis Billings, saw it out behind the restaurant. You should find out about that," she said excitedly.

Sheriff Bryson eyed her with interest, then made a note on her statement. "Any other convenient memories you'd like to add?"

"No one from my crew could have done this. That's the truth," Penelope said firmly.

"So you say," he said, his eyes dropping back down to Francis.

"What is the motive, then? Why would we want to hurt Jordan? I'll tell you this, you won't find anything. We all respected him very much," Penelope said. She felt a small shudder go through Francis.

"We'll see," the sheriff said. "You're both excused." He waved them off and went back to studying his reports.

Penelope pulled Francis by the elbow into the powder room down the hall, closing the door behind him.

"What did he ask you about in there?"

Francis swept his gaze along the tin ceiling tiles. "Nothing. Regular stuff, what was Jordan doing the last time I saw him, how did he seem...why?"

"Did he ask you about the necklace?" Penelope urged.

"Yeah, Jordan's."

"What did you tell him?"

Francis shrugged.

"I said I knew the one he meant, and that I hadn't seen it around anywhere. What's the big deal about it?"

"They found it outside by our truck," Penelope said.

"So he dropped it?" Francis shrugged, palms in the air.

"They say your fingerprint is on it, Francis," Penelope whispered. "Do you remember touching it?"

Some of the color drained from Francis's face. "I don't know...yeah, I did. Now they think I killed Jordan and stole his necklace?"

"When did you touch it?" Penelope urged.

"It fell off one time and I picked it up off the floor mat, handed it back to him. The chain broke. He said it was getting old, that he needed to replace the chain," Francis said.

"Good," Penelope said. "There's a reason your fingerprints were there."

Francis shook his head and laughed bitterly. "Yeah, but it was just me and Jordan who saw it. They're not going to believe me. They just want to make the quickest arrest."

Penelope shook her head and put her palm to her forehead. "It does put you in contact with him, physical contact."

"We were all in close physical contact with him in the kitchen.

I worked close to him a couple of times, and he came out to see the truck now and then. We shook hands, slapped shoulders."

"If they had hard evidence you killed Jordan they would have arrested you already. I've heard that fingerprints can stay on surfaces for a long time. It's not enough." She pulled her phone from her pocket and texted Joey a question about fingerprints to confirm what she thought.

"I can't have this happening again," Francis said. "I haven't been in trouble in a long time, Boss."

Penelope looked up from her phone at his pleading expression. "I know. And that stuff before...you were just a kid."

"I was a stupid kid. I got caught shoplifting twice, and that's on my record. They're going to find out," Francis said helplessly.

"You're a different person now. I've got your back. Just don't answer any more questions without me or a lawyer with you."

"I've managed to land at the top of Sheriff Bryson's suspect list. And insult him on top of it," Penelope said in a low voice after taking a seat next to Ava at the bar. She swept a glance at the tables behind her, half of them full of crew members, a few of them eyeing her with interest. She decided it was best to keep the information about the necklace to herself for now. "Big city versus small town, something like that."

Ava smiled wearily. "He's a good guy, just inexperienced. This is the first murder in Forrestville for something like ten years, which would make it his only one as sheriff. He used to be a park ranger until he took over after the previous sheriff died. People don't bother locking their doors around here."

"Really?" Penelope asked. Unfortunately, she had never lived anywhere where serious crime, even murder, wasn't daily news. It was something she read about in a detached way in the papers that were left around the set. If bad things occurred in neighborhoods she didn't frequent, she could somehow distance herself from the violence, like it wasn't part of her world. She felt a rush of shame about that now. "I'm worried he might be focusing on the out-of-towners because we're unfamiliar."

Ava shrugged. "I don't think he knows what to do. I hope he can handle it."

"What's happened in the past? I mean, how do they normally investigate serious crimes around here?"

"It hasn't really come up, at least since I've lived here. I can't say for sure, but the sheriff doesn't strike me as the kind of guy to turn things over to another department. That's just a guess, but a pretty good one."

"You've known Sheriff Bryson a long time?" Penelope asked.

"It feels like I've known everyone around here for a long time," Ava said. "Maybe too long." She got up and walked behind the bar, gazing at the wine bottles below the mirror-backed shelves and selecting a red. She poured herself a glass and glanced at Penelope.

"Sure," Penelope said, eyeing at the cuckoo clock on the wall and seeing it was just past six.

Jennifer came up to them. "I think that's everyone they wanted to talk to." She held a notepad in her hand and glanced down at the list. "Now it's just the restaurant people." She wandered over to talk to another group at a nearby table.

Penelope put her chin in her palm and closed her eyes. "Did you get that list started?"

Ava squinted at her as she took a sip. "What list?"

"Of people who come in and out of the kitchen," Penelope said. She looked around for a pad of paper and a pen as Jennifer moved through the room, stopping at each table to talk to her crew.

Ava sighed. "It's not going to be anyone like that," she said. "It had to be a complete stranger, someone who happened upon Jordan, maybe someone who was trying to rob the inn."

"Really? Why would a random robber go to the trouble of making Jordan's death look like a suicide? Also, what is there to steal in here?"

Ava looked up at the ceiling. "Lots of things of value up in those rooms." She took another healthy gulp from her glass.

"Whoever killed him probably assumed Jordan's death wouldn't be questioned, that it would be ruled a suicide and they would get away with murder."

"But nothing was stolen," Penelope reminded her gently. "It doesn't seem like a random act, Ava."

Ava's eyes flashed. "Someone came in. Jordan was always leaving the doors unlocked, propping them open even, both here and over at Festa. I told him he shouldn't, especially when he was alone. There was a struggle, and the robber choked Jordan to death. He panicked and tried to cover it up by staging a suicide. Then he ran out without taking anything to cover his tracks."

Penelope considered her theory. "I guess it could have happened that way." The scenario was highly improbable, but she was tired and didn't want another contentious conversation.

Ava nodded quickly. "That's the only thing that makes sense. Because everyone loved Jordan." A tear slipped down her cheek. "It had to have been a transient. Someone who didn't know him, or any of us."

Penelope gently placed a hand on Ava's forearm then picked up her glass, swirling the liquid inside. "We're going to find out who did this."

CHAPTER 14

Penelope sat up in bed, shaken from a deep sleep by a nagging feeling, the wisps of a dream evaporating into the darkness of the room. She heard a dull thud she couldn't quite place outside, a car door maybe. Penelope went to the window that looked down on the courtyard. The clock on the nightstand said it was 3:20, the red numbers glowing in the darkness. Penelope sighed and rubbed her eyes, worrying she wouldn't be able to get back to sleep. She stared out the window at the yellow halo of light that crept across the cobblestones and illuminated the front doors of Festa. The door on the left shifted slightly, blown open at the seam before settling back against the other. At first Penelope thought it was her imagination. She looked again, forcing her sleepy brain to focus. The doors puffed against the wind again and Penelope tried to see if the deadlock was bolted, looking for a glint of silver between the doors. She decided they couldn't be secured if they were moving like that. All the lights were off inside, at least in the front dining room as far as she could see.

"I can't believe the police left the doors open. They couldn't come find me?" Penelope said quietly to herself. She considered texting Ava to see if she'd locked up when they were done, but then decided disturbing her in the middle of the night, especially after they day they'd had, wasn't the best idea. Pulling Ava out of bed and asking her to drive over seemed ridiculous when she had a set of keys and could lock up in two minutes.

Penelope stepped into her fleece-lined snow boots and slid her puffy jacket over her flannel pajamas before heading down the front stairs of the inn. She felt for the keyring in her pocket as she made her way, the wooden steps creaking under her boots. The cuckoo clock chimed once to mark the half hour, causing her to pause. The bar and great room were deserted, and Penelope wished she was still asleep like the rest of her coworkers.

When Penelope reached the front doors of Festa, she pulled one of them open with her gloved hand, confirming they'd been left unlocked. The night air was still, not even sounds of wildlife coming from the forest. The temperature was well below freezing, and Penelope assumed most of the animals were hibernating, or at least tucking themselves away until the sun rose and warmed everything up again. She thought briefly about Randall and Max camping out in the woods and shivered.

Penelope slipped the orange key into the lock, then froze when she saw a flicker of light inside the darkened dining room. Penelope dropped the keys back into her coat pocket and stepped into the foyer, squinting through the inner vestibule door to get a better look. The hair on her arms stood on end when she saw five black pillar candles burning at the far end of the bar. The candle wax dripped down the sides, and they all sat in a puddle of liquid on the bar. They gave off a pine scent that lay thick in the air. Penelope stared at the candles as she approached the bar, certain she'd never seen them in the restaurant before. Jordan used unscented tea lights in small glass votives on the tables, preferring to not have competing aromas from candles or flowers that might detract from the flavor of the food.

Penelope reached the bar and pulled off a glove, gingerly touching the sticky substance under them with her finger and holding it up to her nose. "Whiskey," she whispered. Her stomach did a flip when she heard a thump from behind the kitchen doors. "Ava?" she murmured, then dismissed the thought quickly, considering it was the middle of the night. Penelope reached into her coat pocket for her phone, realizing too late she'd left it on the nightstand next to her bed.

Penelope heard faint laughter and the thud of the kitchen's

back door closing. She approached the doors on shaky legs, moving carefully toward the sound. When she was pretty sure she was alone, Penelope pushed the kitchen door open with her fingertips, slowly at first then all the way. The overhead lights glared in the empty room, and Penelope sucked in her breath. Someone had been in the kitchen, and it hadn't been Ava. Unless Ava had completely lost her mind.

Meat Is Murder! was scrawled in spray paint across the walk-in, and several boxes of food had been dumped on the floor. Penelope let the door swing closed behind her as she took in the scene. Raw steaks and chicken parts were piled on the floor, a bucket of red paint poured on top. The vibrant red was jarring and unnatural, like a cartoon.

The sound of a vehicle pulling out of the parking lot brought Penelope back to the present. She hurried to the door and pushed it open, but only saw the taillights of what she thought was a truck speeding away. Exhaust vapors wafted in the air.

"I can't believe this," Penelope said as she stepped back inside, heaving the door closed and sliding the deadbolt home. She shook out her hands and hurried to secure the front doors too, worrying in the back of her mind that she might be locking herself inside with someone. She dismissed the idea when she thought about the truck pulling away, doubting the vandals would leave one of their accomplices behind. But to be safe, she'd check for anyone who might be hiding. After she called the police.

"Please send someone quickly," Penelope said to a weary-sounding woman at the police station. She tried to explain what had happened in a calm voice, forcing herself to slow down when she thought she sounded frantic. Hanging up the extension behind the bar, she blew out the candles and saw the empty whiskey bottle tucked into the well, which she hadn't noticed until she'd stepped behind to make the call. It had been dumped completely out, the amber liquid pooling on top of the wood and dripping into the reservoir on the service side of the bar.

Penelope picked up an unopened bottle of vodka by the neck

and held it like a bat as she walked to the bathrooms, quietly opening the doors and ducking to look under the stalls, confirming she was indeed alone. Afterwards, she doubled back to the kitchen's office to wait for someone to come.

She called Ava, running her finger down the list of phone numbers pinned to the board behind the desk.

"You've got to be joking," Ava said, her voice groggy.

"I'm telling you, I just missed whoever it was," Penelope said. "The police are on the way. I thought you should know."

"Of course," Ava said with a heavy sigh. "I'll be there in twenty minutes."

Penelope hung up and walked back out to the kitchen. The pile of frozen meat and paint was a disturbing sight, and she fought the urge to start cleaning it up. She looked at the drying paint on the walk-in door, the black drips sliding down from the bottoms of the letters. A small pentagram had been carved in the metal, angry scratches with some type of blade.

"Satanists?" Penelope said, thinking about the black candles on the bar. "Do Satanists not eat meat?" An upsetting image of animal sacrifice from a movie she'd seen flashed through her mind. Penelope tried to match up what she was seeing in the kitchen with what she remembered reading about those who proclaimed to worship the Devil.

Penelope went back to the office and sat behind the desk, staring at the blank computer screen. "Who would do this?" she wondered out loud.

Rubbing her chin with her finger, she turned the computer on and pulled up the admin screen. She clicked on Jordan's avatar and scanned the files, nothing changed since the last time she'd poked around. She quickly searched online for *Forrestville Indiana Satanic Cults* and clicked on the top result, an article dating a few years earlier about a group of devil worshipers in the area being arrested for vandalizing cars in town. Penelope skimmed the article, none of the names sounding familiar. She zeroed in on a picture of three men who looked to be in their late teens or early twenties, the caption below saying they were ordered to pay five thousand dollars each in fines and serve probation. She jotted their names down on a piece of paper on the desk.

Hearing the familiar rapping on the back door of the kitchen, Penelope exited out of the article on the screen and went to let the police in again.

CHAPTER 15

"It doesn't appear to be forced entry," Sheriff Bryson said, eyeing the kitchen doorframe. "Not that I can tell, anyway. Either the door was left unlocked or the perpetrators had a key."

Ava shifted her weight back and forth on her slender legs. She had on a red Indiana sweatshirt and jeans, the puffiness of sleep still on her face. "Do you think what's happened here is connected to Jordan's death?"

Sheriff Bryson's jaw tightened. "It would be quite a coincidence if the two incidents aren't related."

"Maybe it was just kids, someone who knew the restaurant was closed," Penelope said.

"Could be," Sheriff Bryson said. "Except that candle business on the bar looks like attempted arson to me. It's my guess they were hoping that liquor would catch on fire when the candles burned down."

"But why not just start a fire? Turn on the gas stove and set some paper towels on top? That's all it would take."

"That's pretty dangerous. Maybe they were afraid of blowing themselves up. A slow burn like the one out there would do the job and they'd already be gone," Sheriff Bryson said.

Penelope folded her arms. "True. If it was a prank, it was a dangerous one. Have you seen anything like this before?"

The sheriff shook his head and went back to studying the pile of meat on the floor. "You say you locked up last night, right?"

"Yes, after you finished questioning the staff. I remember locking the doors," Ava said.

"And who else has keys?" Sheriff Bryson asked.

"The two managers, night and day shifts," Ava said. "I think that's it. Oh, and Jordan had a set, of course."

"Does Megan have spare keys at the house?" Penelope asked.

Ava's eyes widened. "Yes, I think Jordan did keep an emergency set there too."

"Lots of keys, lots of opportunities for people to get hold of them," Sheriff Bryson said, putting his hands on his belt. "I imagine it wouldn't be hard to slip away, get a copy made from any one of those sets if someone had a mind to."

"I should change the locks, right?" Ava asked.

"I would if I were you," Sheriff Bryson said. "My crime-scene tech is on the way. She'll dust for prints, take a look around outside. I'll keep you in the loop, let you know what we find out. It goes without saying, but the kitchen will be closed until we release the scene."

Ava's face fell and she looked even more exhausted.

"Ms. Sutherland," the sheriff said, pulling her aside. "We were able to independently verify Mr. Moretti's alibi. His bunkmates at the inn all confirmed separately that he never left the room last night. Still doesn't explain his fingerprints on the necklace."

"Actually, he did touch the necklace once when it fell on the floor in here," Penelope said quickly.

The sheriff nodded tightly. "Okay, no way to prove that. He does have a prior record. I wasn't sure if you knew."

"I knew," Penelope said. "From a long time ago."

"Ten years isn't that long. I am going to ask him about this here," he said, sweeping his arm at the mess on the floor.

"There's no way Francis had anything to do with this," Penelope said with a sigh.

The sheriff excused himself and went back through the door as he pulled his phone from his pocket, a puff of frigid air pushing past him.

Ava cleared her throat and looked at Penelope. "Go back to bed. I'll stay here with them, then clean up when they're through."

"Are you sure?" Penelope asked, reluctant to leave but grateful at the chance to go back to bed.

"Yes," Ava said, waving her off and turning around to look for a broom. "You've got a busy day ahead. Morning call, right? Plus you might start receiving inquiries from new chefs."

"Yeah, but after all of this...when do you think they're going to let you reopen the restaurant?"

"I hope soon," Ava said. "We've lost thousands already. We can't afford to stay dark much longer."

"Now there're two crime scenes," Penelope said. Ava's features pinched together and Penelope regretted reminding her. She wondered how long investigating a crime scene like this took, and reminded herself to ask Joey next time they talked. "Do you think Jordan being murdered is going to keep people away?"

"It could," Ava said. "We'll have to be careful how we handle the news of his death, once we're allowed to move forward."

"Handle?" Penelope asked.

"You know, we don't want to appear insensitive, but we need to carry on with the business at the same time."

Penelope made sympathetic noises and tried to imagine how customers might feel, staying in an inn where someone had been killed, eating from a menu designed by a murder victim.

"Festa is a monument to Jordan's success, a tribute," Ava said, seeming to read Penelope's mind. "Who knows, business might increase because of what's happened. His legend might draw more people in. Like when an artist dies and their paintings triple in value."

Penelope nodded uncertainly and gazed at the pentagram on the freezer. She felt cold, even though her pajamas were warm against her skin and she was still wearing her coat. Maybe Ava was right—maybe there would be visits from the macabre. Her tongue tasted bitter in her mouth.

"See you later," Ava said as the sheriff walked back through the kitchen door.

"Yeah, see you," Penelope said.

CHAPTER 16

A few hours later, Penelope sucked down her third cup of coffee, raising the blue and white Greek-patterned paper cup to her lips with one hand and waving at Francis from behind the kitchen truck with the other. He backed toward her slowly, tapping on the brakes until she made a fist and the truck lurched to a spot next to their matching pantry truck.

Francis hopped down from the cab and sauntered over. "The broiler is busted, Boss. I tried reattaching it, but the element has burned out."

Penelope drained her coffee cup, immediately thinking about refilling it from the urn inside. "I'll go online in a minute and order a replacement."

"We doing our regular breakfast today?"

"Yeah, but the restaurant kitchen is...it's not clean. We'll cook out here today, maybe tomorrow too. Maybe the rest of the shoot." An image of Joey flashed in her mind and she had the sudden urge to drive to the airport and head home.

"Sounds good, Boss," Francis said. "You know me, I was born to cook on the trucks. I'm used to living tight."

Penelope punched him lightly on the bicep through his puffy jacket. "Let's just stay close, do our work, and get out of here. You hear from the police again?"

"Nope," Francis said.

"Good. You still might." She told him briefly about the incident the night before.

The rest of her team was huddled nearby, their limbs stiff,

hands wrapped around their coffee cups for warmth. "Yo, let's get set up. Usual breakfast," Francis called to them.

They broke into two teams and hustled under the tents and into the truck. The two in the tents were on salads and cold sides. The truck team would cook off a few sheets of bacon in the oven, whip together the egg mixture they'd use for omelets, and shred potatoes for their signature hash browns. Breakfast was the easiest meal of the day since most crews liked the basics, what was essentially diner food. They'd make pancakes and waffles, get the cast and crew fed, and get them to set for their long morning of filming ahead. Penelope pulled a large chalkboard from the storage area beneath the truck and started writing up the morning menu in colorful chalk pens.

A few minutes later she stepped inside, breathing in the warmth from the grill and ovens and pouring herself another coffee. The radio chirped from her back pocket. "Go for catering."

"Penelope, will breakfast be ready in an hour?" Jennifer's voice crackled.

"Good morning, Jennifer." Penelope sighed. "Yes, no delays."

"Good. Just a head's up, not sure what the day will be like, considering the news. We might get some lookie-loos from town."

"What news?" Penelope asked.

"They ran a story about Jordan's murder in the Indianapolis paper. The news has been picked up by the AP too. It's all over."

"Oh no," Penelope said. Her attempts at putting aside the events of the previous day drifted away.

"Just be on the lookout for press, anyone unfamiliar wandering around on set. Remind your crew to keep comments and opinions to themselves. If someone from the press does show up, refer them to the media coordinator."

"We have stanchions if we need them, right?" Penelope said. "This is the first set I've worked on where we haven't had to keep onlookers behind ropes."

"Another reason Forrestville was an appealing location. It's not so appealing anymore."

"Right," Penelope said.

"I'll be down soon," Jennifer said and signed off.

Penelope clipped her radio back onto her pocket and climbed into the cab of the truck, which doubled as her mobile office. She swiped her iPad to life and searched for the story.

Local Celeb Chef Murdered blared the headline. Penelope read the whole article, which told her nothing she didn't already know. A professional picture of Jordan, his familiar smile in place, accompanied the article. There was no mention of the previous night's break-in or the vandalism at the restaurant.

Sighing, she closed the article and ordered the replacement part for her oven, then sent an email to the placement office at her culinary school, briefly describing the head chef position at Festa. Afterwards she rested the iPad on her lap and closed her eyes, resting her head against the seat. She felt like she was suffocating, that control of things was slipping away, and she had to regain her footing, hold tight to her team and loved ones. The feeling of being accused or held responsible in some way for what was happening was constantly nipping at the back of her mind. She opened her eyes and set her jaw, resolving to regain her footing before climbing back down from the cab and getting back to work.

CHAPTER 17

"You think I'm bad. Admit it," Jackson Wilde said.

"I don't think you're bad. You're my precious little boy," Arlena responded, folding her hands together at her waist and pacing the carpet in her long black dress.

"You don't think I'm evil, then? Possessed?" Jackson asked in a challenging tone.

"How does a child speak of such things?" Arlena asked.

Jackson smiled at her sweetly from the school desk in the corner of the room as Arlena paced, but his smile was tinged with darkness.

Penelope stood next to the craft-services table, holding a silver tray with two peanut butter banana smoothies. She watched the scene they'd been filming all morning unfold again from just behind the camera line along with a dozen other crew members. The clapboard under the assistant director's arm said it was the fifteenth take of the day. The crew was filming on the ground floor of the event space adjacent to the inn. They'd cordoned off a corner and the set designers had transformed the space into a vintage playroom, complete with a study area with bookshelves, desks, and a small chalkboard. The frosty light seeped in from two large picture windows, casting Jackson and Arlena in shades of blue. Stage lights lit the corner of the room from the opposite direction, one of the production assistants holding up large round filters in front of them as Arlena and the children moved around the space.

"Continue your lessons, and don't speak of evil again," Arlena scolded the boy.

Dakota, who had been waiting just outside camera range for her cue, skipped onto the rug and began teasing her brother. "I've just had the most lovely walk with Mrs. Grose, and she gave me some sweets. Too bad for you, in here studying like always."

Jackson shot his sister an evil look, then his face went slack and he looked back down at his desk.

"Take your seat, young lady," Arlena scolded her. "I'll speak with Mrs. Grose again about playing favorites, and what's expected of you both during the day."

Dakota took her seat and smiled sweetly, her eyes cutting across the room to find the camera.

"And cut," Jennifer said quietly from behind the monitor she was staring into. "We're going to do this one again after lunch. Everybody reset before you break." She pressed a button below the monitor and marked the sheet she held in her lap with a red pen, jotting a note in the margin of the script.

The crew members reset the scene, rolling up cables, sliding cameras back to their starting positions, and raising the boom mic in the air.

Jackson and Dakota hurried to Penelope, eyeing the smoothies.

"One second," Sybil said, plucking the straw from one of them and touching the bottom of it to her tongue, shaking her head immediately after tasting it. "This is peanut butter. I specifically asked for almond butter. Peanuts are garbage nuts. Almonds are much more nutritious and better for their skin." She plopped the straw back through the hole in the lid, the plastic on plastic screeching loudly.

Penelope's cheeks burned. "Sorry. Who did you give today's menu requests to?"

"I don't know," Sybil said, waving her hand in annoyance. "One of your people. A man with black hair in a chef coat that said Red Carpet Catering. You're supposed to be the best, according to Jennifer." She smiled sarcastically and sniffed. Penelope was distracted by her perfectly applied makeup and styled hair that cascaded in symmetrical waves over the shoulders of her designer jacket.

"I'm sorry for the confusion. I'll have new drinks made right away."

Sybil huffed, clearly perturbed. Her green eyes darkened a shade as she took a step toward Penelope. "Jackson and Dakota have been working all morning and have earned their treat. Get it right." She turned away and gazed at her children, who were still looking longingly at the smoothies.

"Ms. Wilde," Penelope said. "Would the kids like some tomato soup and grilled cheese for lunch?"

Sybil turned back around and smiled, which somehow didn't feel inviting. "I gave your man a weekly menu for my children. Please don't deviate from my wishes or I'll file a complaint with the studio. Jennifer might think you're the best, but one call from me will get you thrown off this set."

Penelope gave her a small smile and nodded pertly. The children stood perfectly still behind their mom, listening to every word she said. "Of course, Ms. Wilde, whatever you say."

Sybil knelt down to straighten Dakota's socks, tugging the lace flat against her ankles above her Mary Janes. Jackson put his hand on his mother's back and stroked her shoulder. She smiled up at him and he gave her a quick hug. Sybil rubbed her cheek against his and brushed his bangs from his forehead.

"I'll be right back with your smoothies," Penelope said. The children eyed her cautiously, neither of them speaking.

Arlena caught up with Penelope as she walked outside, heading for the food truck.

"What's for lunch?" Arlena asked.

Penelope sighed. "Roast beef or chicken, mashed potatoes, mushroom and leek risotto, shaved asparagus, our usual salad bar."

"Yum," Arlena said, throwing an arm over Penelope's shoulder.

Penelope took comfort from the closeness and let go of the tension from her conversation with Sybil.

"You were good in that scene with the kids," Penelope said. "Very natural."

"I guess," Arlena said. "I can never tell if Jennifer is happy with my work. She's not giving a lot of feedback, and she always seems on edge."

"Well, there's a lot going on, with Jordan and everything," Penelope said.

"True," Arlena agreed. "But she's been like that since we started. She's changing the script and dialogue constantly. What I'm reading and saying now, it barely resembles the book anymore. I read the story and the script before I signed on to the movie, and I could follow the thread. Now she's deviated so much from the original, it's like I agreed to a different project. Or this one under false pretenses."

"Are you unhappy with the way the movie is going?"

"I mean, I guess it's okay," Arlena conceded. "I want to support her, I'm just not sure we're heading in the right direction. We're wearing period costumes, but the rewriting of the dialogue sounds modern."

"Are you having what they call 'creative differences'?"

"Not yet, but..." Arlena tailed off with a nervous laugh. "Hey, have you ever seen those shows about haunted houses...ghosts? They say a place can have bad vibes, that they can radiate from a physical space."

"I suppose that's the definition of a haunted house," Penelope said. "People have been telling ghost stories for hundreds of years." Penelope glanced around the courtyard and thought if she removed the food trucks, the electrical fixtures, and the contemporary clothes of the movie crew that were milling around them, she could picture herself in the 1800s. The cobblestones, the old stone buildings, the remoteness of the location, and the sprawling forest right next to them. She shivered. "I have to get new smoothies blended for the kids. Their mom-ager was displeased with our first effort, so I need to redo them on the fly. See you later?"

Arlena nodded distractedly, lost in thought as she wandered

toward the inn. Penelope knew Arlena liked to immerse herself in the roles she played. The fact that she was thinking the inn and surrounding area might be haunted was not surprising.

Penelope had made it all the way back to the kitchen truck when she heard Arlena scream. Penelope jolted and her arms went rigid, causing her to drop the smoothies on the ground, the lids popping off as they hit the cobblestones. Thickly blended banana and peanut butter oozed at her feet. Looking up from the mess, Penelope saw Arlena being twirled around by her boyfriend, Sam Cavanaugh, her arms wrapped around his neck and her legs around his waist.

Sybil sidled up to Penelope and looked at spilled smoothies, then at Arlena and Sam. "So they really *are* together. Good for her," she said with interested admiration. "I wasn't sure if they were for real or just a publicity couple."

Penelope bent down to pick up the plastic cups, tossing them into the trash can near her truck. "They're the real thing, all right."

"Isn't that nice," Sybil said with a sly grin, openly eyeing the couple who were now hungrily kissing each other in the middle of the courtyard. "Whenever you have those drinks ready will be great. Sorry if I was a little rough on you back there. It's already been a stressful day." She turned on her high heels and headed back to the set, not waiting to see if her apology was accepted.

Arlena skipped lunch with the crew, her first time since she'd been on this set, preferring to spend her break with Sam in the suite. Penelope sent up a tray for them with two lunches, and a note to call down if she and Sam needed anything else. Penelope smiled as she arranged the platter, thinking how happy Arlena had been when she saw Sam after almost six weeks of being apart. Working on location could be fun—it was always an adventure and an interesting way to see different parts of the world. But it did take you away from your loved ones for long stretches of time, months at least, sometimes close to a year, depending on the movie.

Penelope's thoughts moved to Joey. Would their relationship be strong enough to endure her career if she had to be away for months at a time? Maybe she would have to limit herself to taking local jobs, things that kept her close to home. New York was a major filming area, so she thought she could probably work it out if it came to that. Penelope didn't know many married couples who kept the hours she did, and she definitely didn't know of anyone with small children who did on-set catering. She was sure there were a few, somewhere, but imagined it would be hard to balance a personal life and children with the demands of a film schedule. She sucked in a breath and put her hand on her lower stomach.

Her phone buzzed and she felt a twinge of dread when she saw the name. "Hi, Ava."

"Penelope, hi. Just wondering if you've heard from your school about potential replacement chefs?"

"Yes," Penelope said, resisting the urge to roll her eyes. "I got an email this morning listing a couple of potential candidates."

"Great," Ava said. "And will you have time later to come and learn Festa's menu?"

Penelope put her hand to her forehead. "Is it okay with the sheriff? I thought the kitchen would still be closed."

"No, he released it an hour ago. They came through and dusted for fingerprints, did whatever they were doing, poked around. We're not going to open back up to customers right away, but I'm hoping we will in a few days."

Penelope sighed. "Um, sure." She thought about what her evening might bring. Hanging out with Ava for a couple of hours wouldn't be the worst option, especially since Arlena would likely be busy with Sam. "We're supposed to wrap at four. I can come over afterwards."

"Perfect. See you then," Ava said.

CHAPTER 18

Up in her room after Jennifer called a wrap on the day, Penelope slipped out of her Red Carpet Catering sweatshirt and soiled chef pants, dropping them in the hamper outside the bathroom door. Pulling on a clean pair of pants and undershirt from the bureau, she went to the closet and sorted through her chef jackets, choosing her short-sleeved red one. When she put it on, she felt something in the interior pocket.

"Crap," Penelope said, remembering she'd stuck the check she'd found in there and then forgotten about it. She made a mental note to call Denis when she got to the restaurant.

Penelope placed the well-seasoned filet mignons into the smoking hot cast-iron pan. The steaks would only need two minutes on each side and then another three minutes in the oven to reach the perfect temperature. She wrapped a white kitchen towel around the handle of the sauté pan on the next burner and picked it up, flicking her wrist and causing a wave of mushrooms to somersault in the air and land back in the pan. She rolled them around a few more times and threw in a sprig of thyme and a dash of sea salt. Eyeing the menu she had taped beside the service window, she mentally ticked off the items she'd practiced cooking that evening. She felt confident that, with the support of Jordan's kitchen crew, running a service at Festa wouldn't be terribly difficult. If she could stay awake through it.

"Order up," Penelope mumbled to the invisible wait staff on

the other side. "Ava, dinner is served at the bar," she called toward the closed office door behind her, nodding when she heard Ava's faint response. The kitchen floor had been cleaned, but Penelope could still make out the vile scratches on the walk-in door. She hoped Ava was in there looking up how to buff them from the metal. Penelope slid the warm plates through after placing the steaks and mushrooms on top of a smear of golden parsnip puree. She used a towel to wipe the rims, eyeing her work carefully to make sure everything was perfect.

Penelope walked the plates through the empty dining room and sat them on the bar, which had also been cleaned since the break-in. Ava had lost some of her anxiousness after watching Penelope whip through the specials menu, calling on her restaurant line-cooking skills she hadn't used since working in a small restaurant back home during high school. Ava had left it up to Penelope to sort through the refrigerator and pantry to see what they'd need to order for their eventual reopening, tucking herself into the office to work on reports and payroll.

"Dinner's ready," Penelope said again, poking her head into the office when Ava didn't appear at the bar.

Ava pulled her eyes from the computer, her hand clawed over the mouse on the desk. "Smells great," she said, clicking a few more times and standing up.

They sat at the bar and ate, Ava making appreciative sounds as she chewed her steak. The glass shelves along the mirror behind the bar were nearly lined with liquor bottles, the glass reflecting the symmetrical flow of white tablecloths in the dining room. The bottles looked like soldiers awaiting instructions.

"Have there been any updates from the sheriff?" Penelope asked.

"About..."

"The break-in. Does he have any idea who might have done it?"

Ava shook her head and swallowed a piece of steak. "Kids, that's what he thinks. Like you said."

"That's so stupid," Penelope said. "How did they get in?"

"Apparently, one of them had a key," Ava said darkly. "Which reminds me." She pulled a single key from her jeans pocket and slid it across the bar to Penelope. "The front and back are the same now. New locks went on this afternoon."

"So the theory is it's someone who works here?" Penelope asked.

Ava closed her eyes and sighed. "I hope not. I would hate to think someone we have in our inner circle, our family, would hurt us that way. Even if it was just a prank, it was pretty ugly."

"I guess it could be anyone who's ever worked here, or any family or friends of former employees, if they got hold of a key and made a copy," Penelope said.

"I know. The locks hadn't been changed in years, since we took over, actually," Ava said.

Penelope took a bite of parsnip puree and thought about the wait staff. There were four of them, all friendly from what she could tell. They were all in their late teens to early twenties and seemed like a tight group of friends. She'd never noticed anything off about them, but then again, she didn't know them very well either. She assumed that would change by some degree the following evening.

"Jordan's funeral is Monday," Ava said.

"I'll let Jennifer and the crew know. I'm sure some of them would like to go and pay their respects," Penelope said.

Ava nodded. "I already told Jennifer. She acted like she wasn't going to give anyone the time off to go, but I think she thought better of it."

Penelope rolled her eyes.

"She's been under a lot of pressure. I'm not sure what's going on with her."

"I'll just stay quiet," Ava said.

"I'm sure you've known her much longer than I have," Penelope said.

Ava shook her head and ate a forkful of puree. "No, I hardly know her at all. Jennifer, Jordan, and Megan grew up here. I met

Jordan in culinary school in San Francisco. I moved here to work with him on the restaurant, and by then Jennifer had moved."

"You opened Festa together?" Penelope asked.

"Yeah. We started with the diner on Main Street, then took over this place."

Ava waved around the room with her fork.

"You don't cook?" Penelope said, taking another bite of steak.

"No, I manage the business side. I didn't go to school for culinary arts. I have a certificate in hospitality management."

"Do you miss California?" Penelope asked.

"Yes," Ava said without hesitation. "And now with Jordan gone, I feel aimless. He was the reason I came here. Now I don't know what I'll do." She twirled the tines of her fork on her plate.

"It's a lot to think about," Penelope said. "Don't try to figure everything out at once or make big decisions while you're upset. The restaurant is doing well, so you still have that."

Ava looked down at her plate.

"Hey," Penelope said. "I'm sorry. I shouldn't have brought all of this up."

"I'm okay." She smiled weakly. "This is a very grand meal, Penelope, but it's missing something." Ava slid off her stool and walked behind the bar. She bent down and Penelope heard wine bottles clinking together. "This will make it truly fabulous," she said, setting an expensive cabernet on the bar. Penelope recognized the label, the swan with its wings in the air forming a circle.

"That reminds me," Penelope said, watching Ava open the bottle. "Denis left a case of samples behind. I stored them underneath in the corner."

"He's on vacation this week, somewhere near Chicago. He said he was leaving his work phone behind, destressing at some retreat for sales professionals." Ava looked down on the floor then back up at Penelope. "You said it's under here?"

"Yeah," Penelope said as Ava filled two large goblets with wine.

Ava set a glass in front of Penelope and came back around. "There's no wine down there. Someone must have moved it."

"We're the only ones who have been in here, except the police. Do you think whoever broke in stole the case of wine?"

"Why would they only take one case of wine?" Ava asked, looking at the rows of liquor bottles on the shelves in front of the mirror, doing a quick inventory.

"I know, it doesn't make any sense," Penelope agreed.

"Nothing makes any sense right now. Let's not worry about it. If it was just samples, it wasn't in the inventory. Hardly a loss."

"Still, I'm heading into town tomorrow. I'll swing by and tell the sheriff so he can add it to his report."

"Fine, if you want to," Ava said. "I don't want to think about it right now. Let's talk about something more cheerful. What's the latest gossip in the world of entertainment?"

Penelope looked at her incredulously. "You're asking the wrong person. I barely have time to sleep, much less keep up with that kind of thing."

Ava took a sip of wine. "You live with an A-list celebrity actress. I'm sure you hear things."

Penelope shook her head. "Nothing lately. Arlena's not really into gossiping."

"Well, how are things going on the set?" Ava asked.

Penelope groaned. "Ugh, I'd rather talk Hollywood gossip."

Ava laughed quietly. "Sorry. Let's talk about the weather."

"No," Penelope said. "It's going to snow, I think."

"Oh man," Ava said. "Okay, let's just drink wine and forget about everything."

Penelope nodded. They clinked glasses, but Penelope felt less than cheerful. She tried to put off the feeling of dread in her gut, her mind trying to grasp onto something she couldn't quite put her finger on.

"I am going to tell Sheriff Bryson about the missing wine. Maybe it will help."

Ava took a healthy sip from her glass. "Sure, sounds good." She swirled the ruby liquid in her wineglass, not seeming to care one way or the other.

CHAPTER 19

Penelope knew it was going to happen before it did. She thought she might have been the only one who was ready when Jackson Wilde opened his mouth to say his line on the schoolroom set the next morning, then snapped it quickly shut. Penelope saw the boy's stomach lurch in and out, undulating like a snake under his white button-down shirt and gray flannel pants. His face lost all color and his eyes grew wide right before he opened his mouth and barfed all over Arlena's skirt.

"Ah!" Arlena cried, jumping back from Jackson in alarm.

"Sorry," the boy said weakly, putting his hands on his knees and retching again.

A collective groan passed through the crew surrounding the set. Penelope looked away from the pile of vomit at the boy's feet after her own stomach did a lurch. Dakota screamed, and then she threw up too. Penelope couldn't tell if it was a reaction from seeing her brother getting sick or if she was also ill. She ran through what the kids had eaten for breakfast, reassuring herself everything they'd been served was fresh and safe.

"What's happening?" Jennifer shouted as she stood up.

"I'm sick," Jackson whimpered. Sybil rushed to him and hugged him to her side, aiming his face away from her wool slacks as he heaved again.

"My poor darling," Sybil cooed, putting a hand to his forehead. "He's burning up. Call the medic, you idiot," she said to the assistant director, who clearly wasn't prepared to be the target of her anger. Stunned, he looked helplessly at Jennifer.

"Call him. We obviously have a medical emergency," Jennifer said, defeated.

Arlena pinched the fabric of her skirt with her fingers, holding her wet dress away from her legs, and looked sadly at her young costars.

"It must be the flu," Sybil said, placing a palm on each of their foreheads before crossing her arms in front of herself. "They've both got fevers."

"Mommy, help," Dakota said, and began to cry. Sybil wrapped her arms around her children and shuffled them away from the set toward the inn.

"Perfect," Jennifer said, throwing her clipboard to the ground. "I suppose Sybil had no idea they were sick before they came down this morning."

The assistant director spoke quietly into his phone to the medical team on set and gave Jennifer another helpless glance.

"I guess that's a wrap on the day." Jennifer stalked off, not bothering to pick up her notes.

The frazzled AD hung up and retrieved her clipboard, then gathered the crew around. "I'm sorry about this, guys," he said. "Tomorrow will be better." He apologized in general terms for Jennifer's reaction to the situation and instructed everyone on how to prepare the set for the next day.

Skylar hurried to Arlena. Without saying a word, she uncovered the zipper at the back of her dress, pulling it down to her waist and easing the costume from Arlena's shoulders. Sarah stepped forward and opened a thick bathrobe in front of Arlena, shielding her from the room as she stepped out of her soiled dress. After being freed from her clothes, Arlena cinched the robe tightly at her slender waist.

"Poor kids," Arlena said when she caught Penelope's eye. "Jackson said something about not feeling well at breakfast, but when I asked him if he was okay to do the scene he said absolutely."

"It seems like kids get hit with bugs out of nowhere," Penelope said.

Arlena felt her own forehead. "I really don't want to get sick right now."

"You do look a little flushed," Penelope said.

"I just got barfed on," Arlena said, sighing. "Not an experience I'd recommend. I'm going to get cleaned up and enjoy my free time as much as possible."

"You and Sam have fun," Penelope teased her. "By the way, how are your dad and Max doing out in the woods?"

Arlena rolled her eyes. "Daddy's loving it, but Max feels like he's being punished."

"For what?" Penelope asked.

"Maybe not punished—more like Daddy feels like he didn't spend enough time with any of us growing up, so he likes to do these immersive activities once in a while. Make up for lost time."

"It's nice he likes doing stuff with you guys," Penelope said a bit wistfully.

"Yeah, we're lucky. Anyway, they'll be at the inn later. Unless Daddy changes his mind and decides to keep roughing it out there. I'll call and let you know."

Penelope balanced a small tray on one forearm and knocked quietly on the door to the second-floor suite where Sybil was staying with her children. She heard someone padding to the door and stepped back as it opened a few inches, holding the tray in both hands. Sybil leaned out of the door, a look of concern on her face.

"Penelope," Sybil said, glancing back over her shoulder. "What can I do for you?"

"Nothing," Penelope said. "I brought some chicken broth. Organic," she added hastily as Sybil eyed the cloches on her tray. "And some saltines and ginger ale for Jackson and Dakota."

Sybil's expression softened and she opened the door all the way, waving Penelope inside. "That's very kind of you."

"Of course," Penelope said, pushing aside some papers on the desk in the main room and setting the tray down. "How are they?"

Dakota called for her mother from the bedroom. "Excuse me a minute," Sybil said, hurrying to her daughter. Penelope peeked inside when she opened the door and saw the little girl lying in bed, propped up with bright pink pillows and surrounded by stuffed animals. A cold compress lay across her tiny forehead and her cheeks were the same shade of pink as the stuffed unicorn she had tucked under her arm. Sybil closed the door, and Penelope listened to her comfort Dakota with soothing tones. Penelope revised her opinion of Sybil in that moment. Seeing her caring for her children convinced her that she did have a heart.

A folder on the desk caught Penelope's eye and she nudged a piece of paper on top of it over with her index finger. "Herring – Steele" was jotted on the top edge of the folder with a series of numbers underneath ranging from $10,525 down to $5,525. Penelope squinted at the folder, trying to remember where she'd seen the name of the company before. Just as she remembered it was the same name on Denis's check, the bedroom door opened and Sybil stepped back through, squirting hand sanitizer onto her palm.

"Thanks again for the soup," she said, picking up a towel from the floor and refolding it a few times as she talked. "Dakota is nodding off now, my poor girl. Jackson fell asleep almost immediately when we got back. The set medic came up right away, diagnosed it as the flu. He's a kind man, really was concerned for the children."

"That's good. I'm sorry they're so ill," Penelope said, feeling a sudden urge to wash her hands again. Or just take another shower. "Please let us know what they'd like to eat when they're ready. Anything at all, we can do it."

Sybil smiled gratefully, then glanced at the door. "I'm going to lie down myself. You must save your strength when the little ones are sick. It can be very exhausting, especially if they're up all night."

"I'm sure," Penelope said, heading for the door. "I'm heading into town in a little bit. Can I get anything for you or the kids?"

Sybil shook her head and murmured goodbye, closing the door

softly behind her. Penelope heard the lock click and stepped quietly back down the hall. Her phone buzzed in her pocket and she pulled it out to read a text from Ava, telling her dinner service was on at Festa for that evening. Penelope sighed and continued down the hall.

CHAPTER 20

Penelope drove her new company truck into town, the Red Carpet Catering logo painted on the side. The large SUV was a recent addition to her fleet of vehicles, and it came at a good time, since they were working in a location with no other way to get around besides driving. The pantry truck was harder to park and burned way more fuel, not practical when she wanted to zip off quickly to run a few errands.

Main Street in Forrestville consisted of five sidewalk-lined blocks, the post office anchoring the east end of town and the police station on the opposite end. In between sat a vintage-looking diner, a hardware store, a beauty parlor, the newspaper's office, and an old-fashioned general store and produce market that stocked a limited selection of fresh groceries and canned goods. The entire town looked like it had been suspended in time during the 1970s.

Penelope pulled her truck into the space in front of the post office and went inside, the cowbell clanging against the glass door as it drifted closed behind her. No one was behind the desk so Penelope rang the bell, waiting patiently for someone to appear from behind the counter. A corkboard on the wall caught her eye, and Penelope read the various announcements and flyers while she waited. She moved closer when she noticed an array of missing persons posters tacked together at the corners with colorful pushpins. Penelope's eyes moved over the photos and she read the descriptions under each, moving closer and touching the edge of one as she read. There were five missing teenagers on the wall, all from Forrestville, Indiana. They were all similar in age, three girls and two boys, all gone missing in the last five years.

"Can I help you?" An angular woman with dyed blonde hair and a spray-tanned face stepped out from behind the counter, her eyes following Penelope's to the posters. "Looking for someone?"

"No," Penelope said. "I'm picking up an express package, should have arrived this morning."

When she disappeared behind the counter to retrieve their new oven element, Penelope pulled out her phone and took a picture of the flyers.

"Those are the Forrestville Five. Gone missing, all of them," the woman said, placing Penelope's box on the counter and eyeing her phone with a mild look of reproach.

"Who are they?" Penelope asked, tucking the phone back in her pocket.

"Local kids," the woman said, shaking her head. "One by one they up and disappeared. In the forest, most people think. It's not safe up there at night. But try telling the kids that. They don't believe all the scary monster stories our parents used to tell to keep us out of there." She clucked her tongue.

Penelope glanced at the dates again, noting the oldest one was a girl who would turn twenty-two in a few months. The flyer showed what looked like her school photo. "So they all disappeared over a three-year period?"

"Yep. About six months apart, each time," the woman said.

"That's so sad," Penelope said. "What has the town done to find them? They couldn't have just disappeared into thin air."

The postal worker shrugged. "We keep an eye out for them, of course. They had search parties up in those woods for weeks right after each disappearance. There are some strange folks who call the woods their home, transients, homeless camps and the like. Then you have the tourists who come through, hikers out for an adventure, hard to track someone like that. Anyone could have snatched them up. And it's so huge, once you're lost, it's hard to get found again."

"I've been running through there on the trails," Penelope said, suddenly feeling cold. "I've never seen anyone suspicious."

"You go up in there enough times, you'll come across someone. You best be safe when you're out there alone," the woman said matter-of-factly. "You should carry a whistle. If I were you, I'd stick to running through town. Safer." She eyed Penelope up and down, then gazed at the flyers on the wall. "Someone grabs you up there, you're just gone."

Penelope shivered.

"Anything else I can do for you, Ms. Sutherland?"

Penelope took a step back and looked down at the box with her name on it. "No," she said hastily, backing toward the door.

"Okay, you take care now. And watch yourself out there. Trust me, you should."

After placing her package on the backseat of her truck, Penelope slid her hands into her jacket pockets and made her way to the police station. She passed by the *Forrestville Gazette*'s office and peered inside. The lights were off behind the glass window and a tug on the door confirmed they were closed. The latest edition of the paper was in a metal box next to the door and Penelope grabbed one as she walked past, folding the thin tabloid in half and tucking it into her jacket pocket.

Penelope stopped short in front of the hardware store, remembering that they were in need of a new screwdriver for the kitchen truck. She'd watched Francis snap the end off their old one while trying to remove a stubborn screw on a loose sauté-pan handle. She stepped inside and breathed in the scent of sawdust, the wooden floor creaking under her boots. An old man in a plaid flannel jacket and knit hat nodded to her from behind the counter and waved her to the rear aisle when she asked where she could find a set of screwdrivers.

Penelope wandered through the store, glancing at the different shelves, thinking about what else they might need in the kitchen.

When she came to the small selection of household items, she grabbed two sheet pans and a set of metal animal-shaped cookie cutters. Baking cookies would be a fun project on the set, maybe something Jackson and Dakota would enjoy.

When she got to the tool section at the rear of the store, she almost stumbled over a man sitting cross-legged on the floor, sorting through a box and tossing different-sized screws into a collection of plastic bins in front of him.

"Sorry," Penelope murmured as she walked around him.

"No worries," he said, looking up at her with piercing dark eyes. He tossed another screw from the box. "Help you find something?"

"I'm looking for a screwdriver," Penelope said, gazing at the tools, the sheet pans tucked under her arm.

"You're in the right spot," he said in a relaxed manner. He pushed himself up and stood close to Penelope, pointing out the different tools. "This is the best set, if you want to know the truth. Pricy but worth it."

Penelope inched away, putting more space between them, but he immediately moved again, closing the gap she'd created. Penelope picked up the set he suggested. "Thanks, I'll take them."

He turned to her and smiled. "I knew you would. You have a good rest of the day, okay?"

Something about him was familiar to Penelope, something she couldn't quite place. His eyes were so distinctive, she was sure she'd seen him somewhere before. The restaurant, maybe. He began humming a tune and went back to sitting on the floor. Penelope listened as she walked away, the clinking of the screws he tossed providing the beat to the song.

"Ms. Sutherland," Sheriff Bryson said curtly as he emerged from his office. The police station was narrow, uniform in size with the neighboring buildings on Main Street. There was an unmanned reception desk and a few metal chairs lined up against the glass of the front window. A short hallway led to the sheriff's office and a few more closed-off rooms.

"Sheriff," Penelope began, then paused when she saw two young men walk out from the office behind him. Penelope recognized them as one of Festa's waiters and the bartender. "Hey guys," Penelope said. They offered mumbled greetings as they passed by on their way out the front door.

Sheriff Bryson put his hands on his belt and looked at her with a questioning glance.

"What were they doing here?" Penelope asked as the front door swished closed.

"Giving statements," Officer Bryson said. "What are you doing here?"

Penelope shifted the bag from the hardware store into her other hand. "I'm here to report a missing case of wine from Festa. I thought you might need it for your report on the break-in."

Sheriff Bryson motioned for her to follow him to his office. She took the seat opposite him and placed her bag on the floor as he shuffled through the folders on his desk and pulled out what she assumed was the one about the break-in.

"What was it now? Wine?" He closed his eyes and rubbed the lids roughly.

"Yes, from behind the bar," Penelope said.

"You sure it wasn't just misplaced?"

"I don't think so. I thought you'd want to have the complete report of what was damaged and missing," Penelope said.

"Yeah, it's good to have the whole picture," Sheriff Bryson conceded. "Can you describe the case of wine?"

Penelope bit her bottom lip. "No, I'm not sure what the bottles were specifically."

Sheriff Bryson dropped his pen on the desk and leaned back in his chair, hands tucked behind his head.

"Sorry, I didn't look at them," Penelope said. "I can ask Denis, the wine rep, when he gets back to work. Ava told me he's away the rest of the week."

"Okay then, that would be helpful."

"Did you ever ask Denis about the man arguing with Jordan the night he was killed?" Penelope asked.

"We did," the sheriff said cagily. "He says it wasn't an argument he saw, just two guys talking about food. Said you must have heard him wrong."

"What?" Penelope asked. The floor shifted slightly under her feet. "That's not what he told me."

"Sometimes people want to have more of connection to a victim, make themselves important, or part of the events. Happens all the time."

Penelope sat and thought about the conversation with Denis, trying to see where she might have misunderstood him.

"Everything else okay over there? I assume there've been no more incidents," Sheriff Bryson said.

Penelope updated him on the status of the restaurant, Ava's plans to reopen as soon as she could, and about the kids being sick on the set that morning. "I hope it doesn't turn into an epidemic, all of us coming down with the flu."

"Steer clear of them and wash your hands," he said, glancing at a framed photo of his wife and two young sons on his desk. "And if anything else comes up, just give us a call." He pulled a card from his desk drawer and handed it to Penelope. "My cell number is on there. We're a little," he motioned out the door to the reception area, "understaffed at the moment."

"Where's the rest of the team?"

"Edie's at an appointment with her wedding planner. And the rest of the team isn't full-time here in Forrestville. They're a mobile forensic team out of Quincy, a bigger town about forty-five minutes from here. They offer support to the smaller outlying towns."

Penelope prepared to leave, easing up from her chair until a sudden thought made her sit back down and pull out her phone. "Sheriff, I was just at the post office and saw this." She showed him the picture of the missing persons flyers. "Look at this one...her name is Kellie Foster."

The hint of a smile fell from his face. "Terrible thing, all those runaways."

"Is this girl related to Jordan's family?"

Sheriff Bryson rubbed his chin and gazed at the phone. "Yes. She's a cousin, or a niece. Some relation. Not close with the family, from what I remember."

"Really," Penelope said, turning the phone to look at the girl's face. The picture was grainy, and it was hard to make out her features in more than a general way, but she resembled Jordan slightly.

"People run off, troubled young people especially," Sheriff Bryson said, a touch of sadness in his voice. He glanced again at the photo of his family.

"The lady at the post office made it sound like gangs of homeless people are snatching kids off the forest trails."

Officer Bryson sniffed a laugh. "Yeah, Patsy. She does like to spin a tale. Likes horror movies too. I would take whatever she says with a generous grain of salt."

"Have you ever seen anyone suspicious up there? Maybe someone...I don't know, not mentally stable, fixated on Jordan? You know he ran those trails. Someone like that could have vandalized the restaurant. Maybe even killed him."

"Sure," Sheriff Bryson said, nodding. "I guess that's possible, except I doubt a homeless maniac living in the woods off the grid would be organized enough to kill Jordan, then stage it as a suicide, and leave no clues behind." He shook his head and leveled his gaze at her. "More likely this was someone with smarts. Organized."

"If the two crimes are related, the pentagram on the walk-in...doesn't that seem, I don't know, like a hate crime, or like someone who might be unstable?"

Sheriff Bryson rubbed the bridge of his nose. "Kids do stupid things, Ms. Sutherland. Let's not create monsters in our heads when it's probably a much simpler explanation."

"I'm not creating anything. I just feel like there is more than one possibility."

"You know what? I will take what you say under advisement. Now, if you don't mind, I have a lot of work to do." He flicked his eyes at the door of the office.

Penelope rose from her chair and left, mumbling a goodbye on her way out.

CHAPTER 21

As Penelope walked back down the sidewalk, she made a mental list of the things she wanted to accomplish the rest of the day. Lost in thought, she didn't notice the man standing next to her truck until she was half a block away. He bent at the waist with his hands in his pockets and peered through the tinted windows.

Penelope stopped at the front bumper and watched him, a finger of unease drawing a line down her spine.

"There you are," he said when he noticed her standing on the sidewalk. It was the employee from the hardware store who'd been sitting on the floor sorting screws. His fleece-lined denim jacket was buttoned to the top, the cloth apron that read *Fenton's Hardware* still tied at his waist. A memory clicked together in Penelope's head. He was one of the hikers in the courtyard the other morning, the one who held the door for her and told her she was pretty while she struggled with the heavy coffee urns.

"What are you doing?" Penelope asked, clutching the bag from his store in both hands in front of her. He smiled easily and took a few steps toward her.

"Nothing, just saying hi," he said. He closed the space between them quickly and Penelope took an awkward step backwards. "What's wrong?" he asked.

Penelope looked around, but there was no one else on the sidewalk. "Nothing," she said quietly.

"I'm Bailey," he said. "What's your name?"

Penelope hesitated. She stepped around him and walked quickly to the back of her truck.

"Oh, you're shy," Bailey said. Although he made her uncomfortable, Penelope noticed his tone of voice remained conversational, friendly even. "You don't have to tell me. I can find out from the credit-card receipts."

"I'm expected back at work now," Penelope said, flipping up the hatch to the truck and slipping her bag inside. A toolbox was tucked into the side panel of the storage area. She thought about what she could use from it to defend herself if it came to that.

"You're one of the out-of-towners staying at the inn," Bailey said. "From the movie." He pulled a piece of gum from his pocket and folded it into his mouth, tossing the wrapper on the sidewalk.

Penelope looked at the ball of foil and then met Bailey's eyes. "Yes. I'm a department head. I manage one of the crews on the set."

"Nice. You look like someone who takes charge."

Penelope relaxed, deciding Bailey might just be a little off or socially awkward. She didn't feel as threatened as she had a few moments before.

"I'm up that way a lot. I'll look for you next time," Bailey said, chewing his gum and smiling widely at her.

"That's, um...I have a boyfriend," Penelope responded in a clear voice. She wasn't sure if Bailey was hitting on her, or if this was his idea of a normal conversation.

"That's okay, I don't mind," Bailey said, smiling even wider. "You're nice. And pretty."

A sharp whistle caught Bailey's attention and caused him to turn around, much to Penelope's relief. The old man from the hardware store stood in the doorway, hands crossed over his chest. He put his fingers to his lips and whistled again.

"My old man says break's over," Bailey said. He turned on the heel of his tan work boot and started toward the store, then stopped suddenly and turned back around. "You never told me your name."

Penelope just stared, saying nothing.

"Not going to say, huh?" Bailey said. For the first time his expression darkened, a momentary flash of something else beneath his boyish features. "That's okay. Like I said, I can find out."

Penelope watched until he stepped inside the door, shrugging his shoulders at his father when asked a question Penelope couldn't hear. The old man adjusted his knit hat and shot a glance at Penelope, openly gaping at her from the doorway. Penelope fought the urge to scramble inside the truck and speed away. She made a U-turn on the deserted main drag and drove slowly back toward the inn. When she glanced in the rearview mirror, she could see the old man was still watching her.

CHAPTER 22

That evening, Penelope's first dinner service at Festa was underway. Several of the guests had cancelled their reservations, which was unusual. But these weren't usual times. Ava said some of them gave vague answers when asked why they wouldn't be coming in, but she figured Penelope had been right about some people being uncomfortable about Jordan's murder, even though it hadn't happened in the restaurant.

Jordan's crew slowly re-acclimated to the kitchen, working their first shift without their head chef at the helm. Their mood was subdued, but they worked well, with no major issues for Penelope to handle. Two hours in, with things in the back running smoothly, Penelope went around to the service area to observe the wait staff. The whole staff was on the floor, not saying much, at least when they were around Penelope, once in a while throwing her a curious glance.

Conversation among the guests in the dining was hushed, the diners speaking in reverent tones. Penelope had only dined at Festa on the occasional night off, but she remembered the mood inside the restaurant being more jubilant.

One of the waitresses bumped into Penelope as she hurried to pick up one of her table's dishes from the window.

"Sorry," Christine mumbled, not looking at Penelope.

"It's okay," Penelope said. "How's it going out there?"

The girl's expression was stony. Her shoulders rose beneath her starched white uniform shirt. "Okay, I guess."

"How do you think everyone is holding up?" Penelope asked. "You're the senior staff member, right?"

Christine eyed the plates of food in the window. "I don't know. Good, okay? I have to get this to my table." She swept around Penelope and loaded up a large oval tray, expertly propping it on her shoulder and hurrying through the swinging doors into the dining room.

"This place is like a funeral home," Penelope whispered to herself as she headed back into the kitchen. She unlocked the office door and slipped inside, telling the sous chef to come get her if they got a sudden rush, which she doubted. He agreed, keeping his eyes on the ticket machine in the window just below a picture of himself and Jordan, laughing and holding up glasses of wine.

Penelope closed the door and called Ava's cell phone. When she didn't answer, Penelope left a message. "Ava, hi. Things are going okay at Festa tonight, although the mood is pretty somber. I think the staff is unhappy. It's not affecting the service, just wanted to let you know. Maybe we've asked them back too soon. Things might change after tomorrow, when they can pay their respects and Jordan is laid to rest. That's it. Call if you need me."

Penelope sighed and hung up the phone, then logged onto the computer on the desk. She thought about her afternoon trip to the hardware store and creepy Bailey and his equally creepy father. Something about the young man seemed so familiar, but she couldn't put her finger on it. His personality was off-putting, but he was handsome in a dark hawkish kind of way. She Googled him, but without his last name she didn't get a good result. She sat back against the office chair and thought, then leafed through some paperwork on the desk. Suddenly it hit her and she sat up straight.

Penelope typed "Forrestville Devil Worship" into the search tab and the article she'd already read appeared again. She scrolled to the photos of the three men and looked into Bailey's eyes, his picture the one on the far left. She read the article more carefully, a feeling of dread building in the pit of her stomach with each word.

Bailey Fenton was the ringleader, it seemed. He and his

friends vandalized several cars in Forrestville and spray-painted pentagrams on dozens of trees in the forest, as well as an abandoned barn. The crimes were misdemeanors, and they were fined and ordered to perform community service as punishment. The one on the left was named Kevin Helmsley, which also rang a bell. Someone had mentioned something about a Helmsley to her recently, and she filed through recent conversations to remember. She then remembered that was the name Megan said caused the most recent scandal in town, the one who died with illegal pictures on his computer. She made a note to look up the Helmsley incident, find out if there was a link.

Penelope found Sheriff Bryson's card and stared at his cell number. She had no proof it was Bailey who broke in and vandalized Festa's kitchen, but she had a strong suspicion it was him. She sat the card on the desk, deciding she'd call him in the morning. It wasn't an emergency. Plus, she wasn't sure of what she'd even say. A man had made her feel uncomfortable on a public sidewalk. It wasn't a crime, however edgy the interaction made her feel.

She folded her arms on the desk and tapped her fingers against the wood, then typed in one more name: Kellie Foster. Several images popped onto the screen in a row, of very different-looking women. Penelope added "Forrestville Five" to the search box, which narrowed it down, the photo Penelope had seen from the flyer appearing first. She clicked on the first link listed, an article from the Indianapolis paper. She read quickly about the high-school basketball player and her sudden disappearance, and the background about the other missing young people from the area.

Penelope whistled quietly as she read, clicking on different articles to try and find out more about Kellie. A picture appeared of the high-school basketball team, which Penelope figured had been taken around the time of Kellie's disappearance, five years earlier. She was standing in the middle row on the end, her long thin arm hooked around a basketball propped on top of her hip.

"Troubled kids?" Penelope whispered. She sat back in the chair and gazed at the photo, her eyes drifting over the other faces until they stopped on one. Penelope sat forward and squinted to read the caption again, confirming the girl in the back row's name: E. Collins.

A sharp knock on the door startled her. "Come in," Penelope said after clearing her throat.

"Someone here to see you," the sous chef mumbled through the crack.

"Thanks," Penelope said. "Wait, who is it?"

He opened the door wider and shrugged, flipping a kitchen towel over his shoulder. "No idea. Christine said someone at the bar is asking for you."

The ball of unease in Penelope's stomach turned into a hard fist. She stood up and squared her shoulders. "It's a crowded restaurant," she said to herself as she watched him walk back to the line. She decided she'd peek out through the service doors, and if it was Bailey she'd turn around and call Sheriff Bryson after all.

Penelope pressed the swinging doors open with her fingers and peered through the gap. Her face broke into a smile when she saw the man sitting at the end of the bar.

"Joey!" Penelope said, rushing to his side.

Joey stood up from his stool, arms open wide. Penelope crushed herself to his chest, feeling his strong arms wrap around her tightly. She tilted her head up to him and they kissed.

A smattering of applause made them both laugh and Penelope stepped back from him. Her cheeks burned red and she said, "Thank you," to the nearby diners, who smiled appreciatively at the couple.

"What are you doing here?" Penelope asked. "I thought you were getting in tomorrow."

"I couldn't wait," Joey said. "I switched to an earlier flight."

Penelope took his hand. "I've never been so happy to see you. Honestly. The last few days have been..."

"I know. Whatever you need, you know I'll help."

Penelope kissed his cheek and squeezed his hand. "Hungry?"

"Always," Joey said.

"1 only have to be here another hour or so," Penelope said. "This is the last reservation block."

"I'll wait for you, of course," Joey said.

Penelope kissed him quickly and nodded at the bartender as he slipped a menu in front of Joey. "He's a VIP."

CHAPTER 23

Penelope woke the next morning and gave Joey a sleepy hug before getting out of bed. Her throat was dry from staying up late and talking for hours, so she drank a bottle of water while she looked out the window at Festa. Penelope had filled Joey in on everything that had been going on the past few days, while he updated her on how things were going back home.

"Where'd you go?" Joey murmured from under the down comforter.

"I have to get ready for work," Penelope said, her voice raspy. She got back in bed and slipped under the covers, pressing herself into him. After a few minutes of bonus cuddling, Penelope reluctantly pulled open the drawer on the nightstand and retrieved her phone, sitting up in bed as she read the long list of messages that had come through during the night. The first one at the bottom of the list was from Jennifer. *No work today (Monday). Arlena, Jackson, Dakota and I are under the weather. Flu. Please take precautions and stay healthy. Jen.*

Clearing her throat, Penelope swallowed, feeling tenderness in her throat and trying to judge if she was also coming down with a bug.

"They're all sick?" Joey asked, pulling the sheets up comically over his mouth and nose and widening his eyes.

Penelope swatted the sheet away playfully. "Unfortunately, yes. Your stay at the Forrestville Inn must be taken at your own risk."

A thought coming to her, Penelope grabbed her iPad and

searched for the Forrestville Helmsleys, the ones she had come across the previous evening.

"Oh man, this is awful," Penelope said. "The sheriff prior to Bryson had a heart attack at his desk while looking at underage pornography on a state-owned computer."

"What a scumbag," Joey said, playfulness forgotten.

"Yeah, and his son was one of the ones arrested with that Bailey kid for vandalizing cars and trees." Penelope continued to read through the article. She'd told Joey the night before about her encounters with Bailey.

"Good thing that Helmsley guy is dead," Joey said. "He wouldn't have had a fun time in prison. Where's his kid now?"

Penelope sighed. "Looks like he's in jail for some other crime in Indianapolis. Attempted robbery and kidnapping. Jeez." She tilted the screen toward him so he could read along.

"But Bailey is out walking free," Joey said. "These articles are all from other cities—this one's from the Chicago paper."

"I know." Penelope reached back over to the bedside table and pulled out the thin tabloid she'd picked up in town the day before. "This is the local paper. More like a flyer, mostly ads."

Joey took it from her and scanned the front page, then leafed through a few pages.

"Do you think you can do me a favor?" Penelope asked. She pulled up the photos on her phone of the missing persons flyers and showed them to him. He sat up and rested the newspaper in his lap on the comforter. "Can you look into these kids, I don't know, more officially than I can? Particularly Kellie Foster. I think there's something happening here."

Joey looked at her, his eagerness to please her dampened by doubt.

"And you think it might tie in with Jordan's death?"

"Maybe," Penelope agreed. "The restaurant, the inn, the forest, they're all so close together, and Jordan was such a big part of the community."

"I can try, but I'm probably not going to find much more than what's already known. If they're registered on the national missing persons list...you're looking at the info there."

"No, I don't mean we should try and find them. Wait, I take that back. I'd actually love to try and find them. I'm really curious about who they are, what they did here in town before they vanished, what they might have had in common. Is there a way we can do that?"

Joey pulled her close and kissed her. "Yes. We can ask questions. You're good at that," he teased.

"Hey," Penelope said. "This is really important." Her eyes fell to the newspaper and she picked it up. "That's Jacob Pears," she murmured, looking at the small photograph of the bald man in round wire glasses.

"Who's Jacob Pears?" Joey asked, looking at the photo. "Besides editor-in-chief of this...paper?"

"All I know is he's not a fan of Festa," Penelope said, eyeing the picture more closely.

"Okay, you've convinced me. I want to help."

"I know," Penelope said. "Oh, Jordan's funeral is later today."

"I'll go with you," Joey said.

Penelope thought about the old church across from the police station on Main Street, and then about Bailey at the hardware store. She'd told Joey about her suspicions that Bailey was involved in the restaurant break-in and vandalism, and Joey agreed she didn't have enough evidence to pursue the issue with the sheriff. He was concerned for Penelope's safety and suggested she steer clear of Bailey.

"I'd really like to be there for Jordan and his family," Penelope said. "And maybe we can find out something about Kellie Foster too."

Penelope texted Francis, making sure the crew knew they had another unexpected day off, then popped her phone back in the drawer. "I'll check on Arlena later, make sure she's okay. I don't want to wake her up if she's resting."

"Too bad she's sick on her birthday," Joey said.

"Yeah," Penelope said. "The birthday celebration will have to wait, I suppose. For a few reasons now."

"I can't believe Randall and Max are camping in this weather," Joey closed his eyes and a shiver passed over his body.

Penelope grimaced. "I'm still waiting for them to come in from the cold."

"I'd be back inside after an hour," Joey said. "Your work is done for the moment, right?"

Penelope put her finger to her chin and thought. "Yep."

Joey pulled her back down next to him under the comforter and flipped it over their heads.

CHAPTER 24

Penelope and Joey entered through the paint-chipped double doors of the church and slid into a pew on the left side of the aisle. Mourners settled in their seats around them, whispering hushed greetings to each other as somber chords played from an organ in the corner. The front two pews had black ribbons clasped to the ends, sectioning them off for Jordan's family and close friends.

Penelope recognized a few faces, but there were many more she'd never seen. All four members of the wait staff from Festa walked up the center aisle together, easing into a pew on the right. Once they were settled they sat very still, a contrast from how she'd seen them in the weeks before, happily rushing around the restaurant and laughing easily with each other.

Joey laced his fingers with Penelope's and gave her hand a squeeze.

The music suddenly got louder as the organist launched into a choppy version of "Amazing Grace." Megan, her four children, and a few other relatives filed into the church from the vestibule behind the altar and silently took their seats. Megan wore a black suit and a small tasteful hat with a thin black veil atop her stiff blonde hair. She appeared calm, her back rigid against the wooden pew, with Karen and Kyle on either side of her, clutching her hands.

Penelope glanced around, noting most of the pews were nearly full. A few members of the film crew were in the back rows, including the assistant director, who appeared to be staring at something in his lap. Penelope hoped he wasn't texting, or if he was, that he would stop when the service began. Sheriff Bryson sat across the aisle from them in his uniform, serenely gazing at the podium on the altar.

The doors of the church opened and Penelope's eyes widened when she saw Bailey enter and saunter up the aisle. He tucked into the end of a pew a few rows behind Penelope and Joey.

"That guy is here," Penelope whispered.

"Who?" Joey asked.

Penelope squeezed his fingers. "Bailey, from the hardware store. He's in the gray flannel shirt, black hair, a few rows back."

Joey looked around casually, then pulled a hymn book from in front of him and flipped it open. "He's staring at you."

The back doors clattered shut again and Penelope resisted the urge to turn around. The song ended and an uneasy silence fell across the congregants as the pastor took his place behind the podium.

"Friends, we are gathered here today to say farewell to one of our own, Jordan Foster, as he passes from this place on to the next."

Penelope watched Megan bow her head, and her shoulders began to shake. Karen circled her arm around her mother's shoulders. Penelope closed her eyes and bowed her head, bringing to mind an image of Jordan, one that was happy and full of life. Thinking of him brought an unexpected wave of emotion over her, and she lightly chewed the inside of her cheek to keep from crying. She couldn't understand how someone could kill him and cause so much sadness for his family. Penelope opened her eyes and looked at Karen, deciding then she would try to help them in whatever way she could to find out who had done this to them.

The hair on Penelope's arms raised when she heard someone behind them trying to suppress a laugh. She and a few other people turned to see Bailey, his face bright red, clearly muffling giggles behind his hand.

Bailey caught Penelope's gaze and he lowered his hand, then grinned at her. Penelope's eyes swept to the sheriff, who she saw had also turned to see what the commotion was.

"We want Megan and the whole Foster family to know our community holds you in our hearts during this time of tremendous sadness," the pastor continued, squinting at the pews through his black-framed glasses. His silver hair was parted on the side and slicked down, his forehead shiny from the billowing heat from the furnace.

Another round of choked laughter caused a few people behind Penelope to shush Bailey, which only caused him to go into further hysterics.

Penelope felt a building anger warming her chest. She glared at Bailey, then caught sight of his father tucked behind one of the doors in the entryway. His face was inscrutable as he stared stonily at the back of his son's head.

"Excuse me, Mr. Fenton, but you might be more comfortable outside," the pastor said, breaking from his prepared remarks.

More people turned to look as Bailey wiped tears of laughter from his eyes. Bailey's father stepped out from behind the doorway and walked to the pew, hitching Bailey up to his feet by his elbow. The old man's expression was one of alarm, but Penelope thought she also saw fear or maybe embarrassment there.

"Let's go, son," he said firmly as he led Bailey out of the church.

Penelope's heart pounded and she turned to Joey, who raised his eyebrows, silently questioning if she was okay. She nodded and inched closer to him, pressing her side into his. A weight lifted from her shoulders when the church doors rattled closed again. Megan hadn't moved from her seat or turned around during the episode with Bailey, although all of her children had, their reactions ranging from irritation to sadness.

"I'm very sorry for that terrible interruption," the pastor said, shaken. He looked down at the podium and cleared his throat, steadying himself before continuing.

He waved to the organist, who looked back at him in alarm, not sure what he was asking her to do. After another rigid wave from the pastor, her fingers flew to the keyboard. A soft hymn rose from the pipes while the pastor shuffled his papers and took quick apologetic glances at the Fosters.

"Fenton," Penelope said in a whisper.

"Hmm?" Joey asked, straightening his tie.

"I just remembered I know someone else with that last name." Penelope craned her neck around and looked for Marla, the innkeeper, not seeing her anywhere in the pews.

CHAPTER 25

Penelope caught up with Sheriff Bryson outside the church as the mourners filed from the doors to the line of cars waiting to follow the late-model hearse out front to the nearby cemetery. The sheriff peered down at Penelope from beneath his wide-brimmed hat.

"Have you thought about questioning Bailey about the break-in at the restaurant?" Penelope asked. Joey stood off to the left, listening to their conversation.

Sheriff Bryson glanced at Joey, waiting for an older couple to pass by before responding.

"Look," Sheriff Bryson began after a beat, "I know what happened in there was inappropriate. He's a troubled kid. His dad does the best he can with him, keeps a close eye." He threw a glance in the general direction of the hardware store.

"You have his prints on file, right? Can you check and see if they match up with any you took from the restaurant?" Penelope asked.

Sheriff Bryson sighed. "We didn't get any usable prints out of Festa's kitchen that night. Whoever it was must have worn gloves."

"Well, there's the connection of the pentagram, like in his previous case, and he could've gotten the paint from the hardware store. Can't you at least talk to him? Maybe ask his dad where he was both nights?"

"Excuse me," Sheriff Bryson said, beginning to walk away. He turned back and said, "I've known the Fentons all my life. Bailey's a little...he's no criminal, not the way you're saying."

"If it's not him, then who did it?" Penelope asked, taken aback.

The sheriff shook his head. "I know you're trying to help, and I'm sure you think you're doing just that. But you need to stay out of our investigation." He threw Jocy a glance then stalked away, heading in the opposite direction of the police station.

Penelope hoped some of what she said had gotten through and that he was going to the hardware store after all.

Megan Foster emerged from the church surrounded by her four children, linking arms with the two younger kids. Penelope caught her eye and Megan excused herself, walking stiffly over to her and Joey.

"Thank you for coming," Megan said in a calm voice. She'd folded her veil down to shade her red-rimmed eyes.

"Megan, we're very sorry for what you've been through," Penelope said.

"Jordan is gone now. Hopefully he can be at peace. But his legacy will live on." She glanced at her children. "You're helping with that."

Penelope looked at Joey, unsure how to respond.

"You're a lifesaver," Megan said. She put her hands on Penelope's forearms and pulled her closer into a not-quite-touching air hug.

Megan's oldest son, Kyle, who looked like a younger, thinner version of Jordan, appeared at his mother's side and placed a hand on her elbow. "It's time to go, Mom," he said gently, steering her toward the waiting limo.

"Thank you, Kyle. Penelope knows how important your dad was," Megan said, motioning at Penelope. "She knows."

"It's okay, Mom," Kyle said. His twin sister, Karen, joined them, taking her mom's other arm. Once they got Megan inside the limo, Karen closed the door and walked back over to Penelope.

"Can I come by the restaurant?" Karen asked.

"Sure," Penelope said, confused. "It's your family's place, you're welcome anytime."

"There's something I want to talk to you about," Karen said, before sliding into the limo next to her mother.

* * *

Penelope and Joey walked back toward Penelope's truck. She'd parked on the opposite side of the street, as far from the hardware store as possible.

"Let's stop in here for a coffee," Joey said, peering in the diner's front window.

"Okay," Penelope agreed a bit reluctantly.

The restaurant had a retro feel, but Penelope thought that was how it always was, not remodeled to look that way. She darted glances at the stools and under the counter, noticing that although the space must have been over sixty years old, it was clean and looked to be lovingly cared for. Penelope caught their reflection in the chrome linings of the stools as they passed, which had all been polished to a sparkle.

As a gray-haired woman in jeans, a sweatshirt with the diner's logo faded on the front, and a loosely tied apron led them to a booth along the wall, Penelope noticed Festa's wait staff in the rear booth next to the kitchen doors.

"I'm going to say hi," Penelope said as Joey settled onto the cushioned bench and picked up the plastic menu.

"Sure," he said, flipping through the pages.

"Hi, guys," Penelope said as she approached the table. "Everyone doing all right?"

Dressed all in black, the four of them looked up at her with wide eyes and blank expressions, except for Regina, who stared at the table. Her dark red hair was parted severely on the side, her pale bluish scalp showing through.

"Rough day, huh?" Penelope said when they didn't answer.

"Yeah, you could say that," one of them said.

Penelope glanced back toward her table, seeing Joey was still reading the menu. "I'm going to be working at the restaurant for a little bit. If any of you need anything, please ask. I know no one can take Jordan's place, but if I can help..." She felt awkward, as if she was speaking a different language based on their reactions.

Regina put her elbow on the table and rested her head on her palm, looking up at Penelope with a doleful expression. Christine, who was sitting across from her, kicked her under the table, causing her to sit up straight and throw the girl a dirty look. Regina immediately went back to resting her head lazily on her hand.

"Okay, got it," the youngest waiter said with a smile. He picked up his coffee mug and took a sip, flashing his bright blue eyes at Penelope. The waitress emerged from the kitchen door balancing several plates on her arms. Penelope stepped aside as she set the food down, cheeseburger platters with fries for the boys, a tuna melt for Christine, and a spinach salad for Regina, who reluctantly sat upright and gazed at the bowl of greens in front of her.

"Okay, I'll see you guys," Penelope said, turning to go.

"See you," Christine said, sticking a French fry in her mouth and chewing hungrily.

As Penelope walked away, she heard hushed laughter from the group but didn't react, choosing instead to make them think she hadn't. She slid into the booth across from Joey.

"This is such a strange place," Penelope said.

Joey looked around at the walls of the diner.

"I don't know, looks pretty standard to me. A little old, maybe."

"Not this place. This place," Penelope said, motioning with her arms in a wide circle. "This whole town."

Joey smiled and set his menu down. "Penny Blue is homesick."

Penelope sighed and picked up the menu, trying to put aside all of the awkward encounters she'd experienced lately. "You still want coffee?" She looked at the pictures of French toast and burgers beneath the plastic cover.

"Yeah, and a BLT," he said.

"What can I get you?" the waitress said, tapping a pen on her light green pad. They made their orders, Penelope sticking with coffee, her appetite gone. "Be right out," the woman said and turned to go.

"Wait," Penelope said. "You look familiar."

"Been working here all my life, feels like anyway," the woman chuckled. Her teeth were a lighter shade of gray than her hair.

"No, I saw you the other day, on my way to the Foster house," Penelope said. "You're their neighbor?"

The woman hitched her apron up and nodded.

"Yep. Well, up the road a piece. That's the mail drop there at the end of the lane. That also feels like forever, us living on that icy road."

"How long?"

The woman blew out a sigh. "Thirty years, next June."

"That is a long time," Penelope said.

"You know, it's a terrible thing that's happened to that family," the waitress clucked, glancing in the direction of the church. "Just terrible."

Penelope remembered the woman's slow wave by the mailboxes, her eyes sweeping over the car, studying them as they drove past.

"Your sandwich will be right up," she said before walking away to greet a newly arrived customer.

When Penelope and Joey walked past the newspaper office, the lights were on.

"Hang on a second, I want to stop in here," Penelope said.

"I'll wait for you at the truck. I'm going to call in to work," Joey said.

"Hello?" Penelope asked from the empty reception area.

"Back here," a man's voice called from the rear.

Penelope walked past a gathering of empty desks into an office at the rear of the building.

"How can I help you? Want to take out an ad?"

"No," Penelope said. "I'm the chef on the movie set over at the inn. Are you Jacob Pears?"

His expectant expression stayed in place as he acknowledged her question with a nod.

"I was wondering...I saw a restaurant review you wrote about Festa several years ago."

He didn't speak and continued to stare.

"Did you happen to come in the other night to update your review?" Penelope asked. "I'm curious because I'll be helping out there for a while. If we can put together a special dinner for you..."

Mr. Pears shook his head and waved his hand. "No, that won't be necessary. I don't backtrack on my reviews." His head was completely round, his silver hair combed over to complete the circle effect. Even his glasses were round.

"I see. Isn't that a little— "

"Mrs...."

"Sutherland. And it's not Mrs."

"Ms. Sutherland. This is my newspaper. I run it as I see fit. The review stands. If I decide to review again, I will not let you know. It will be a surprise, as all impartial restaurant reviews should be. I hardly think my opinion of a restaurant is what you should be focusing on, especially on a day of mourning such as this."

Penelope shook her head. "You were seen arguing with Jordan that night."

"And?" Mr. Pears said. He remained defiant, but Penelope could see doubt behind his eyes.

"What were you arguing about?" Penelope asked.

"None of your concern," he said. He rose from his chair and motioned her toward the front door. "And it wasn't an argument. It was a discussion."

"A discussion about what?" Penelope persisted, standing her ground.

He sighed when she didn't make a move to leave. "If you must know, he asked me to retract my earlier review, replace it with a positive one. I told him no. He didn't like that."

"And then?" Penelope asked.

"Nothing. I left. And he went back inside and continued to push overpriced food on unsuspecting diners, take advantage of his community, and live up to his self-proclaimed hype."

"Mr. Pears, it sounds like you have a personal problem with Jordan, beyond what you think about his restaurant," Penelope said. The bell on the front door jangled and he looked expectantly toward the sound.

"Thank you for stopping by, Ms. Sutherland," he said, more forcefully ushering her out this time. Penelope reluctantly turned to go, nodding to a woman waiting in the foyer before going back outside.

CHAPTER 26

When they arrived back at the inn, Joey headed upstairs to change out of his shirt and tie and Penelope went to look for Marla. Not finding her in the office, she checked the kitchen, which remained empty and unused. Penelope opened the door to the basement in the hall opposite the kitchen door, an earthy wet smell greeting her as she descended the stairs. Marla was tucked in a corner of the large room doing laundry, wringing out a set of sheets and hanging them from a line suspended in the air.

"Marla," Penelope said, causing the shadow behind the sheet to jump. The industrial washer hummed in the corner, drowning out other noises.

"Penelope, you gave me a start," Marla said. She wiped her forehead with her sleeve, sweat glistening her short hair. "We've got twice the laundry to do today, what with all the sick people upstairs."

"Who else is sick?" Penelope asked.

"Let's see, there's at least ten of your folks up there now with different degrees of the flu. Some just feeling lousy, some who can't get out of bed." She shrugged. "It's that time of year, I suppose."

Penelope put her hand to her throat and swallowed again, grateful for not feeling any soreness. "We just got back from Jordan's funeral." She looked down at her black dress, as if it would explain perfectly where she'd been.

Marla picked up a wet sheet and shook it out, jerking it to and fro in her thick hands. "I'm not much for funerals, myself," she said as she worked. "Ask me, families should be left alone at a time like that, not have everyone they know come and gawk at them while they try not to cry." She hung the sheet across the line, inching the first one over to make room.

Penelope glanced at the dryer in the corner. "The young man from the hardware store, Bailey, was there. Made kind of a scene during the service. Do you know him?"

Marla's face tightened. "Of course I know him. He's my nephew."

"So, his father is..."

"My brother," Marla said. "That's typically how that works."

"Right," Penelope said, taking the woman's sarcasm in stride. "Have you ever known Bailey to be...violent?"

"Can't say that I have," Marla said quickly, snapping another wet sheet in the air. "Why would you ask a thing like that?"

"I read an article about him getting arrested and was wondering if he might have had something to do with the recent break-in at the restaurant," Penelope said matter-of-factly.

Marla scoffed. "Well, I can see how you might think that, you trying to put two and two together and whatnot." She shook out another sheet from the basket, a frown on her face. "Bailey just fell in with the wrong crowd. He's impressionable, got talked into doing something stupid. He's made up for it."

"The article I read made it sound like he was the ringleader," Penelope said.

Marla snorted a laugh. "That's a lie. You must know you can't believe everything you read in the paper." She picked up a wet towel and wrung a few drops of water from it onto the floor. Penelope took a step back.

Marla turned to the washer as it stopped spinning, pulled the door open, and dropped a pile of damp sheets into the wicker basket at her feet. She twisted her mouth into a smile and softened her voice. "Bailey's no threat to anyone, Penelope. He's a good boy, wouldn't hurt nobody. Now, go on back upstairs. There's lots to be done."

"Okay," Penelope said. "Thanks." When she was halfway up

the wooden staircase she looked back down at Marla, who was shaking her head and muttering under her breath, twisting the last drops of water from the sheet in her hands.

CHAPTER 27

Back upstairs, Penelope found Joey on the bed with his eyes closed, her iPad on the comforter next to him. She stepped quietly out of her shoes and unzipped her dress, laying it across the back of a chair and shivering as she pulled on a pair of yoga pants and a sweatshirt. She eased onto the bed next to Joey, pulling the crocheted blanket at the edge of the bed over both of them after setting the iPad gently on the nightstand. Penelope inched closer to him and closed her eyes, listening to his regular breathing and feeling the warmth between them build beneath the blanket.

Penelope tried to clear her head and relax, but her thoughts kept slipping back to Bailey, the way he stared at her and his maniacal laughter at the church.

After a few minutes, she gave up, deciding she was too keyed up for a nap. She slid over a few inches so she wouldn't disturb Joey, whose breathing had slowed as he'd fallen into a deeper slumber. Grabbing the iPad from the nightstand, she swiped it to life and searched "Herring – Steele Inc." Over three hundred results came up, so she added "Indiana" to narrow it down. She clicked on a few of the links, pulling up a car dealership, a stationary business, and what looked like a lawn and garden company. They all had one or two elements of the name, but not the whole one.

Penelope then pulled up the article about Bailey she'd found in the *Forrestville Gazette*. She read it more carefully this time, searching for any similarities to the vandalism at Festa. The only thing both crimes had in common was the pentagram, which

Penelope had to admit was a common symbol for rebellious kids, not at all unique to rural Indiana.

Penelope's eyes stopped mid-sentence when she came across something she had missed the last time she read the article.

"Bailey Fenton identified himself as *Defensores Cibum* to arresting officers, and demanded the name be used by his attorney. Mr. Fenton would not respond unless addressed by his self-appointed alias."

Joey stirred next to her and opened his eyes. "Hey, there you are," he said sleepily. His eyes slipped closed and he reached out for Penelope, pulling her into a hug under the blanket. Penelope set the iPad aside and snuggled into him, breathing in his sandalwood cologne.

"I tried to nap with you," Penelope said, "but I can't rest."

"I know, you're not a good napper," Joey said. "What were you reading?"

"The article about Bailey's arrest a few years ago," Penelope said. She suddenly felt drowsy, like she could actually fall asleep. "He called himself something weird, *Defensores Cibum*. Like a superhero name or something." Her voice trailed off and she pulled the blanket up to her chin.

"Come on, you remember Latin class at Immaculate Heart, don't you?" Joey asked, nudging her a little.

"Stop," Penelope said, burrowing under the covers. "Kind of, not really."

"Cibum is meat," Joey said. "I remember that much."

Penelope's eyes popped open and she sat up in bed. "Defender of Meat? That's what he called himself?"

"Sounds like it," Joey said, trying to pull her back down.

"Then it's got to be him," Penelope said urgently. "That fits with the animal-rights messages, the whole paint as blood thing."

"So the kid doesn't like to eat meat," Joey said. "That doesn't prove he trashed the restaurant, Penny."

Penelope sat up and swept the blanket back. "Jordan was a hunter, served meat that he killed himself at Festa," she said, her words coming quickly. "If Bailey thought he could save more animals by killing Jordan..."

Joey propped himself up on an elbow. "Okay, you might have something there," he admitted. "But how do we prove it? I didn't get the feeling that sheriff was interested in pursuing Bailey as a suspect."

"I'm not sure," Penelope said. Her phone buzzed on the table and she grabbed it. "Text from Arlena. She's feeling better, but not one hundred percent. Sam isn't sick."

"He's made of steel, that guy," Joey said.

Penelope started to text her back when another message came through. "See you later?" from Ava.

Penelope blew out a sigh and responded a quick "yes" before putting the phone down and flopping backwards onto the bed. "I never should've agreed to this. I'm needed at the restaurant again tonight."

CHAPTER 28

Penelope dreaded going into Festa that night, not a feeling she was used to at all. She loved working as a chef, spending days with her crew on different sets. The time she was spending at Festa confirmed she'd made the right career choice after graduating from culinary school. Penelope had a lot of respect for restaurant chefs, but her preference was to be on the go, not working in the same kitchen night after night. Even though it was temporary, Penelope couldn't wait for this particular favor to be over.

She took a breath and reset her attitude, deciding her feelings were more to do with Jordan's death, and the fact that Joey, not to mention Arlena, her best friends in the world, were in town and she couldn't spend as much time as she'd like with them. She decided to stay positive and help Festa get through another dinner service, then have a talk with Ava about stepping aside and letting the current staff take over. She was confident they could.

Christine and Regina were in the service area adjacent to the kitchen, huddled in the corner and speaking to each other in low voices. Regina pulled the strings of her apron tightly around her waist as Christine adjusted the collar on her shirt. When Penelope got closer, they stopped talking and hurried to finish getting themselves together.

"How are you guys doing?" Penelope asked. She picked up an almost empty box of the dark green half-sized straws Jordan preferred to use at Festa and grabbed the remaining few. She handed an unopened box to Christine and motioned to her to add the ones in her hand to the full one. "Marry these up, will you?"

"Sure," Christine said, taking the straws from her with an overly enthusiastic smile. Regina remained quiet, averting her gaze from Penelope.

"What are tonight's specials?" Penelope asked them.

"Um," Christine said, looking up at the ceiling to recall. "Venison stew?"

Penelope shook her head and directed her next question to Regina. "What's your guess? We went over this week's specials last night, remember?" Penelope wasn't sure why, but putting them on the spot made her feel some sense of power shift back to her.

Regina looked up from the floor at Penelope, and, to her surprise, burst into tears. She sprinted from the service area through the dining-room doors. Christine's mouth hung open as she watched her friend hurry away.

After an awkward moment, Penelope said, "I'll go check on her."

"Regina's just…" Christine paused. "She's taking everything really hard."

"That's understandable," Penelope said. "I think we all are. I'm not just asking how you're doing to make conversation. I'm concerned about you guys."

"That's…thank you. It's been hard to be here, you know?"

"Yeah," Penelope said. "I get it. I'm going to go check on Regina."

Penelope scanned the dining room and saw no sign of her, only Jeremy behind the bar cutting lemons and limes into wedges. He waved his knife and rolled his eyes in the direction of the ladies' room when Penelope asked if he'd seen Regina come through.

"Hello?" Penelope said, entering the room.

"I'm in here," Regina answered testily.

"What's going on?" Penelope asked, keeping her tone light.

"Leave me alone," Regina said. She was leaning against the pink-tiled wall next to the sinks clutching a paper towel. She wiped her eyes and nose angrily every few seconds.

"Would you like to go home?" Penelope asked, meeting the

girl's eyes in the mirror. "If you're too upset to work, you're excused."

Regina wiped her nose again. "Don't you think it's messed up any of us are here at all?"

Penelope didn't want to admit to her the thought had crossed her mind. "Look, I know things aren't easy right now, but they will be again. The family wants to keep things going, make sure you all continue to get paid regardless of their personal tragedy."

Regina rolled her dark green eyes, swiping a smear of mascara from her cheek as she glared into the mirror. "Right. The family. Bunch of money grabbers, if you ask me. They're probably hoping Chef Jordan gets more famous now that he's dead so they can squeeze even more cash from his corpse."

Penelope crossed her arms in front of her and leaned on the bathroom wall. "That's a little harsh, Regina. You can't know how Mrs. Foster or any of them are feeling."

Regina scoffed. "Yeah, right. I know exactly."

"You know, you don't have to stay. If you don't feel comfortable working for the family, no one can stop you from leaving."

Regina tossed the wet ball of paper towel into the trash and pulled off a fresh sheet from the dispenser. "You can stop talking to me like you're my boss," she said, raising her voice. She pulled a tube of eyeliner from her pocket and began to draw thick circles around her eyes.

"Speak to me respectfully, regardless of what you think is fair," Penelope said, maintaining her gaze in the mirror.

"Whatever," Regina said dismissively. "You'll be gone soon, like everyone else."

"You know what? You should go home," Penelope said. "You're obviously too upset to work a shift on the floor."

"You can't send me home," Regina said. "You're just some bitch from New York."

"Get out," Penelope said, keeping her voice even. "I'll let Ava know you won't be working."

Regina turned and stared at Penelope, a small smile playing on her painted lips. "Fine. Good luck without me tonight."

She pulled off her apron and dropped it on the bathroom floor before taking a wide arc around Penelope and stomping through the door.

Penelope felt the sudden urge to laugh, a surge of adrenaline making her skin feel tingly. She'd never fired anyone before, and even though she hadn't officially done it now, it felt like she had. Penelope ran her hands through her hair and retied her ponytail before heading back into the dining room. She caught a bit of conversation as she got closer.

"...thinks she can tell me what to do," Regina was saying. A murmured response came from Jeremy, noncommittal from what Penelope could make out. "She's a bitch," Regina complained.

"That's enough," Penelope said. "You should be going, Regina."

Jeremy busied himself by polishing a glass, looking like he wanted no part of the conversation.

The girl slapped the handle on the front door of the restaurant and went through, throwing one last dirty look at Penelope through the glass.

CHAPTER 29

Halfway through dinner service, Penelope handed the service window over to the sous chef and went out into the dining room. They were down to two servers who had to cover all the tables on their own. Luckily for them, but maybe unluckily for the restaurant, the seating was sparse, with many more cancellations that night than the one before.

Christine looked at Penelope apologetically when she saw her on the floor, but kept her expression neutral when speaking to the guests.

Joey sat at the bar, a frosted glass of amber-colored beer in front of him. He talked easily with Jeremy, who leaned straight-armed on the wood between filling drink orders.

Penelope stepped up behind Joey and tapped him on the shoulder.

"There's my girl," Joey said. "Jeremy here was just telling me he's taking a semester off school to save money, working here as much as he can."

"Good for you," Penelope said. "What are you studying?"

"Criminal Justice over at IU," Jeremy said.

"He's going to be a lawyer," Joey said, taking a sip of beer. Some foam stuck to his upper lip and Penelope resisted the urge to wipe it off.

Jeremy chuckled. "Maybe, or a police detective. We'll see if I can save up enough to pay for law school. By the way, I'm running low on a few things." He held up an empty bottle of wine, then rattled off a couple of other items he needed. Penelope squinted at the label then jotted down the name on a small pad in her apron and headed back toward the kitchen.

"Penny," Joey said catching up to her and pulling her into the restroom hallway.

"What's up?" Penelope asked.

"Something weird. I ran those five names you gave me in all the usual places. There are no files to be found on any of them."

"That is weird. What does it mean?" Penelope asked.

"Besides the national registry of missing persons, there are no local police files on those missing kids, none that I can find anyway. I have a call into a guy on the job in Indianapolis, a friend of a friend."

"So it's like a clerical error?"

"I could see a clerical error if it was one, maybe two files. Not all five," Joey said. "Anyway, I'll keep looking."

"It's such a well-known case," Penelope said. "Seems like there should be lots of records on the missing kids."

The front door opened and Randall and Max Madison blew inside, shaking the cold from their coats. Max headed immediately to the bar with Randall right behind him. Jeremy froze when he saw the two famous actors approaching.

"Hey, guys," Joey said, coming back around the corner with Penelope. He shook Max's hand. "Wow, you're freezing."

Randall's laughter boomed as he pulled out a stool and eyed the bottles of liquor behind the bar. Max sat down next to his dad and hugged himself, his teeth chattering.

"What are you doing here?" Penelope asked. The few tables scattered nearby ceased their conversations and stared openly at the father and son duo at the bar.

"I told Dad if we didn't get inside and have a decent meal, and a decent drink, that I was going back to New York tonight," Max said.

Jeremy found his voice. "What can I get you, gentlemen?"

"I'll have a bourbon, neat," Randall said, shrugging out of his coat.

"Same," Max said. He took his father's jacket and his own to hang in the outer vestibule while Jeremy slid menus in front of their seats.

"Poor kid," Randall said, chuckling. "He made it a couple of days. Pretty good, I have to admit, with this cold."

"Are you going back to your campsite after dinner?" Penelope asked.

"Um, no," Max said, still chattering after returning to his stool.

"I think I got the general idea of what it's like to almost freeze to death," Randall agreed. "I feel I'm prepared for the role."

"Better you than me," Joey said.

Randall picked up his tumbler of bourbon. "Max has been complaining the entire time, but I think overall it's been a good experience. Crazy enough, we're not the only ones out there."

"Who have you seen?" Penelope asked.

"We've come across a couple of camps on our hikes."

"You see any bears?" Joey asked.

"No," Randall said with clear disappointment.

"These camps," Penelope said. "Were they campers like you guys or more like homeless people?"

Randall considered. "A little of both, now that I think about it. You know, you'd like it out there." He flipped open the menu. "It's good to unplug once in a while, get back to nature."

"That's not a bad idea," Penelope said.

Max rubbed his hands together and took a sip of his drink. "Arlena said everyone is sick at the inn, but that you were over here cooking. A Penelope-cooked meal is just what the doctor ordered."

"You got me there, kid," Randall agreed. "I do love your food, Pen."

The front door whooshed open and Sybil walked in, clutching a dark green scarf with a matching leather-gloved hand.

"Sybil, how are Jackson and Dakota feeling?" Penelope asked, helping Sybil off with her camel coat and hanging it in the vestibule with the others.

"Much better, thank you," Sybil said with relief. "I talked the assistant director into keeping an eye on them tonight so I could venture out for a proper dinner."

Penelope laughed when she pictured the nervous young man, who always seemed at a loss for what to do around the kids, wrangling the two young actors into bed.

Sybil stopped short when she noticed Randall at the bar. "Randall Madison, after all these years."

Randall did a half turn on his stool and eyed Sybil, his face breaking into a wide grin. "Have we met?"

Sybil blushed and adjusted her scarf. Penelope thought she looked lovely, considering she'd been holed up in a room with two sick children the last couple of days. She was dressed casually in skinny jeans and a sweater, but Sybil always looked pulled together.

"We were in a movie together many years ago," Sybil said.

"Wait, I remember," Randall said. "Sybil Wilde. You're on that soap opera, right?"

"Was," Sybil said, waving a hand. "And I can't believe you actually remember me. I had a bit part with one line in *Murderous Night*. I was on the set for two days, playing the hotel clerk who checks you in during the opening scene. It was my first movie."

"But I do remember. I never forget a beautiful face," Randall said. He stood up and took her hand, bending to kiss the back of it. Max tossed Penelope an amused glance from behind his back.

"Sybil," Randall said, releasing her hand. "My son, Max, and I were just about to have dinner. Would you care to join us?"

Sybil smiled gratefully. "That would be lovely, if you're sure I'm not intruding."

"Of course not," Randall said, not consulting Max before answering. "And this is our friend, Joey. Four is a nice round number. Let's all of us get a table."

Penelope led them to a spot near the fireplace. After they were seated, Christine handed them menus and told them about the specials, her hands tucked pertly together at the small of her back.

Penelope retreated to the kitchen to check on the chefs and let them know about the newly seated VIP four top.

"Ava's here," the sous chef said as he pulled an order ticket from the machine.

Penelope stuck her head inside the office. "Celebrity-laden table has just been seated by the fire. They're causing a bit of a stir in the dining room."

"Really?" Ava said, looking up from the screen. Her eyes were puffy and she'd pulled her hair into a messy bun on top of her head.

"Randall and Max Madison, my boyfriend, Joey, and Sybil Wilde," Penelope said. "Also, we need to do a wine order. They're low on a couple of bottles at the bar."

Ava sat up in her chair and pulled the elastic band from her hair, letting the dark locks spill over her shoulders. She pulled a mirror and a tube of lipstick from the desk drawer, applying the dusty-rose gloss to her lips then rubbing them together to smooth it out. "I'm going to send them a complimentary bottle."

Penelope was used to people acting star struck around Arlena and her family, but it still amused her when it happened. "Sure. I know they'll appreciate that."

Ava brushed a few strands of loose hair from her sweater and headed to the dining room. Back at the service window, Penelope slid tickets across the silver strip, expedited orders, and dressed the plates for the servers, stepping back to the grill to sear off steaks and pork chops when needed. The kitchen hummed along with the sounds of clanging pans and low chatter, the crew moving like a well-oiled machine. Penelope glanced down the line at the chefs, dressed in crisp white, and knew for certain they didn't need her. A head chef would eventually have to be brought in to guide them, keep the menu fresh, and create new specials, but maintaining where they were right now wouldn't be difficult for this crew.

After calling out the order for Randall's table and watching Christine load up her tray, Penelope followed her out to the dining room to oversee the service. Ava was standing at the table, and Penelope watched her laugh and toss her hair over her shoulder. Her hand rested on the chair behind Sybil's back as she listened to one of Randall's stories.

When the food was served, Ava stepped back, telling them to enjoy and thanking Penelope. She brushed Sybil lightly on the upper arm as she left, and Penelope watched the actress glance at her sleeve after Ava departed.

"I'm so happy right now," Max said, eyeing the plates in front of him. He looked hungry enough to polish off his own dinner and everyone else's too.

Penelope topped off their glasses, emptying the bottle of wine Ava had brought them as she listened to Christine explain their entrées. When she'd finished, Penelope carried the empty bottle to the bar and set it down. "Another of these, Jeremy."

"That's not one of our usual bottles," Jeremy said, shaking his head at the label. "Must be from Ava's private stash."

"Private stash?" Penelope asked. She recognized the swan logo and the name of the wine, *Cygne Reseau*, as one of Denis's brands, and thought again about the missing box of wine samples.

Jeremy slapped a towel over his shoulder. "It's not in my stock."

Penelope took the empty bottle back to the kitchen. When she saw the office door was closed, she went to knock, then paused, glancing down and rolling the green glass back and forth in her palm. She opened a cabinet below the service window and tucked the empty bottle out of sight, then headed back out to the bar to select another label for her friends.

CHAPTER 30

The next morning on the set, Penelope fought back her third yawn in five minutes, putting the back of her hand to her mouth and squeezing her eyes tight. She opted for another cup of coffee, which would be her fifth, and scanned her email inbox on her phone. Her Red Carpet Catering crew was busy setting up for breakfast, their illness-induced break over with all of the talent back on their feet again, including Arlena.

An immense feeling of relief passed over her as she read an email from someone who wanted to try out for the head chef position at Festa. Penelope hoped he would be the one. She'd already decided the previous night was her last official shift. She was still willing to help Ava, but it was time to step back and let her handle things going forward. She thought about the empty bottle of wine now stashed in a cabinet in her kitchen truck. She didn't know exactly what it was that bugged her about it, but something was off. At the very least, it wasn't above board to serve wine that hadn't been brought into the restaurant through a licensed distributor. Something like that could put Festa's liquor license in jeopardy. Even worse, Ava had potentially lied to her about the missing case of wine. Penelope couldn't figure out why she would do that. She'd left another message for Denis to call her the next time he checked his messages.

She typed a quick response to the email, inviting the auditioning chef to come at his earliest convenience.

"Penelope," Jennifer said crisply as she poured herself a cup of coffee from the urn near the truck.

"Good morning," Penelope said, holding back another yawn.

"We've got some suits coming through today," Jennifer said darkly.

"Thanks for the heads up," Penelope said. "Lunch or dinner?"

"I don't know," Jennifer said. "I get the impression they'll be here awhile from the messages I've gotten. Honestly, what they want to eat is the least of my worries."

"Yeah," Penelope said wearily, "but it's good for me to know, right?"

Jennifer sighed. "I know, Penelope. I'll find out. Janie Levinson is the point person, the executive producer they're sending to check on the production. She's bringing a team, like a triage unit." Sarcasm dripped from her words.

"Isn't she married to...?"

"Brock Taylor, yes," Jennifer said, nodding. "She marries a big movie star and gets to be an EP now, I guess."

"I read she was producing before they met," Penelope said. "She hired him on a project after he couldn't get insured by anyone else because of his..."

"Drug problems, yeah," Jennifer said. "He's clean and sober now, funds a treatment center for celebrity clientele. And Janie's been optioning all the hot books lately. Bestsellers, the books everyone is talking about. It's not like she's uncovering obscure material."

"Is it true she and Brock are totally vegan, like almost religious about it?" Penelope asked.

Jennifer shrugged. "Who cares? I just don't want Mrs. Taylor," she sniffed a laugh, "to decide our movie isn't a sure bet, isn't trendy enough to continue supporting."

Penelope watched her stalk away, still half talking to herself and stewing about the executive visit. Penelope had been on a few sets where the money people came through, and it wasn't always a bad thing. Sometimes they just wanted to see how the set was working, if the actors were gelling, and if they were on track to get a return on their investment.

"Each of you come up with your best vegan recipe," Penelope said inside the kitchen truck a few minutes later.

Francis nodded. "You got it, Boss."

"We're getting an important visitor from LA. I'm pretty sure she's strict. And let's think of a variety of options, please. I don't want a bunch of variations on beans and rice."

CHAPTER 31

After filming wrapped for the day, Penelope and Joey sat at the bar of the inn having a drink and deciding what to do with their evening. Penelope had let Ava know about her decision to step back at Festa and offered to help interview the candidates for the new chef. She'd maxed out her energy level, and she was missing too much time with Joey, which was really the deciding factor.

Joey and Penelope clinked their wineglasses and kissed as the fire crackled behind them.

"Get a room already," Sam Cavanaugh said behind them.

Penelope laughed. "Sam! I've hardly seen you at all since you got here. How are you?"

"I'm great," he said, shaking Joey's hand. "I'm glad I found you guys. Arlena's still getting ready for dinner. We're heading," he waved in a general way out the window, "somewhere. Listen, did you still want to do something for her birthday? I know things are weird here right now."

Penelope thought about it for a minute. "I think she'd like to do something with the family. Just you guys, you know? The mood on the set is subdued, to say the least."

Sam nodded, agreeing with Penelope. "I've got something in mind," he said, winking at her. "I'll keep you in the loop."

After he left, Penelope took out her phone and searched the nearby towns for what they could do without going too far. "I don't have to be on set early. We're just doing lunch. Jennifer's scheduled a half day of shooting due to some special visitors. We could get dinner somewhere, come back and watch a movie?"

"Perfect," Joey said, looking down at her phone also.

Ava came through the front doors and into the bar and headed straight for Penelope and Joey. Penelope's heart sank, but she resolved to hold fast to her decision not to work that night.

"Something's happened," Ava said, her eyes wide.

Penelope sighed. "What now? Ava, I'm off work and we're heading out—"

"Regina is gone," Ava said, holding her palms in the air in a helpless shrug.

"Yeah, she probably thinks she was fired," Penelope said. "By me, last night."

Ava shook her head. "No, gone. Like really gone. Her mom just filed a missing persons report."

"Slow down," Joey said. "Tell us what happened."

Ava took a breath before speaking again. "Regina's mom came into the restaurant asking about what happened during the dinner shift. The girl has run off. She's not answering her phone and her car is gone. No one knows where she is. She's underage, only seventeen. When she didn't come home last night her mother called Sheriff Bryson."

"Christine might know where she is. They're close."

"No, she's saying she doesn't," Ava insisted.

"Look, she was upset when we talked, and she left angry. She's probably just blowing off steam somewhere," Penelope said.

"You were the last person we know she talked to," Ava said.

Penelope thought about the young girls on the missing persons posters at the post office and an alarm went off in her mind.

"I'll keep an eye out for her," Penelope said. "What else should we do?"

"I don't know," Ava said, defeated. "I guess pray that you're right and she just took off in anger. I don't want to think about it being something worse."

CHAPTER 32

Penelope had a fitful night of sleep, even though she usually slept well next to Joey. The first rays of sun were peeking in through the window, and she decided a run would help clear her mind. She hadn't been on a good run in two weeks, which she knew always made her feel antsy and out of sorts.

After pulling on her running gear and slipping from the room without waking Joey, Penelope synched her phone's running app and headed to the main trail through the forest, the one she had run a couple of times with Jordan. She had another motive for making the trip. She planned to keep an eye out for the camps she'd heard about from Randall and the sheriff.

Penelope warmed up with a light jog, picking up her pace when she arrived at the edge of the forest. The air was crisp and clean, and she felt her arms and legs fall into their familiar pattern as she increased her strides, her running shoes scraping against the pebbled sandy path. The sun warmed her face as she ran through the pockets of light peeking through the trees, and she felt joyous for the first time in days.

The image of Jordan hanging in the walk-in flashed into her mind and she tripped, correcting herself to keep from falling at the last minute. She slowed her pace and pushed the picture from her mind, trying again to focus on the trees and the beauty of nature around her, concentrating on the scent of the pine and the crispness of the cool air.

After the first mile, something to the left of the path caught her eye and she pulled up to a stop, jogging in place for a moment as she peered through the trees. A shiny black box was tucked between two trees next to what looked to be a makeshift tent, a camouflage-colored sheet strung between some branches. Something about the box was familiar. Penelope hadn't seen any other runners or hikers that morning, and the campsite appeared to be abandoned. At least right now. She took a few tentative steps away from the path, pine needles crunching under her shoes as she went.

She pulled her hood up over her damp hair and took a few more steps. It then became clear to her why the box was familiar. It was the case of wine that had gone missing the night of the break in at Festa. Penelope's heart had slowed when she stopped running, but picked up again as she glanced around the campsite. The wine box was empty, and several bottles were strewn across the ground.

"Maybe this is Denis's hunting campsite," Penelope muttered, hoping there was some innocent explanation for what she was seeing. Her heart sank when she peered behind the sheet and saw a box of Festa's straws and pint glasses with the restaurant's logo painted on the side. She found scraps of food too, and a few dinner plates. Her mouth turned bitter when she looked to the right and spotted Jordan's missing boots. They were thrown in the corner of the tent, partly obscured by a white tablecloth, which was streaked with mud and food stains.

Penelope backed out of the tent, not wanting to disturb what looked like important evidence. She was suddenly freezing, the icy air permeating her damp clothes. She'd been idling too long and her body temperature had dropped. She pulled her phone from her pocket, the words *Poor Connection* showing on the screen. She swiped open the camera and started snapping pictures, positioning her phone at different angles to capture the entire area.

When she heard the crunch of pine needles behind her, Penelope froze, then looked carefully around her, the discomfort she was feeling immediately forgotten, replaced by fear.

A spray of giggles made her turn sharply to look to her left. She could see the edge of someone's jacket poking out from behind a tree about fifty yards away. Penelope took a few steps back toward the trail, putting distance between herself and whoever was there. A second sharp laugh made her think it was a man, but she couldn't be sure. Another footstep from a slightly different direction caused the hair to raise on her arms under her shirt.

Penelope summoned her courage and willed herself to remain calm, even though adrenaline was running through her, urging her to run.

The arm behind the tree shifted and whoever was hiding stepped into view. Penelope squinted to see, but when the person revealed their face, all she could do was stare. They were wearing a dark hoodie with something obscuring their face. It looked painted on, a ghostly white see-through mask that obscured his features with a grotesque black smile. She definitely see now that it was a man, and was almost certainly Bailey.

Penelope took a few more backward steps as the man slid back behind the tree. She saw someone else moving close by, a smaller figure, most likely a woman. Neither of them revealed themselves to her, and she wasn't going to wait for them to. She spun around and sprinted back to the path, running at her top speed back to the inn.

CHAPTER 33

"I found something out in the woods," Penelope said as she entered her room. She watched Joey's face morph from excitement to worry and settle somewhere in between as she told him what she'd stumbled upon.

"Sheesh, Penny, I'm glad you're okay," Joey said, hugging her tightly.

"I was rattled," Penelope admitted. She peeled off her damp shirt and picked up her phone, dialing the sheriff's cell. "Now hopefully he'll listen to me," she said as she counted the rings. When she got his voicemail, she left a message for him to call her back right away. She tossed her phone on the bed and headed into the bathroom to get cleaned up for work.

An hour later, Penelope was on the set, getting things underway for the day ahead. Lunch service would be busy, it being the first time in days the entire crew was up to full speed with everyone working. There were a few sniffles here and there, but it looked like the flu epidemic had left the set.

"Yo, Boss," Francis said through the window of the food truck. Penelope was inside butterflying chicken breasts and tossing them into a silver bin to marinate for the grill later.

"What's up?" she asked, still focused on cutting the chicken. She was using her sharpest butcher knife. The last thing she needed was to get distracted and cut herself.

"Sheriff's here to see you," Francis said, picking up a crate of apples and heading toward the prep tent.

Penelope put the chicken she was working with in the fridge and washed her hands, scrubbing under her fingernails to get all the raw chicken off. She stepped down from the truck and greeted the sheriff as she dried her hands on a service towel.

"You found something for me?" Sheriff Bryson asked. He seemed cheerful today, something Penelope wasn't used to.

"Sure did." She waved for him to follow her as she walked to the rear of the inn. "About a mile down the main path there. I found a stash of stolen items from the restaurant, and most importantly, Jordan's missing hiking boots."

Sheriff Bryson put his hands on his belt and considered the trees. After a moment, he shrugged and said, "Guess I better take a look."

"Did you come by yourself?" Penelope asked with surprise.

"Yeah," Sheriff Bryson said, nodding. "Edie's looking at yet another wedding spot. I'm all there is today."

"I don't think you should go alone," Penelope said.

"Don't worry about me," he said defensively. "I know these woods like the back of my hand. I grew up here, remember?"

"Yeah, but whoever is hiding out there is obviously dangerous. I'll go with you," Penelope said, untying her apron.

Sheriff Bryson gave her an amused glance. "A caterer for backup. That's a new one. I appreciate the offer, but I think I can manage."

"Wait," Penelope said, pulling her phone from her pocket. She stepped away to have a murmured conversation and then returned. "Joey and I will both go with you. He's police, he knows how to handle himself. It's not safe for you to go alone."

The sheriff looked doubtful, but Penelope saw a glimmer of thanks behind his eyes.

"And I know exactly where the camp is," Penelope added, "so I'm going."

He nodded reluctantly and remained silent.

A few minutes later Joey appeared, his ski jacket zipped to the top and a knit hat pulled down over his ears. Penelope had grabbed her own coat and let Francis know she was stepping out.

The three of them headed up the forest trail, Penelope leading the way.

"So you still think your town is safe, that nothing happens here?" Penelope asked after they'd walked in silence for a while.

"It's as safe as it can be," the sheriff said, puffing a little bit. He'd quickened his pace to keep up with Penelope and Joey, who walked briskly up the path. "Everywhere can be dangerous. That's just a reality of life."

As they got closer, they agreed to keep quiet and only talk if necessary so they wouldn't alert anyone to their presence. When they arrived at the spot Penelope recognized from that morning, she stopped and pointed at the black box of wine.

The two men nodded and made their way up the slope to the partially hidden campsite, the sheriff leading the way, pushing aside branches, with Joey close behind. They'd agreed Penelope would hang back on the path, watching the surrounding area for any movement. The woods felt abandoned, but Penelope remembered thinking the same thing earlier that morning when she first came across the camp.

Joey and the sheriff ducked out of her sight. Penelope waited, standing still and listening to the sounds of the forest. She thought about how peaceful and serene some places were, and then she thought about Jordan's boots and wondered how someone could do such horrible things in a place so beautiful.

A sharp yell from the tent brought her back to full attention. Squinting at the campsite, she saw two figures wrestling just behind the tent, the flaps jerking against the taught rope strung between the trees. More shouting followed and then a heavy thud of metal, like the sound a shovel made when it hit a rock in the earth.

"Joey!" Penelope shouted.

There was so much commotion and yelling in the tent, she doubted anyone heard her. Penelope hesitated a second, then started up the hill toward them, ducking behind a large tree when she heard another clang of metal.

The rustling of leaves and the crack of a branch sounded on her left and she quickly took cover on the right side of the tree, peeking out from behind. A man in a black sweatshirt and clear plastic mask was running wildly down the embankment, heading toward the path. Penelope braced herself until he came level with her tree.

Right as he passed, Penelope stepped out behind him and shoved him between his shoulder blades, sending him hurtling headfirst into a pine tree. The man crumpled to the ground and lay still, knocked out cold.

Penelope took a few tentative steps toward him then nudged his leg with her boot. It rolled back and forth, but he stayed still. She put her hand to her mouth and spun around, running on shaking legs up the hill to find Joey.

"And this is where we've set up catering."

Penelope heard Jennifer's voice before she saw her. Her tone was uncharacteristically upbeat as she led a group of unfamiliar faces through the prep tent and past the kitchen truck. "Where is Penelope?"

As she led Joey and Sheriff Bryson back through the set, their handcuffed prisoner shuffling slowly in front of them, she watched Francis say, "Here she comes," while motioning toward them. Jennifer's eyes widened when she saw Bailey in handcuffs, smirking at her, a clear mask hanging from a rubber band around his neck.

"Penelope, Janie Levinson is here," Jennifer said, recovering with an artificial smile. "What in the world is going on?" she mouthed as she attempted to block the view of the short dark-haired woman who was clearly in charge of the group of visitors.

The sheriff and Joey headed off toward the parking area with Bailey while Penelope stayed behind.

She stuck out her hand, but Janie just nodded. "Too many germs," she said as a way of explanation. "But it's nice to meet you. I've heard good things."

Janie was petite, the down coat she wore looking more like it was wearing her. She eyed the sheriff's back as he retreated from the set.

"Thank you," Penelope said. "We'll be setting out lunch shortly. We've provided a few vegan options for you to choose from."

"Perfect," Janie said in a clipped voice. She perused the menu on the sandwich board in front of the kitchen truck, a brief look of disgust passing over her face as her eyes scanned the meat-heavy options. She turned without a word, her team behind her, and ducked into the prep tent to inspect the inner workings of the kitchen.

"She's making me nervous," Jennifer said, reverting to her normal tone of voice, which was more of an irritated hiss. "Where were you?"

"Catching a thief," Penelope said quietly.

"Good thing you came back in time. This is an important day," Jennifer said, throwing a worried glance at the tent.

"Don't make more out of it than it is," Penelope said. "I was helping the sheriff. That's important too."

"That's easy for you to say," Jennifer said, her irritation growing. "You'll get a job right after this one. This could be my last chance of getting hired on a wide-release film."

Penelope stayed silent to avoid another biting remark.

"That woman has the power to pull the plug on this whole production," Jennifer said, throwing a furtive glance at the tent. "Everyone should understand that."

Janine and her team emerged from the tent. "Things look good in there," Janine said. "Let's go and speak with the talent before lunch." One of the men standing behind her raised his phone to take a picture of Penelope and Jennifer. "By the way, what was that we just witnessed, with the police officer?"

"Nothing, just a local issue that's got nothing to do with us," Jennifer said. She started toward the event space, motioning for them to follow. "Let me show you the main set. I think you'll be happy with the design."

Skylar sidled up to Penelope, grasping a cup of tea in her hand. "Who was that?" she asked.

"An executive from California," Penelope said.

"No, the handcuff guy," Skylar said, rolling her eyes.

Penelope could tell she was curious, but was trying to act like someone being led away in handcuffs was a daily occurrence for her.

"I came across a camp on my run with some stolen stuff from Festa. The sheriff is looking into it," Penelope said. She held back from sharing Bailey's name or her more serious suspicions.

"That was that weird guy from town," Skylar said, nodding. "He asked me and Sarah out to the woods the other day when we were getting lunch at the diner."

Penelope turned to her.

"Really?"

Skylar nodded. "I think Sarah was into going, you know? Just for something to do since it's so boring around here. But I was like, no way."

"What did he ask you specifically?" Penelope urged.

Skylar shrugged, but became more serious when she saw Penelope's expression. "I don't know. He was telling us everyone hangs out there at night, drinking and stuff. But that's not really what I'm into."

When Penelope asked if she remembered anything else, she said, "The guy said it's the only place to get away from parents. Something like that. Meanwhile I've been away from home for years now. Like I said, there was no way I was going, so I kind of tuned him out. I told Sarah not to go."

"Thanks," Penelope said with fresh concern. Remembering there were two people at the campsite that morning, she thought about what to do. She supposed it could have been Sarah, but then again, if Bailey was inviting random girls from the diner into the woods, it could be anyone.

A thought suddenly occurred to her as Skylar wandered over to read the lunch menu. She pulled out her phone and texted Joey: "Tell Sheriff we need to check the campsite for Regina, the missing waitress."

CHAPTER 34

Penelope sat at a table at Festa after work, reading over the résumé of the new potential chef, Paul Gustafson. He had cooked at a number of well-regarded restaurants in the Midwest and had graduated with honors from Penelope's culinary school ten years before her. Penelope listened from the dining room as he put together a dish for her to try, the initial aromas already convincing her he could be the perfect replacement.

Karen walked through the front door, heading directly to Penelope's table when she saw her.

"Karen," Penelope said, rising from her seat. "It's nice to see you. But I wasn't expecting you today."

Karen unwound her scarf and slipped out of her coat, hanging both on the back of one of the barstools. "I know. Mom told me you were interviewing chefs, and..."

Penelope looked at her expectantly, eyebrows raised.

"...and I want to be considered for the job."

"Karen," Penelope said, inviting her to sit down. "I had no idea you were interested. Aren't you going back to school soon?"

Karen settled into the chair. "I don't want to go back to college. I want to stay here and cook at my father's restaurant."

Penelope met her gaze and recognized something familiar behind her eyes. "This is the first time I've heard you wanted to be in your family's business."

"I've been practicing at home, making all of my dad's dishes," Karen said. "My mom doesn't agree with my decision, but working here is my dream. Please, Penelope, give me a chance."

Penelope wished Ava would come back out and help her with this situation. Her instinct was to let Karen audition with the other candidates, but she didn't want to get in the middle of a family issue between Megan and her daughter.

"Wait here," Penelope said to her, then headed into the kitchen. She nodded at Paul, who was still working on his audition plate.

"Ava," Penelope said, poking her head into the office. Ava looked up at her warily, fatigue wrinkling her almond-shaped eyes.

"What?" she said testily.

"Sorry," Penelope said. "I didn't mean to bother you, but Karen is here, asking to try out for the head-chef job."

"Really?" Ava said, brightening.

"Yeah, but I get the impression it's not what her mom wants," Penelope said.

Ava waved her off. "If she's here, let her try out. Can't hurt anything."

Penelope invited Karen back to the kitchen and set her up at the station across from Paul, giving her identical ingredients to his and asking her to create whatever she wanted.

"You have thirty minutes. Ava and I will blind taste your dishes and give you feedback," Penelope said. "Good luck," she said to Karen.

Karen sorted through the ingredients on her cutting board, then glanced around the kitchen at the ovens, grill, the hanging pots and pans. Penelope saw her eyes land on the photos of her dad around the service window. Her expression froze in a mask of pain and sadness.

"Hey," Penelope said. "You don't have to do this if you're not ready."

Karen cleared her throat. "No, I'm okay. I want to do this for my dad."

Penelope nodded and stepped back outside.

*   *   *

Paul poked his head out the kitchen door and let Ava and Penelope know they were ready to serve. Ava had opened a bottle of the house red and Penelope went to retrieve the dishes. Paul smiled widely and Karen watched nervously as Penelope set down the plates. Penelope had to admit she couldn't tell just by looking which dish had been put together by the professionally trained chef and which by the passionate amateur.

"Thanks, chefs," Penelope said. "Please wait in the kitchen. We'll call you back when we're through."

"Wow," Ava said after Paul and Karen had left. "These both look wonderful." She slid some of the pasta from each serving platter onto her own, then handed the spoon to Penelope.

They ate in silence, taking several bites from each plate. "I like the boldness of this one, and the meatiness of this one. To be honest, they're both excellent," Penelope determined.

Ava wiped a smear of red sauce from her chin. "Agreed. This is a tough choice."

"Karen seems very interested in the job, Ava," Penelope said after taking a sip of wine.

Ava nodded. "Yes, she's always been the one kid from the family who took to the kitchen. But Megan thinks Kyle should have the restaurant passed down to him, not Karen. Kyle doesn't appear interested. But he's only halfway through college—they both are."

Penelope looked at her with surprise. "Why not hand it over to the child who really wants it?"

Ava looped more spaghetti around her fork. "Megan wants Karen to be a teacher. She thinks both girls should be. The boys should be in the business."

"But what about what they want?" Penelope said.

"I don't know, Penelope. It's hard to understand, but Megan is traditional when it comes to her kids and the careers she thinks they should have."

Penelope felt a stab of pity for Karen, thinking of her going against her mother's wishes to follow her dream. "What did Jordan think of Karen becoming a chef?"

Ava laughed darkly. "I don't know. He didn't talk about the kids much with me."

"That seems odd," Penelope said.

"Yeah. I was his work wife, he said. He didn't talk about the restaurant at home, and he didn't talk about home at the restaurant. Two worlds," Ava said, taking another big bite.

"Well, I recommend you bring Karen on as an apprentice and hire Paul as executive chef," Penelope said definitively. It would help solve their staffing issue, and it would be the quickest way to separate herself from Festa and the drama that went along with it.

"I think you're right," Ava said.

She went to the kitchen and asked Karen and Paul to join them.

"Who made this one?" Penelope asked. The subtle flavors of the sauce were so good, they had Penelope wondering what little twist of special ingredient had been used.

Paul raised his hand.

"Spot on. We loved it," Penelope said.

Karen visibly deflated, but turned to shake Paul's hand and congratulate him.

"And this one," Penelope interrupted her, "was amazing too."

Karen's face lit up and she did a little jump in place. Paul patted her on the back and she gave him a grateful smile.

"We're offering the job of executive chef to Paul," Ava said, excitement in her voice, "and we'd like to bring Karen on as apprentice to the head chef."

Penelope noted Ava's use of the word "we," but didn't mind when she saw how happy it made Jordan's daughter.

Karen squealed with delight and almost jumped into Penelope's arms. She hugged Ava too, rocking back and forth a few times. She even hugged Paul, who stooped down and returned the hug, keeping a respectful space between them and patting her on the back.

"I think we know how Karen feels about our decision," Penelope said, laughing. "What about you, Chef?"

Paul nodded, suppressing a grin. "Absolutely. I can start almost immediately."

"Almost?" Ava said, a pinch of alarm breaking through the happy moment.

"I just have to pack my things and find a place to live up here, or close by at least."

"No worries," Ava said. "We're throwing in a relocation package for you. I can find you somewhere to live in no time."

CHAPTER 35

Penelope felt a huge sense of relief when she got back to her room at the inn. She pulled off her chef coat and went into the bathroom, locking the door behind her. Francis had a key to her room and sometimes popped upstairs if he needed to use the computer or print out a menu, so she had gotten in the habit of securing herself in the bathroom to avoid any embarrassing encounters.

She plugged in her hairdryer and curling iron and stepped into the shower stall. Penelope stood under the hot water, allowing her hair to soak all the way to the ends. It hung down in long strands as she stared at her feet and the water swirling around the drain. She was glad to be free of Festa and happy to end things there on a high note. She smiled when she thought about how excited Karen had been, and she refused to worry about how Megan would react, grateful she didn't have to be part of that conversation.

She heard a thump from the bedroom. "Hey, Joey. I'll be out in a minute."

Penelope heard another thump and a mumbled response, which she couldn't make out over the noise of the shower. Lathering up her hair, she turned her face to the water, letting the tension from the day fall away and disappear down the drain. Turning around to let the water beat on her shoulder blades, she heard a crash and her eyes flew open.

"Ouch!" Soap ran into her eyes and she squeezed them tight, throwing water on her face to rinse them out. "Joey, you okay out there?"

When she got no response, Penelope turned off the water and

rubbed the remaining soap from her eyes with a towel. Wrapping a larger towel around her, she stepped out of the shower and onto the floor mat. "Joey, what's going on?"

Penelope reached out to touch the doorknob and heard heavy footsteps approaching on the other side and then heavy breathing. She pulled her hand away from the knob, fear causing her stomach to flip. Her eyes darted around the small bathroom, looking for something she could use to defend herself. She touched the end of the hot metal of the curling iron, then picked it up and yanked the cord from the socket.

"Who's there?" Penelope asked. Drops of water splashed onto the tiles at her feet.

The labored breathing continued, then the footsteps retreated from the door. Penelope strained to hear, waiting until she was certain she'd heard the bedroom door open and close quietly before emerging.

Penelope opened the bathroom door and stopped in her tracks. Her suitcase, which had been sitting on a stand in the corner of her room, was open on the floor, the contents strewn across the bed. All the bureau drawers had been opened and her clothes rifled through. Whoever had been in her room had been looking for something in a hurry.

Penelope's eyes darted around the room. She still grasped the curling iron in her hand. "What in the heck is going on?" she asked out loud. She padded to the door and saw that it was slightly open. She couldn't remember if she'd locked it behind her when she'd come in, but was almost certain she had. Being a single girl in the big city, that was second nature. Penelope took a quick look down both directions of the empty hallway. She closed the door and spun the lock, listening to the click.

Penelope tightened her towel then gathered her clothes. She had no idea what someone could have been searching for, but she was positive she hadn't packed anything worth stealing.

"Oh no," Penelope said aloud. She pulled open the lid of her suitcase and felt for the interior zipper. She kept her jewelry stashed there in a small velvet bag when she traveled. None of the pieces were worth much; they were mostly gifts with sentimental value. Her heart sank when she found the pocket empty, the velvet bag gone.

A jiggle on the doorknob caused her to stand up straight and pick up the curling iron from where she'd left it on the bed. She held it up, ready to strike any unwelcome visitor.

"What are you doing?" Joey asked, an amused grin on his face. His expression quickly changed when he stepped into the room. "Looking for something?"

"No," Penelope said, dropping the curling iron back on the bed. "Someone came into our room while I was showering and went through my things. They stole my jewelry."

"What?" Joey asked sharply. He closed the door firmly behind him. "This place is nuts."

Penelope shrugged. "They're aren't worth anything, except to me."

"Except to you," Joey repeated. He pulled her into a hug and sighed. "I don't have a good feeling about this place at all, Penny. I'm not saying you can't take care of yourself, because you can. But I'll feel better when you're back home with me."

Penelope pulled away from him and looked him in the eyes. "Really?" Part of her wanted to leave right that minute, get on a plane with him, and never look back at Forrestville, Indiana again.

"Yeah," Joey said. "This kid, Bailey—the sheriff says he's harmless, but I don't know. There's something going on, something the sheriff isn't seeing it, or refuses to see." He bent down to pick up a pair of her jeans, folding them and tucking them back in a drawer.

"What happened down at the station?" Penelope asked.

"Bailey says he didn't have anything to do with Jordan's death or the break-in," Joey said, shaking his head.

"How does he explain the wine bottles and the supplies from the restaurant? Not to mention Jordan's boots."

"Bailey says he camps out up there on a regular basis, and

people come in and out of his tent all the time. Sometimes friends, sometimes kids just passing through. He remembers drinking the wine, but not who brought it," Joey said. "Says it just showed up one day."

"And Jordan's boots?" Penelope asked.

"Same thing," Joey said. "They just appeared. He didn't know anything about them."

"So he either doesn't know or doesn't want to tell on a friend," Penelope said. She bent down to retrieve a pair of socks that had rolled under the bed. "Skylar, one of the younger crew members on the set, said he invited her and another girl up to the woods to party with him."

Joey pinched the bridge of his nose. "Anyway, he's locked up for the night. That's something, at least."

"Was he hurt? From me pushing him into a tree?" Penelope asked.

"Nah, just a lump on his head. He'll be fine. Physically."

Penelope did feel relieved to know she wouldn't run into Bailey and that she hadn't seriously hurt him. She was still proud of her mini-ambush, at how she'd taken down a fleeing suspect. She didn't know exactly what it was about Bailey that set her on edge, but she'd felt uncomfortable around him every time they'd come in contact.

After putting away the rest of her clothes, Penelope pulled on a pair of black pants and a silky shirt. She talked with Joey while he showered and she swiped mascara onto her lashes.

"You look nice," Joey said, stepping out and cinching a towel around his waist.

"So do you," Penelope said. "I assume we're going somewhere nice tonight. By the way, I called the sheriff to report the break-in. He's going to follow up tomorrow."

He'd actually asked Penelope to come to the station right then, but Randall had invited her and Joey to celebrate Arlena's birthday in Quincy. They were all in the mood to escape Forrestville for the evening, even if it was only to a well-reviewed steakhouse less than an hour away. It looked like a hole in the wall in the pictures, but even if the food was just average, it would be a welcome change of scenery.

"We have to leave in twenty minutes to make it on time," Penelope reminded Joey as he rubbed the water from his hair with a towel.

Penelope looked around the room for her iPad, her heart quickening until she found it. "This they leave behind," she said, shaking her head. "Oh no," she added, as she pawed through the contents of the drawer.

"What?" Joey asked.

"I stuck a check in here and it's gone," Penelope said.

"Call the bank," Joey said.

"No, not one of mine. I found it at the restaurant and the guy, he's out of town, so I was holding it until I saw him again."

"So they left the tablet but took a check. Not a blank check, either," Joey said. "Why?"

Penelope picked up the Bible that was tucked in the drawer and fanned through it, then shook her head, closing the drawer slowly.

CHAPTER 36

"This place is great," Max said as they entered the steakhouse in Quincy. The walls were decorated in a music motif, guitars and other instruments nailed in place over wallpaper with famous song lyrics and vinyl records. A five-piece band on a small stage played a funky version of "Blue Suede Shoes."

The hostess led their party to a quieter room in the back and sat them at a large round table near the bar. Penelope and Joey brought up the rear behind Max, Arlena, Sam, and surprisingly, Sybil Wilde, who Randall guided to the table with a hand on the small of her back. After everyone was settled, the owner came over to introduce himself and take drink orders.

"Cool place, Daddy," Arlena said. She looked radiant in a black V-neck sweater and jeans, with silver hoop earrings matching the silver necklace around her neck, her birthday gift from Sam. She held his fingers loosely in her own.

"Happy birthday, Baby Girl," Randall said, raising his glass of wine and toasting his daughter. "I couldn't be more proud of you. I love you to the moon."

Arlena smiled and raised her glass too. "I love you too. All of you," she said, her eyes landing on Sybil last. Her smile stayed in place, but her eyes lost a bit of sparkle. Sybil toasted her back and placed her hand on Randall's forearm.

"Your father has been telling me all about what you were like when you were little," Sybil said, setting her glass on the table.

Arlena smiled at her father. "Really?"

"Oh, yes," Sybil said. "He says you were a spitfire."

Randall laughed as Arlena blushed. "She was a perfect little girl in every way. And now look at her."

"Stop," Arlena begged. "Someone talk about something else, please." She threw Penelope a pleading glance.

"Sybil, how are Jackson and Dakota liking show business?" Penelope asked, taking a piece of bread from the basket in the center of the table.

"Oh, they have good days and bad, like all of us. But overall, they really do love it," Sybil said.

"If they ever decided to stop acting and do something else, how would you feel about that?" Penelope asked, ripping the bread into smaller pieces.

Sybil's smile faltered for a second, then became bright again. "Well, I suppose that would be fine. I love my children, and they should pursue whatever career they choose."

"These two took to acting like a fish to water," Randall said, pointing at Max and Arlena. "But some of my other children are interested in other things."

Penelope considered what Sybil was saying. "How would you feel though, Sybil?"

Sybil met her gaze. "As long as my children are happy and thriving, I'm happy."

Penelope nodded, satisfied.

The owner returned and took their orders, promising them the best steaks in the state of Indiana.

"Randall, did you guys notice a camp in the woods about a mile up the main path with a bunch of kids hanging around it, with a green camouflage tent?" Penelope asked.

Randall thought for a moment. "Maybe. We did see some different folks out there, right?"

Max nodded. "You know, there was one group, kind of rowdy, near one of the caves. They were just hanging out, drinking."

"Did you notice anything unusual about them?" Penelope asked.

"No," Max said. "It was just kids hanging out. It's not like they have a mall to go to. It's probably the only place to spend time away from home."

"Yeah," Randall said. "I only saw them twice. Didn't pay much attention. Ah..." He rubbed his hands together when the appetizers arrived. A bunch of fried things Penelope had never seen Arlena eat before and was surprised to see her digging into now.

"Hungry?" Penelope asked, laughing.

"You have no idea. That flu wiped me out," Arlena said, nodding and grabbing a potato skin off the large platter. "I don't want them to have to take my dress in again. That might send Jennifer right over the edge."

"If she survives that long," Penelope said. She gave them a brief rundown of her encounter with the executives that morning.

Sybil looked at Penelope with alarm as Randall refilled her wineglass from the bottle on the table. "Do you think they're here to kill the project?"

"Oh, I'm not sure about that," Penelope said, backtracking. "I just know Jennifer is worried, that's all."

"Well, I'm worried too," Sybil said. "It's not often a brother and sister role in the same film comes along, and that real siblings are cast. I looked for a project like this one for a while."

"Wow," Penelope said. "I guess one or the other of them will be working separately at times, right?"

"I guess." Sybil sighed. "The business is so fickle, you could go years without work." She glanced at Randall. "Well, not all of us. But middle-of-the-pack working actors have to fight for roles. That's why I'm always careful with our money. I'm a big believer in saving and investing in real things, getting ready for the lean times."

Sybil turned to Randall when he lowered his voice to ask her a private question.

Penelope turned to Joey. "Having fun?"

"Sure," Joey said, rubbing her shoulder. "Want to dance after dinner?"

Penelope laughed. "I can't dance."

"Sure you can," Joey teased. "A night on the town might be just the thing you need."

"Okay, I'll try," Penelope agreed.

After they finished dinner, Arlena's party moved to the main bar room of the restaurant. Randall ordered a round of drinks and spun Sybil out on the dance floor, the two of them moving to the music so well it looked like they'd been practicing beforehand.

The band was encouraged by the enthusiastic response and seemed to step up their game, launching from one upbeat classic rock number to another, keeping the energy going on the dance floor.

Randall signaled the band and they launched into a choppy version of the Beatles' tune "Birthday." Arlena joined her father and they danced together, Arlena shaking her hair at her dad and Randall laughing out loud as he spun her around the floor. Sam and Max watched from nearby barstools with the rest of the crowd. Sybil sidled over to Penelope and, surprisingly, put an arm over her shoulders. She was a little tipsy, but Penelope thought it was more from the good time and being around Randall than the wine she'd had with dinner.

"You're enjoying yourself," Penelope said.

Sybil nodded quickly and took a sip of something pink from a straw. "He's quite a man." She watched Randall and Arlena dance together with clear admiration.

"Yes, he is," Penelope said. "Hopefully he'll stick around a while so you can get to know each other better."

"I hope so too," Sybil said. "So far, so good." She glanced behind them, eyeing a set of drums that had been nailed over the bar. "This isn't usually my kind of place, but I have to admit it's fun."

Joey sidled up to Penelope and handed her another glass of wine.

"Surprisingly, the food was good too," Sybil said, bopping her head slightly to the music. "I mean, Festa is good, but how many times can you eat at the same place and not go crazy? I could never live here year round."

"I know what you mean," Penelope said.

"And that Ava woman is all over me every time I'm in there. It's hard to relax and enjoy a good meal with her hovering," Sybil said.

Penelope stopped short and looked at Sybil. "What do you mean?" Penelope raised her voice to be heard over the music.

Sybil waved her hand, as if she was sorry to have brought it up. "She's very nice, I didn't mean that. She's just been pitching me on an investment, and I haven't had a chance to review it. She's like a dog with a bone, never lets a visit go by without bringing it up."

"Really?" Penelope asked, glancing at Joey. "She's never said anything to me about an investment opportunity."

Sybil laughed sharply. "You're lucky. I'm sorry I ever said I'd look at the information. I was just being nice, really. Excuse me," she said as Randall waved her over. A new song came on and she took Arlena's place, swaying with Randall during a slower number. Sam took Arlena's hand and pulled her back onto the dance floor, rocking with her to the music.

"It's now or never," Joey said, taking Penelope's glass and setting it down on the bar. "Dance with me."

Penelope smiled and followed him onto the floor.

When they arrived back at the inn, Penelope was exhausted, but her head was still buzzing from the music. She'd never danced with Joey before, and she couldn't remember the last time they'd laughed as hard as they had shimmying together in front of the band. Joey had some moves he'd obviously been holding back, and Penelope decided she'd start practicing so she could keep up with him the next time. Arlena had enjoyed her birthday surrounded by her favorite people. And Sybil.

When they reached the Forrestville Inn, their headlights swept across the edge of the forest, and Penelope swore she saw someone at the edge of the main path.

"Wait," Penelope said as they drove past.

"What?" Joey asked, tapping his fingers to invisible music.

"Someone's there," Penelope said, pointing at the trail.

"So what?" Joey soothed her. "If some hiker wants to go out there and freeze their tail off, that's their business, right?"

Penelope relaxed back against the seat. "Right, I'm sorry."

"No need to be sorry," Joey said. "It's a regular hangout—you're just more aware of it now because of this morning."

"I suppose," Penelope said. She wished she was still dancing in Quincy and not back home at the inn.

CHAPTER 37

Penelope went to the sheriff's office first thing the next morning and filed a report for her missing jewelry.

"Never a dull moment," the sheriff said.

Penelope sighed and rose to leave after he assured her he'd keep an eye out for her things.

"Well, I don't have a lot of hope of seeing them again, but thank you," Penelope said. "I wanted to ask you..."

The sheriff looked at her with his familiar wary gaze.

"How well did you know your predecessor, Sheriff Helmsley?"

Sheriff Bryson's face fell. "Not at all. I never met the man. I came on board after he...passed away. I was a forest ranger, reported to Quincy, didn't have a lot of contact with the sheriff's office."

"I read that his son is in jail. And that he used to run with Bailey."

"I read the papers too," he said, not offering any further information or encouraging the conversation.

Penelope looked at him expectantly.

"Helmsley won't be back for a long time, if ever," Sheriff Bryson said. "Now, if there's nothing else..."

When she stepped back onto the sidewalk, she almost ran into Edie on her way into the station.

"What are you doing here?" Edie asked casually. Penelope thought she still looked at her suspiciously.

"There was an incident at the inn. Someone broke into my room, stole some things," Penelope said.

Edie's expression softened. "Sorry to hear that." She hitched her purse strap higher on her shoulder after it slipped down her coat sleeve.

"I've been meaning to ask you...you knew Kellie Foster, one of the missing Forrestville Five?"

"Yeah, I knew her," Edie said. "Whole reason I became a cop in the first place."

"Really? So you guys were friends?"

"Arc friends," Edie said. "I still think we'll find her somewhere."

"What do you think happened to her? Or to any of them?" Penelope asked.

Edie looked down at Penelope, considering. "Something happened, I think, something that made her want to disappear."

"Like something at school or at home?" Penelope asked. "Was she being bullied?"

Edie shook her head. "No, she comes from a good family—her folks are the best. I was over there all the time and still see them. She never said what it was, but that last year, when we got back from spring break...she was different somehow. Then she skipped practice, didn't come to school. Then she was gone." Edie swiped at her cheek and hardened her stare at Penelope.

"Did you know all the files from back then are missing?" Penelope asked.

Edie paused, allowing a man to pass by before responding. "How do you know that?"

"I found out," Penelope said. "Why is that?"

Edie pulled her away from the front of the police station. "Walk with me."

They walked slowly, stopping in front of the diner. "This is where she worked after school," Edie said. "She was saving up for her first car. She had dreams of playing ball at IU; she practiced all the time." Edie paused. "Those files are somewhere."

"Is there an archive somewhere?" Penelope asked.

"That's the thing. The computer copies were wiped, and the paper files in police storage are gone. Someone tried to erase the cases, get rid of the Forrestville Five."

"I want to help," Penelope said.

Edie put a hand on Penelope's shoulder and smiled weakly. "I can see that. I've been trying to figure this case out ever since I passed the police test. I'll get there eventually."

"I hope you do," Penelope said. "I really do."

CHAPTER 38

Penelope stood next to Sybil the next afternoon on the set. She was armed with correctly made smoothies for Dakota and Jackson for when they wrapped up their scene.

Jackson seemed out of sorts that day, and had more than the usual number of missed cues and forgotten lines. Dakota played happily outside of camera range like she always did, spinning herself around or using her fingers as pretend puppets to talk to each other.

"Cut!" Jennifer yelled, then looked guiltily at Janie, who gazed at the set from a director's chair. "Let's take twenty and reset."

The crew members wandered away for their short break, heading to the craft-service table for a snack or stepping outside for air.

Janie waved Jennifer over to her chair and pointed to something on her copy of the script. Jackson and Dakota hurried over to Penelope and she gave them their smoothies. She watched their cheeks sink in as they sucked the strawberry and almond milk concoctions through the wide straws.

"Jackson," Sybil asked when he took a break from his drink, "what's going on today? Are you feeling all right?"

Jackson rolled his eyes at his mom, which caused her to put her hand to her throat. "Excuse me, young man, but you will not roll your eyes at your mother."

Penelope took a step backwards, not wanting to intrude on the private mother-son moment. Just then Randall strolled onto the set, making his way to Arlena and giving her a quick hug. Jackson rolled his eyes again and stalked away, sucking harder on his straw.

"Thanks, Miss Penelope," Dakota said, keeping an eye on her brother.

"You're welcome, sweetie," Penelope said, giving Sybil a sympathetic glance.

"He's upset I went out last night," Sybil said, waving it off. "He'll get over it."

Penelope nodded silently. She couldn't pretend to know what it was like to be a single mother, or to even have children for that matter.

"Sybil," Penelope said, "remember that thing you said last night about an investment opportunity?"

Sybil nodded as she tightened Dakota's pigtails, tugging gently on them until the girl protested and scurried away. "Yes, it's restaurant shares or something. I'm a bit fuzzy on the details. Ava pitched me after a few glasses of wine at the bar, then dropped off some paperwork at the inn. To be honest, I haven't looked at it. Like I said, I was just being polite."

"Thanks," Penelope said. "See you at dinner later?"

"Maybe," Sybil said, throwing a glance in Randall's direction. Arlena gave Sybil a tight smile. Penelope got the impression Arlena wasn't thrilled at the idea of sharing her father either, even though she was twenty years older than Jackson. Penelope figured some things between parents and children never changed.

"Herring – Steele," Penelope mumbled, swiping open her iPad in the cab of her truck and searching up the company's website. She was curious why Ava had never mentioned anything about an investment group to her at the restaurant, considering they had been working so closely the past few weeks.

Penelope searched the company name again, this time adding on "restaurant" to the keywords. No official website appeared, but a link to a PDF on the state of Indiana's property registry caught her eye. A deed inched open on the screen listing Herring – Steele Inc. as the seller and Jacob Pears as the buyer of the address 227 Main Street in Forrestville. Penelope tried to picture which building that was. Not able to place it, she searched it and found it was the diner.

"Jacob Pears," Penelope said out loud in the truck. "The owner of the newspaper owns the diner too?" She wasn't sure what that meant, if anything, but it certainly was interesting that the man who had the only competing eatery in town had attempted to tarnish Festa's reputation. "At the very least that's a conflict of interest. At most he was intentionally trying to damage Jordan's business."

She thought back to Ava in the kitchen telling her that she and Jordan bought the diner before Festa was renovated and opened.

"Maybe they made a bad deal," Penelope pondered out loud. "Or he just really doesn't like Festa's food." Penelope tried to imagine which scenario made more sense and failed to come up with a logical reason for either. She hopped down from the cab and locked up, then walked over to Festa to ask Ava herself.

As she crossed the courtyard, Penelope's phone buzzed in her back pocket. "Sheriff Bryson," Penelope said. "What can I do for you?"

"I was wondering if you could come down to the station," he said. "I've got some paperwork for you. Some new information has come to light regarding the restaurant break-in."

"You should talk to Ava," Penelope said, happy to have washed her hands of all things Festa.

"Well, I could," the sheriff answered cagily. "But I prefer speaking with you. Would you mind heading over?"

Penelope sighed. "Sure, I'll let my team know I'll be off-site for a bit."

Sheriff Bryson hung up without saying goodbye. Penelope turned and walked to the parking lot.

CHAPTER 39

Penelope was surprised to see Regina sitting in Sheriff Bryson's office, a sweatshirt hood pulled up over her dark red hair. Her magenta lipstick was freshly applied, but the rest of her face looked oily and unwashed, her usual dark eyeliner faded. She still sported her standard bored sneer. Penelope sat down in the chair next to her in front of the sheriff's desk.

"Regina," Penelope said. "What are you doing here? Everyone's been looking for you."

"I don't know what for." Regina sniffed, rolling her eyes. "I'm allowed to go off if I want to."

"Your mother was worried. You still live under her roof," Sheriff Bryson said. "The right thing to do is to call."

"So you weren't missing, just...hiding?" Penelope asked.

"She was up at Bailey's campsite."

Penelope leaned forward in her chair. "I told you I saw someone else."

"Yes, you did," the sheriff said. "The forensic investigators from Quincy came across a lot of interesting things up there, Regina included."

"What else did they find?" Penelope asked.

"Food, a couple of bottles of liquor from the restaurant. At least that's where I assume they're from."

"I'm glad you found Regina," Penelope said. "But why are you telling me? I'm not involved with the restaurant anymore."

He pulled a small manila envelope from his desk drawer and handed it to Penelope.

She pulled open the flap and slid one of her necklaces out, rubbing her thumb over the pendant and her etched initials. A wave of emotion passed over her and she decided then to make a trip down to Florida to see her parents the next time she had a break. Getting her necklace back reminded her how much she missed them.

"You made the first complaint, brought all of this to my attention," Sheriff Bryson said.

Penelope nodded, keeping her emotions in check. "Why did you break into my room?" she asked the girl.

Regina shrugged, but Penelope saw what looked like regret behind her defiant mask. "I know where they keep the room keys. I used to be one of the part-time maids, before I finally got a better position at the restaurant. At least I thought it was better. I was just getting back at you for firing me. I only wanted to scare you, but..."

"Old habits kicked in," Sheriff Bryson said.

"Old habits?" Penelope asked.

He nodded. "Regina here has a knack for palming personal items. This isn't her first arrest for theft. Her mother is on the way to get her, sign her out." He ducked his head and looked up at the girl, his fingers interlaced on the desk in front of him. Regina stared back and slid down in her seat, her hands stuffed firmly in her sweatshirt pockets.

"Tell her what you told me earlier," he said sternly.

Regina sighed dramatically. "Fine. I never should have opened my mouth. If I'd known I'd be stuck here all day, I never would have."

"Right, I know," the sheriff said. "Now talk."

"It's no big secret we're up in the woods at night," Regina said. "Everyone knows about it at the restaurant."

"It's your hangout. Big deal," Penelope said, looking at the sheriff.

"Yeah, that's it," Regina said, picking at some lint on her sleeve.

"No, there's more," the sheriff said.

After a long pause, Regina began again. "Ava knows we take stuff sometimes," Regina said. "She'll tell you she doesn't, but she gives me food, liquor, stuff we can take over to the campsite."

Penelope looked at the sheriff again, frustration beginning to build. "What does that have to do with anything that's happened?"

"Because," Regina said, sitting up straight for the first time. "She's acting like she didn't know, trying to make people think Bailey's the one who killed Jordan."

Penelope looked at the sheriff. "Can I talk to you alone for a minute?"

Sheriff Bryson escorted Regina to a room across the hall and closed her inside. Leaving his office door open, he sat back down. "She's saying it wasn't Bailey."

"You're going to take the word of a troubled young girl who spends her time hanging at a campsite in the woods as evidence? And you're telling me she has a record already?"

"At the very least, I can get Ava for supplying alcohol to a minor," Sheriff Bryson said.

"I can't believe what I'm hearing," Penelope said, standing up. "Ava is an adult, a business owner in your community. What is it with you and Bailey that you need to protect him all the time?"

Sheriff Bryson's expression faltered. "Bailey hasn't gotten a fair shake in life. I'll admit, our department hasn't been fair to him in the past. He's easily talked into things, then he gets left behind when his friends run away or think of better stories to get themselves out of trouble."

"You've arrested him before when he shouldn't have been?" Penelope asked. "If that's true, then drop the charges or throw out the case."

"That's not how it works. Once you go through the system, that stays with you," he said. For the first time, Penelope sensed real regret from the sheriff.

"The article I read made him out to be the ringleader," Penelope said. "He didn't talk those other boys into vandalism, malicious destruction of property?"

"That's how it was reported, but after getting to know the kid better, I don't think that's what actually happened. But all of that is in the past; we can't undo it. I can, however, not send him up because someone more savvy knows how to position him into the spotlight."

"That may be true, but you can't discount evidence because of personal feelings or to make up for some mistake from your past," Penelope said. She wished there was more room in the cramped office to pace. "Can you separate the two or are you set on protecting him?"

When he didn't answer right away Penelope said, "I should go. Thanks for finding my things."

"Wait," Sheriff Bryson said, standing up from his desk.

Penelope stopped, her hand resting on the doorknob.

"Those kids were going missing around the time Bailey was up to no good with those other boys," he began. His face turned red and he struggled to find the right words. "Lots of people in town thought he had something to do with the disappearances."

Penelope pulled out her phone and scrolled to the photos she'd taken of the missing persons flyers. "Which one?"

"The last one to go. The Foster girl. Bailey admitted he'd seen Kellie before she disappeared," he said, shaking his head. "He told folks she went off on her own into the woods, wasn't part of the messing around with cars or spray painting trees. She stayed for a while at the camp, then wanted to get back home. But she never made it. No one has seen her again. Still, suspicion has never left him. I know that kid. He wouldn't hurt an innocent girl."

"What about the other two boys?" Penelope asked.

"Both were seen in town, one at his job," the sheriff said, deflating. "Bailey was the only one who didn't have anyone to account for him."

"Where are the files on these kids?" Penelope asked.

Sheriff Bryson gave her a cold stare. "I don't know."

"Then how do you know this?" Penelope asked.

"I've talked to Bailey, trying to rebuild the information."

"Well, that's not good enough," Penelope said. "Who were the other officers? What else can you find?"

"It all disappeared with Helmsley," the sheriff said.

Penelope considered his words. "Your answers lie with him, then."

"Believe me, I know."

"Why is Bailey always hanging around up in the forest?" Penelope asked, not sure what to think. A headache was beginning, right behind her eyes.

"His daddy's been taking him up there since he was a boy. A lot of people around here spend time in the woods. His aunt has a cabin out on the edge." The sheriff shrugged. "Bailey knows the area well, says he feels at home there. He's not ready to live on his own, but it's a place for him to go and be alone."

"Did you investigate if he was connected to the rest of the Forrestville Five? Or are you giving him a pass on that also?" Penelope asked, slipping her phone back in her pocket.

Sheriff Bryson let her comment slide.

"We looked for the kids, of course we did," he said. "As far as anyone knows, they just ran off. It happens, small town like this with not many opportunities."

Penelope thought about the one-hundred-acre park and all the wildlife that lived just beyond the town. "What are the chances, if something did happen to one or more of the missing, they'd be found in those woods? If Bailey knows the area as well as he says, wouldn't it be easy for him to dispose of a body without anyone ever finding it?"

"I won't argue you there, he would have the skill for that," Sheriff Bryson said. "But he's not that kind of person." He motioned to the closed door across the hall. "Big groups of kids, boys and girls, hang out up there without anything improper happening."

"Except theft, and underage drinking, and who knows what else," Penelope said, looking at the door also.

"Kids will be kids," Sheriff Bryson said by way of explanation.

"If Regina's telling the truth and Ava was supplying them the stuff, you can take theft off the list."

"Why are you telling me all of this?" Penelope asked, exasperated.

"Thought you'd want to know," he said. "You're the one with all the concerns. Ava hasn't filed one complaint with my office, which makes me think this is all a big fuss over nothing."

The front door opened and Sheriff Bryson stepped out into the hall. He waved Regina's mother into the room where she waited, grabbing a folder from his desk.

"Thanks for coming in," he said to Penelope before heading in behind Regina's mom. He closed the door most of the way but left it slightly ajar. Penelope could hear their mumbled conversation, Regina's defiance hanging strong and her mother's weepy relief mixed with anger.

Penelope stuck her hand in her jacket pocket and rubbed the edge of the envelope containing her jewelry. Her eyes moved over the paperwork on the sheriff's desk and a folder caught her attention. She glanced back over her shoulder and saw the sheriff had taken a seat, his back to the door, his broad shoulders hunched over the table as he went through the arrest paperwork for Regina.

Penelope inched closer to the desk so her thigh was touching and craned her neck to read the folder's tab. *Autopsy Results: Foster, Jordan.*

Her heartbeat picked up as she leaned over and flipped the folder open, spinning it halfway around so she could read it better. She scanned the sheet, stopping at the entry for stomach contents. Listed were venison, steak, potatoes, cabbage, carrots, pineapple juice, wine, and brandy. The next line listed toxins found: Doxylamine.

Penelope thought about the combination of food and spirits, attempting to link them to menu items at Festa, but failing to place them. Chefs tasted all night long, so it wouldn't necessarily have to be one specific dish.

At the bottom of the page was a drawing representing the back and front of a body. Someone had sketched two circles on the lower back of the figure and jotted the word "bruising."

The phone trilled on the desk and Penelope's heart leapt into her throat. She closed the folder and spun it back around just before Sheriff Bryson came back into the office.

"I thought you'd gone," he mumbled before hooking the receiver with his thumb and stretching the phone to his ear.

Penelope made for the door, grateful he hadn't caught her looking through his files. She spelled the name of the toxin over in her head once more so she wouldn't forget it.

"Hold up," he said in a low voice.

Penelope froze, thinking she'd been caught after all. She straightened her shoulders and turned around. The look of alarm on the sheriff's face froze her in her tracks.

"Okay, be right there," he said before hanging up. "The forensic team found human remains in the woods."

CHAPTER 40

Penelope stepped inside the diner and smelled the fresh roasted coffee brewing behind the counter. The older woman who had waited on them a few days earlier offered her a tight smile and nodded at the counter stools. "Nice to see you again."

After filling a mug for Penelope, she sauntered down the counter to check on a customer at the other end while Penelope pretended to look at the menu. She pulled out her phone and searched Doxylamine, finding it to be the main ingredient in several over-the-counter sleep aids.

"What'll it be?" the woman asked when she returned.

"Um, a piece of lemon meringue." Before she could step away again, Penelope said, "You mind if I ask you something?"

Penelope watched her defenses go up, but her smile stayed in place. "Sure, hon. What can I do for you?"

"Is Mr. Pears here?" Penelope asked. "He's not at the newspaper right now."

"No, he's out on assignment somewhere. But I'm his wife, Shirley, if you want to lodge a complaint or fill out a compliment card." Shirley smiled wider, revealing a silver bridge along her gums.

"In that case, maybe you can help. I've been approached to invest in a company called Herring – Steele, and I was told Jacob was one of the first investors. I wanted to ask him about the company," Penelope lied—she'd thought up the story right before she walked in the diner.

"Well, I believe that's our mortgage company," Shirley said.

"Can't say either of us would know much more about it than that."

Penelope deflated. "Do you expect Jacob back soon?"

Shirley shook her head. "No, today is his reporting day. He mentioned something about visiting that movie set at the inn. You're one of them, aren't you?"

"I am," Penelope said. "I'm one of the chefs."

"Well, la-di-da," Shirley said, with a small laugh. She wandered away and returned, sliding a good-looking piece of lemon meringue pie in front of Penelope. "How much longer do you reckon you all will be hanging around? Not that I'm complaining— we've had a nice little bump in business."

"Not much longer," Penelope said vaguely, spearing a piece of lemon curd.

Shirley grabbed the orange handle of the coffeepot and whisked over to a newly seated booth, taking orders and bringing the ticket to the kitchen window. When she came back Penelope said, "I thought Herring – Steele was a privately held restaurant investment company. Are you sure that's where you pay the mortgage?"

"Let's see," Shirley said, thinking. "I suppose 'mortgage' isn't the correct term. They're the folks we bought the diner from, in a lease-to-buy arrangement. We've got years left to pay, a lot of years, if we live that long." She put her hands on the small of her back and did a little stretch. "I guess it's what you call an umbrella company. Lots of businesses represented by an overseeing management team."

Penelope thought about the arrangement. There wasn't anything obviously criminal about it, even if it was a bit unorthodox to sell shares of a company privately.

"Can I get you anything else?" Shirley asked, ripping off a green ticket from her pad.

Penelope shook her head. "Great pie."

Shirley smiled widely again. "Glad you like it. You can take a whole one back for the movie stars. Just $12.99 each."

* * *

Penelope walked out of the diner and saw Denis walking up the sidewalk.

"Denis," Penelope said.

"Penelope," Denis said. "How are things? Oh, I meant to tell you I'll be by on my usual day next week with some new bottles."

"Good, but you won't be meeting with me. There are some changes happening at Festa, which will probably involve you eventually. They're bringing on a new chef."

Denis's face went blank for a minute, then he seemed to catch up. "I've been off this week, out of town. It's funny Ava didn't let us know though. I haven't checked my messages yet. I just got back."

"It's a fairly recent development," Penelope said, wondering why a vendor, someone who wasn't an employee of the restaurant, would expect to be kept in the loop on hiring decisions. "Did you get my message about your check? The one that was stolen from my room?"

"No," he said, confused. "What check?"

"I found a check in that box of wine you left the morning after Jordan died," Penelope said. "I've been trying to call you."

Denis put his hand to his forehead and stared at her. "This retreat thing, it's supposed to be a complete destress experience. Rule one is you have to unplug. Oh man. If I'm late on my payment, I lose my share of the equity."

"So Herring – Steele is your mortgage company too?" Penelope asked.

"No," he said slowly. "It's my shares of Festa." Denis looked at her as if she should already know this. "I'm listed in the portfolio as part owner, bronze level."

"Oh," Penelope said. "I didn't know they sold shares."

"I'll have to explain to Ava, get a new check to her today," Denis said. "If I miss a payment, or I'm even a week late, I get thrown off the portfolio, lose out on all of the returns I have coming to me."

"Returns?" Penelope asked.

"Yeah, I get a quarterly return on my investment," Denis said, nodding. "It's not much right now, but Ava says down the road the revenue will be huge."

"Sounds like a good investment," Penelope said, trying to work it out in her mind. Was Ava crowd-funding Festa's operation? "I've got to head back to the set."

"Sure. See you at the restaurant," Denis said.

CHAPTER 41

When Penelope got back to the set, Jennifer hurried over to her.

"Where have you been?"

"I was in town talking with the sheriff. I left Francis in charge. What's up?"

"Oh, I don't know—someone put a piece of chicken on Janie's plate and she almost threw up," Jennifer said. Her cheeks were pink, her eyes flashing.

Penelope looked at her doubtfully. "I'm sure she didn't throw up from looking at chicken."

Jennifer sighed. "Fine. You're right. I'm just freaking out over here."

"Relax," Penelope said, putting a hand on her shoulder.

"I just wish she would leave, but it looks like they're staying a week at least. They've lost confidence in me as a director."

"Did they say that?" Penelope asked.

"No," Jennifer said. "But I can tell."

"I think you're imagining things," Penelope said.

"Maybe you're right. I should be more confident," Jennifer said. She barked a quick laugh and hugged her arms across her chest.

"Hey, have you been approached by Ava about an investment opportunity?" Penelope asked.

Jennifer shook her head. "No. Thank God," she added. "I have enough going on without getting pitched by a quasi-friend and business partner."

"You're right about that," Penelope said. After Jennifer

wandered away, Penelope thought about Denis. He was a regular guy, unfussy, didn't wear flashy clothes or drive an expensive car. He knew a lot about wine, but shared with Penelope he didn't have the wallet for some of his most expensive bottles, which was why he enjoyed his job. He didn't strike her as an obvious client for an investment portfolio.

Sybil, on the other hand, was a well-known actress with an established career. Shirley and Jacob Pears appeared to be comfortable, but they were still working full-time close to retirement age. And she herself was a business owner with a more than substantial income, yet Ava hadn't breathed a word about investing in Herring – Steele to her or Jennifer. Something wasn't adding up.

Penelope checked in with her crew and found they were finishing up their final meal of the day. "I'm going to head into the woods for a bit, check on something."

Francis looked at her with amusement. "I think I'm the boss on this one, Boss."

Penelope smiled at him. "You are. And I appreciate it."

She trekked up the main path toward Bailey's camp, keeping an eye out for the sheriff and his team. She spotted them a few hundred yards before she arrived and stopped to watch as a few members of the Quincy team stepped gingerly around the woods.

"What are you doing up here today?" the sheriff asked, coming down to meet her on the path.

"Taking a walk."

He looked at her skeptically.

"Okay," Penelope sighed. "I wanted to see what you found."

The sheriff folded his arms and looked down at her. "You should get back to work. This isn't related to our other case."

"How can you say that?"

"Look," he said, turning his back to the team. They were too far away to hear them, but Penelope appreciated he wanted to stay discreet speaking to a civilian. "We may have uncovered a burial ground."

Penelope put her hand over her mouth.

"I'm only telling you because I don't want you coming back here and poking around yourself."

"Do you think it's the missing kids? The Forrestville Five?" Penelope reached for her phone to look at the posters again.

"Too soon to tell," he said.

"Someone lured those kids up here and killed them," Penelope said. "Then buried them in the woods. That's a serial killer. Now Jordan's dead. For a place with no murders in it, now you might have six."

"Miss Sutherland, please let me handle this."

"Bailey invited two girls from the set to come and party with him in the woods."

"I've heard you; now I'm going to ask you to leave and let us do our jobs."

Penelope reluctantly turned away and headed back toward the inn.

CHAPTER 42

Joey, Max, Randall, and Sam were sitting at the bar in the inn, laughing and sharing a bottle of wine. The sight of them together caused a warm feeling to spread in Penelope's chest.

"Hey, guys," she said. "Mind if I join you?"

"You done for the day?" Max asked.

"Yeah, we just wrapped," Penelope said. "They're cleaning up now. I have to do a few more things, but for the most part I'm done."

"We're heading out in the morning," Max said, crooking his thumb between himself and Sam. "Catching the same flight to LA first thing."

"I've offered to give them a ride to Indianapolis, stay overnight," Joey said. "I'll stop in and meet with that contact I told you about in the morning. He says he might have found something out."

"Oh, that's great, Joey," Penelope said. She turned to Randall and Max. "I'm glad you guys were able to visit. It means a lot to Arlena."

"It's been fun, but I have to get back to my set up in Oregon," Sam said.

Penelope nodded and took a sip of wine.

"So, Max, you're quitting the road trip?" Penelope asked.

"The road trip has stalled in Forrestville, Indiana," Max said, jerking his head in his father's direction.

Randall leaned back in his chair and stretched his arms over his head. "Yeah, I'm sticking around for a while. See what happens here, you know?"

"You wouldn't be sticking around for anyone in particular, would you?" Penelope teased.

"Nah," Randall said reflexively. "Well, maybe."

"I'm here two more days after I get back," Joey said.

"Thank goodness. Let's make the most of them," Penelope said.

Max told them about three different auditions Randall helped to set up for him when he got to California. His excitement was contagious, and they all listened as he described the different roles he was up for.

"I hope you get the British one," Penelope said. "I love all those historic shows with the servants and the pretty dresses."

The front door opened and Karen rushed in, looking around the inn. When she saw Penelope, she hurried to the table, excusing herself while trying to catch her breath.

"Karen," Penelope said, standing up and putting her hands on the girl's forearms.

"Penelope," Karen said, unable to stop the tears from coming. "Mom still doesn't want me to do it." She crumpled into Penelope, who wrapped her arms around the girl. She sobbed quietly as the four men at the table looked on, concerned.

After she'd calmed down, Penelope pulled over a chair and eased Karen onto it.

"Tell me what happened," Penelope said.

Karen's words tumbled out, increasing with speed as she went. "I told Mom this is what I really want, that I want to apprentice with Paul. I could take some time off school or commute on the weekends to put my time in. She told me it was the wrong choice. What should I do? I really want her support right now."

Penelope let her finish as she basically repeated the same things over again. "What does Ava say?"

"Ava says she'll talk to her again," Karen said, sniffling.

"Karen, everything is going to work out," Penelope said. "You can always start out in a kitchen in Bloomington near your school, work weekends, and then when you graduate come to Festa. Maybe your mom would agree to a compromise."

Karen shook her head. "Mom's against the restaurant life. Says it's too hard to have a family. It's okay for men, but women chefs can't be good mothers. I don't even know if I want to be a mother!"

Penelope wasn't sure what to say. She looked at Joey, who averted his gaze, then met her eyes again and shrugged.

"Kyle doesn't want the restaurant. I do. It's all I want to do. My family makes no sense."

"Karen," Penelope said, "this isn't the end of the world. Follow your passion and your mom will come around when she sees how happy you are. I'm sure of it."

Karen cleared her throat and wiped away a stray tear. "Would you talk to her for me?"

Penelope felt a prick of dread before Karen finished talking. "I suppose, if you think it would help."

"She respects you," Karen pleaded. "You're a good example. If you could answer any questions for her, let her know it's a great career...I would be so grateful."

Penelope paused, looking into Karen's bright green eyes, then hugged her. "Sure. I'll have a talk with your mom. No promises though."

"Thank you," Karen said, a smile breaking across her face. "I knew you'd help."

CHAPTER 43

Penelope said goodbye to Karen and walked over to Festa, letting herself in the front door with the key. She heard voices coming from the kitchen and headed toward it, surprised to see all four members of the wait staff, including Regina, prepping the service area all dressed in their uniforms for the evening.

She offered a greeting and received a few mumbled hellos in response and a smile from Jeremy. "Ms. Sutherland, it's been a while."

"A day or two," Penelope agreed.

"Feels longer than that," Jeremy persisted.

Penelope knew he was making small talk, but didn't know how much further this line of questioning could go. "Ava in the back?"

"No," Christine said as she wiped down one of the large oval trays. "She had to go into town for something."

"Okay," Penelope said. "Hey, Regina, can I talk to you in private?"

Regina looked at her warily, then followed Penelope slowly into the empty dining room. "You're back at work," Penelope said. "I'm surprised."

Regina shifted her weight and glanced at the bathroom door. "Let's talk in there."

Penelope reluctantly agreed.

"Look, I'm sorry about what I did up in your room," Regina said. "I was pissed, and I wanted you to know it."

Penelope nodded. "Okay. Does Ava know you were charged with theft?"

Regina sniffed a laugh. "Yeah, she knows. She hired me when I got caught stealing over at the inn. Nothing big, little things. Mostly change, cigarettes. I only got caught when I scooped up a money clip that was some kind of family air...air...something."

"Heirloom?"

"Yeah."

"But why does Ava let you stay? You know most places wouldn't let you in the door. You have access to cash here, expensive inventory. Why does she keep you on the staff?"

Regina shrugged. "She and my mom have a deal. I can't get fired. I'm not going to school, and like you said, I can't get hired anywhere else, not like there are hundreds of jobs to get in this crappy town anyway."

"What kind of deal? Who is your mom?" Penelope asked. She felt like she was on the verge of learning something valuable.

"She works at the bank." Regina said. "All I know is she told me I don't have to worry as long as I don't screw up too bad."

"What does that mean, Regina?"

"Like I said, I don't know the details. Mom says she's seen all the accounts. And that's all I have to say to Ava to keep my job. Mention Herring – Steele, and watch her squirm. And I have to keep my job or my mom throws me out. I've got it pretty nice: she's at work all day, I work at night. It's not a bad house. I'm set up."

Penelope put a palm to her forehead. "Okay, then. Hey, did you steal that check from my room?"

"Yep. It's in a safe place," Regina said.

"It's not worth anything," Penelope said.

"I saw it said that company's name. Figured it was one more piece of protection for me."

Penelope sighed. "Get back to work."

Regina checked her eyeliner in the mirror and smiled at Penelope before heading back into the dining room.

Penelope walked past the group of servers again, the other three listening to Regina make up a story about what they talked about in the bathroom. Jeremy gave her an uneasy glance when

Regina did her impression of Penelope giving her a talking to. The girl was quick to spin a cover story, that was for sure.

Checking out back for Ava's truck and seeing an empty lot, Penelope closed herself into the office and turned on the computer. Logging on, she started opening folders she'd never gone to before, looking for anything resembling financial records for the restaurant. She was hoping to find a balance sheet or the check register, something to help her make sense of the different pieces of information she'd gathered over the past couple of days.

She found an out-of-place folder in the orders tab that looked promising and clicked on it. Her curiosity turned to excitement as the spreadsheet began to load, but faded when it asked for a password to unlock it.

Penelope tried her login first, which unsurprisingly failed. She typed in Ava's full name, which didn't work either. She put her chin in her palm and stared at the screen, trying to think what Ava might use. She thought about the Ava's favorite wine with the swan logo and slowly typed *Cygne Reseau*. The spreadsheet opened and Penelope's eyes grew wide. On the left was a long list of names, over a hundred at least, and dollar amounts in subsequent columns matching months. She scrolled down and found the entry for Denis, her eyes moving to the right, quickly adding up the amounts in her head. According to the sheet, he had contributed bi-weekly with a total reaching over seven thousand dollars.

Penelope clicked on the tab at the bottom of the sheet designated as the previous year. It contained a similar sheet with slightly fewer names, and similar dollar amounts filling columns every two weeks to the right.

"Where are the payouts?" Penelope muttered, clicking more tabs. The last one was labeled *Remit* and listed roughly thirty names with debit amounts in rows next to their names. The payouts that had been made to the investors didn't come close to what they had put in.

A thump at the office door made the hair stand up on Penelope's neck and she froze, listening for voices. She heard who she thought was the kitchen staff, coming in from out back, slamming closed the closet next to the office after putting their coats away. She drug her eyes back down to the screen and jotted down a few names. She contemplated emailing the spreadsheet to herself or to the sheriff, but knew that company email was monitored. Another thump from outside the door convinced her she should stop her snooping, at least for the moment. Right before she closed the program, her eyes found Jacob Pears. She scanned across his row. His entries added up to over thirty thousand dollars, just in the past three years. Penelope quickly hit the *Remit* tab, looking to see if they'd received any payouts in return. Confirming they hadn't, she went back to the current sheet, scanning it quickly once more.

Her eyes landed on a number and she blew out a sigh. The office door opened and Ava appeared in the doorway.

"What are you up to?" she asked.

"Just putting a food order in for the set. Hope I'm not intruding," Penelope said, clicking the mouse a few times.

"Of course not, help yourself," Ava said, unwinding her scarf from her neck and hanging it on the back of the door.

Penelope slid open the top drawer to grab a pen, making herself look busy by jotting down some notes. She flicked her eyes up at Ava as she finished writing and smiled.

Penelope pulled into the driveway of Megan's house and slung her messenger bag over her shoulder. She knocked loudly on the front door and greeted the housekeeper, Cynthia, with a smile when she opened it a few minutes later. "Just leave your boots here," she reminded her when she stepped inside the foyer. Penelope's stomach tightened as she looked down at the row of boots, some that must have been worn by Jordan.

Megan was in the kitchen, her bare feet propped on the bottom rung of a stool and a tumbler of juice on the island in front of her. "Penelope, nice to see you again."

"You too. How are you doing?" Penelope asked. She settled herself at the counter.

"I'm getting there," Megan said. "They say grieving is a process. I have to tell you, I do not like the process."

Penelope looked at her with a sympathetic glance.

"Ava tells me the chef you found is going to work out perfectly," Megan said. "We can't thank you enough." She took a sip of her juice and set her tumbler back on the counter.

"Yes, I think Paul will be great," Penelope began. "Speaking of cooking at the restaurant..."

Megan's face tightened, but she didn't interrupt.

"Karen is really passionate about it, and she shows a lot of potential in the kitchen," Penelope began cautiously.

Megan's spine stiffened, her smile remaining in place. She tapped her gelled fingernails lightly against the glass.

"She says she wants to be a chef, like her father."

Megan sighed. "I know, and of course I want my oldest daughter to fulfill her dreams. But school has to take priority now."

"Right, of course," Penelope said. "But maybe she could apprentice on weekends, or intern at a spot closer to campus and come to Festa after graduation."

Megan stood up and stretched, then walked around the island. She reached overhead and pulled out a matching tumbler, her sweater rolling up to show red stripes on her stomach from the waistband of her jeans. She brought the glasses to the counter next to the stove and Penelope watched her mix a cocktail, tipping several bottles over ice. Glancing at the clock, Penelope saw it was just after five.

"You really think Karen would enjoy working at Festa?" Megan asked over her shoulder. Her clothes reminded Penelope of yacht wear, something she'd seen in fashion magazines during the summer months.

"I do," Penelope said. "I think she's got the determination. She's young and has lots of energy, which you need to be a full-time chef."

"How is the life of a chef for you?" Megan asked. "Do you have a family?"

Penelope's cheeks reddened. "No," she admitted. "But I have friends who do."

"I still think the perfect job for a young woman is a teacher, or a librarian," Megan said, stirring the cocktail. "You're home with your children, off summers, or work short days. What's wrong with that being a dream?"

"Nothing, of course," Penelope said. "But it's not Karen's passion."

"She's too young to know what she wants," Megan said. She slid one of the tumblers in front of Penelope.

"I knew very early what I wanted. I started training when I was still in high school, matter of fact," Penelope said. She eyed the drink in front of her and thought about the last time she'd eaten, hours before, and her drive back to the set.

"And your parents were okay with you doing that?"

"Yes, they encouraged me," Penelope said. "Now I'm a business owner, doing really well."

Megan sighed, considering.

"I guess there are worse jobs. Tell you what, I'll think about it. If she wants to intern for a little while, on a trial basis, she'll either take to it, or decide it's not for her."

"Right, a good compromise," Penelope said.

Megan's hair bobbed along with her head as she nodded and swirled her cocktail. "I guess if she ever does meet someone and wants to start a family, she can figure out what to do about it then. Hopefully she'll marry well, like I did, and not have to worry about having a career. Cheers," she said, taking a healthy sip from her glass.

"Thanks," Penelope said. The smell of pineapple juice wafted up from the counter. "What's this, a Greyhound?"

Megan laughed. "No, it's a Wicked Game. Pear schnapps, mezcal, lemon, ginger, and pineapple juice. Jordan and I had them on our honeymoon in Guadalajara. We have..." she paused, and held her finger up in the air, "*had* them every Sunday, sun or snow, rain or shine, ever since."

Penelope waited for Megan's unexpected wave of emotion to pass, remembering too it wasn't Sunday.

"Cheers," Megan said again, urging Penelope to pick up her glass.

Penelope toasted Megan and took a sip.

"What do you think, Chef?" Megan said, a laugh on her lips.

"Yum," Penelope said, taking another taste. "I'm no mixologist, but these flavors are good. I like the ginger."

Megan hummed in agreement.

Penelope took a breath. "There's another thing I want to talk to you about."

Megan smiled and leaned on the counter, swirling the ice in her glass.

"What's that?"

"I think Ava is running an investment program...scheme...tied to the restaurant, using Festa as a front. She's selling shares in the business through a dummy corporation she's set up."

"Wait, what does that mean?" Megan said, looking alarmed.

"From what I can tell, Ava has gotten a bunch of people to put money into Festa, invest in what she calls futures, in anticipation of large payouts over time." Penelope took another sip of her drink, pineapple strong in her nose.

Megan's face became serious. "I don't know anything about business, Penelope. If people want to invest in a restaurant, what's wrong with that?"

"Because the majority of the money is going to pay Festa's bills. And the small number of payouts she's made are only going to the very first group of investors. It's a classic pyramid, a Ponzi scheme. Ava is offering fake shares, but there isn't going to be a payout for the people on the bottom of the list. They're set up to lose everything they've put in."

Megan stood up straight, her face flushing, either from surprise or from the alcohol. "I had no idea."

Her face appeared soft, almost fuzzy around the edges. Penelope concentrated on her pink lipstick.

"How many people are involved?" Megan asked.

"A lot. Herring – Steele isn't a real company. She's set up a crowd-funding receptacle, but didn't tell people they were donating instead of investing, or in reality funding the business."

"How can we prove this?" Megan asked doubtfully. "This is why I never get involved in the business—it's too complicated. Jordan and Ava run that side, I run all of this."

"I've been researching. There's no business registered in the state with that name." Penelope blinked a few times, clearing her vision.

"And you're sure about all of this?" Her words slurred at the edges and Penelope shook her head.

The bottles in the wine rack started to hum and the wallpaper turned overly bright. Penelope had a hard time forming her words, her thoughts falling behind. She tried to stand up, but couldn't get her legs to do what she wanted.

"Oh dear," Megan said. "What should we do now?"

"Oh no." Penelope's vision began to dim. "You knew."

Penelope pushed herself up from the stool, resting her hands on the counter.

"You should sit," Megan said, coming around the island.

Penelope shrank back from her as the room started to spin.

"Sit down. It's going to be okay," Megan said.

Penelope's heart began to race and she slid to the floor, everything going black around her.

CHAPTER 44

Penelope woke to the sound of rushing water. She was in an awkward position, her legs cramped, a seatbelt holding her upright. She opened her eyes with effort, fighting the overwhelming urge to fall back asleep. Her arms were heavy and she had a hard time lifting her head. The sound of water and the cold damp soaking her jeans motivated her to try again.

Rolling her head onto the seat rest behind her, Penelope realized she was behind the wheel of her truck, which was tilted at an odd angle. She looked in the rearview mirror and saw blood from a cut over her eyebrow.

"Help," she whispered hoarsely into the cab, unable to yell. "Help."

The icy water inside the cab rose to her thighs, reviving her some more. She undid the seatbelt, feeling it fly off, the metal buckle clanging loudly against the window. Outside, all she could see was water rushing against the driver-side door.

"Help!" she called, louder this time, panic taking over. She crawled toward the passenger side, her legs tingling painfully, and reached across. She yanked on the door handle, pushing against the passenger door with all her might. It opened an inch, then closed. She felt the water rise farther up her chest.

She screamed again and kicked the passenger door, getting it to open a few more inches. The thought of Joey popped into her head and gave her the strength to pull herself to her knees. Her throat hitched when she saw a log hurtling toward the car. She closed her eyes and turned away just before it smashed through the window.

An icy wave followed the log inside, filling the car until there were only a couple of inches of air left at the roof. Penelope kept her nose and mouth out of the water and grabbed the door handle once more. Taking a deep breath, she ducked under and, with all her might, shoved on the door, almost crying out with relief when it opened. She swam toward the surface, her pushing her panic and exhaustion aside.

"Help!" she gasped after breaking the surface. It was pitch black and the water was numbing her from the inside out. Uncontrollable shivers took over and she worried she'd be unable to keep her head above water.

"I'm here!" Penelope thought she heard someone, then figured it couldn't be. Her head dipped under the water and she held her breath, struggling to swim to the surface again.

Two strong arms hugged her chest, pulling her to the surface. "Hold on!" a man's voice shouted as her body went limp in his arms. As he pulled her onto the riverbank, Penelope felt cold mud under her fingers and took long painful breaths of the frigid air.

"Let's get you inside," the man said, picking her up in his arms.

Penelope laced her fingers together behind his neck and rested her head on his shoulder. "Thank you for saving me, Bailey," she whispered.

CHAPTER 45

Penelope sat in front of the fireplace at the inn, still shivering. She clasped a mug of hot cocoa in her palms while Arlena gently rubbed her hair with a towel. The on-set medic checked her over, determining she'd be okay after warming up and resting. Bailey had called Marla from his campsite, letting her know he'd fished Penelope from the creek in the woods and to come get them. When she'd driven them down the trail to the inn, Marla and Arlena had stripped Penelope's wet clothes off and wrapped her in warm blankets from the dryer.

"Slight hypothermia," the medic said, taking another look at Penelope's fingers. Bailey and Regina sat together at a nearby table, watching Penelope and drinking their own mugs of hot chocolate. Marla came up from the basement with freshly warmed blankets thrown over her arm and fussed over Penelope, swapping out the cooled ones and draping fresh ones around her.

"Thank you, Marla," Penelope said, still shivering. "And thanks for calling the sheriff."

"You'll get warm soon," Marla said abruptly. "More cocoa?"

Penelope nodded and she bustled away, bumping into Sheriff Bryson in the doorway.

"So, you got lost in the woods and ended up in the river?"

"Hello to you too, Sheriff," Marla scolded.

The sheriff looked at her sheepishly. "Sorry, Marla. It's been a rough week."

"You're telling me," she said, hurrying away.

The medic left after giving Arlena instructions.

"I was drugged. By Megan Foster. She served me a Wicked Game. Pineapple juice!" Penelope shouted. Everyone turned to look at her.

"What?" Sheriff Bryson asked.

"She said that was their special drink. Jordan had pineapple juice in his stomach when he died. Megan drugged him and strangled him. If he was lying on his stomach on the floor, she would put her knees on the small of his back and pull the rope. That's what made those bruises."

Everyone stared silently at Penelope.

"I'm not crazy. That's what happened. Megan drugged me the same way she drugged Jordan, then she drove me to the river to make it look like I had an accident and drowned."

"This is so hard to believe," Sheriff Bryson said. "This kind of thing doesn't happen here."

Penelope's eyes flashed. "You can't say that anymore, because it does. You know I'm right. This is what she does...drugs people and stages accidents, or suicides."

Bailey raised his hand from his seat at the table.

"Yes, son?" the sheriff asked.

He shook his head. "It wasn't Mrs. Foster in the truck. It was Ava." Regina nodded as he spoke. "We saw her drive by."

"Can you help me get dressed?" Penelope asked Arlena. "And I have to stop by Sybil's suite too."

CHAPTER 46

"Ava," Penelope said. She stood at Festa's bar, holding onto one of the stools for support. Jeremy stared at her after he called back to the office to summon Ava to the floor.

"Penelope, are you okay?" Ava asked as she approached. "What's happened to you?"

"You know what happened," Penelope said. "You were there."

Ava's face paled. "I don't know what you're talking about."

"Yes, you do," Penelope said, then coughed. Arlena had helped her into her jeans and sweatshirt before she headed over to the restaurant. The front door opened and Arlena came through, followed by the sheriff.

"I found the financial records for Herring – Steele," Penelope said.

Ava smiled tightly. "I know, I have tracking on the computer. I can see what everyone's been up to. Pretty nosy of you."

Penelope let go of the stool and approached Ava. "You've been stealing, promising people a return on investment when you know there never will be one. You've funded all of these renovations, at the business and at the Foster house, with the money."

"It's not illegal to ask for funds from investors," Ava said defiantly.

"It is when you present it like you're doing something to benefit the community, but instead you're just funding your own business."

Arlena placed a folder on the bar, the one Penelope had seen in Sybil's room a few days earlier. Penelope pulled a sheet from the back.

"Here's your mission statement," Penelope began.

"Jeremy, go in the back," Ava ordered. He stood frozen in place until she asked him again.

"Herring – Steele, a charity set up in partnership with Jordan's businesses to prevent suicides among young people in the community," she read from the sheet. "Indiana has one of the highest suicide rates in the country, and our goal is to fund outreach programs in the schools to help." Penelope dropped the paper back on the bar. "Herring is the last name of Jordan and Jennifer's friend back in school who took her own life, and Steele is the name of a student that died a few years ago at the high school."

"And we are doing those things," Ava said. "Making a difference in the community."

"Except you're not," Sheriff Bryson weighed in. "There aren't any programs in place."

"We're still in the planning stages," Ava said.

"You have to register charitable activities with the state. There are no records or Herring – Steele," the sheriff said.

"Which will be taken care of eventually. We'll be in compliance." Ava's voice wavered as she pleaded with them.

Penelope looked around her. "Your records show all of the donations taken so far have gone right back into the business, or into your own pockets, none allocated to any charity of any kind. What happened, Jordan found out what you were up to, cooking the books?"

Ava glared at them. "Yes, he found out by accident from Denis, even though Denis was told Jordan wasn't involved in the charity piece. He never concerned himself with the finances or how the business was run, even his budget at home. I explained to him eventually we'd fund the suicide-prevention programs, but we had to build the business up first in order to do that."

"He refused to let you continue duping people, so you killed him?"

"Jordan didn't understand. This is how business is done," Ava whined.

"Not legally," Penelope responded. "You told people different things with one goal in mind, to take their money, with either a promise of a return on investment or to raise money for charity. But it was really just to line your own pockets."

Sheriff Bryson led Ava out of Festa in handcuffs with Penelope and Arlena right behind. Penelope's head was pounding, a side effect from the drugs she'd been slipped, according to the medic. She thought it was also an excess of adrenaline from the confrontation with Ava.

"I can't believe she would do this to Jordan," Arlena said, her arms crossed. They watched Sheriff Bryson help Ava up into the backseat of his jeep.

"Megan too," Penelope said. "His work wife and his home wife killed him together."

CHAPTER 47

The next morning, Penelope woke with a slight headache, but overall felt renewed after a long night's sleep. She got herself ready for work, the hot shower reviving her further. Joey returned from his trip to Indianapolis right before lunchtime. She'd called him the night before, and he wanted to come back right away, but she insisted she was fine and really wanted him to find out what he could from his contact there.

"I have to go to the sheriff's office again," Penelope said.

"I'm driving you," Joey insisted.

"Not going to argue with you about that," Penelope agreed.

They made their way into town and took the seats opposite Sheriff Bryson's desk.

"How are you feeling?" he asked after they were settled.

"I'm fine, thanks," Penelope said.

Sheriff Bryson sighed and shook his head. "You helped solve the murder of Jordan Foster. Megan and Ava should never have tried to get away with it again."

"Did they confess?" Penelope asked.

"Oh, yes," the sheriff said. "Right away. The investment scheme you uncovered is collapsing like a house of cards the more people we talk to. The Quincy team has a forensic accountant. She's going to be very busy uncovering the money trail."

"And the losses," Penelope said, shaking her head. She thought about Megan's newly renovated house and all the updates to Festa and the inn, most of which were apparently paid for under false pretenses.

"Jordan found out," the sheriff said, sighing. "Long after I'm thinking he should have. But he always left everything up to those two. He didn't involve himself in the inner workings of the business, let Ava make all the deals and sign all the papers. As far as he knew, he was making enough money to pay for everything."

"And then he found out from Denis," Penelope said.

"Yes, he let it slip at the bar one night, congratulating Jordan on all his success and implying he couldn't wait to get his share."

"What about Jacob and Shirley Pears, the mortgage at the diner?"

"From what we found, the Pearses signed an interest-only loan, thinking they would eventually own the property, but in reality it was still owned by Ava. She created a lease, which they signed, and would be paying for eternity for something they would never own."

"They didn't have a lawyer review the sale?" Joey asked.

"Nope," the sheriff said. "It was for sale by owner, a neighborly transfer, no lawyers or agents involved. Ava knew how to pick her marks."

"How did she decide who to ask for investments?" Penelope asked.

"Not sure," the sheriff said. "They all seem to have a personal connection to tragedy, or she simply chose people she thought wouldn't ask too many questions."

"So Jordan confronts Ava, who lets Megan know Jordan will be coming home with financial questions about the house..." Joey began.

"And they bump him off, make it look like a stress-induced suicide," Penelope said. An overwhelming feeling of sadness washed over her and she took Joey's hand. "The ironic thing," Penelope continued, "is they were starting to do well. Once Ava got started, the money and debt just snowballed. The people at the bottom of the pyramid, the early investors...she had to keep finding new investors to cover their returns. Eventually the whole scheme just collapses."

"But who vandalized the restaurant?" Joey asked. "Wasn't it the kids?"

Penelope shook her head.

"That was Ava," Sheriff Bryson said, "trying to throw us off track, make us think Bailey was behind everything. She admitted to planting Jordan's boots at his campsite, figuring that would be enough to get him arrested. Megan strangled her husband on the kitchen floor then loaded him into the car, too rattled to remember he didn't have his work boots on. Then Ava met her and helped her hang him in the walk-in," the sheriff said.

"So Ava went back for the boots, but you had already shown up at the inn by then, so she opted to take them to the campsite?" Penelope asked.

Sheriff Bryson nodded. "Bailey is an easy target. She was trying to throw all the suspicion on him."

"It worked," Penelope said. "She had me fooled."

"She's had a lot of us fooled, for a long time," the sheriff said.

"Can I ask what you found in the woods?" Penelope asked.

Sheriff Bryson's expression became pained. "We found the remains of at least two bodies. The forensic team is still there, with a backup one from Indianapolis, conducting a more advanced search."

"Do you think it's the missing kids? The Forrestville Five?" Penelope asked.

"I sure hope it's not, but I'm thinking it may be," Sheriff Bryson said.

"I was in Indianapolis, at Penny's request," Joey said, squeezing her hand, "looking into the case, the missing files, and the Helmsley connection. My contact said they've had Kevin Helmsley in a cell with a snitch, and he's been talking. You might be getting some company here, maybe federal help soon."

Sheriff Bryson's expression remained calm, but Penelope could see he was pleased at the news. "Is that right?"

Officer Collins emerged from her office and stood in the doorway, her expression hopeful.

Joey turned in his seat to face her. "From what I understand from my contact, Helmsley the younger is a psycho. And his father was in a position to cover for him and destroy other evidence. Who knows, if he hadn't had that heart attack, more kids might have disappeared."

"But where does that put Bailey?" Penelope asked.

"He swears to me he had no part in it, that Helmsley was crazy, leading them around. Bailey swears he never hurt anyone," the sheriff said.

"I hope you're right," Penelope said. "You'll be sure he has a good lawyer, I hope. You know the authorities will have lots of questions for him."

"The guys said the third kid is going to testify, cut himself a deal for his testimony, which should help," Joey said.

Officer Collins pressed her fingers to her lips and stared at Sheriff Bryson.

"We're finally going to have the answer to this awfulness, God willing," the sheriff said.

CHAPTER 48

Penelope and Joey sat in the great room of the inn in front of the fire, enjoying a few moments of peace.

Jennifer came through, Janie trailing behind her. "Penelope, there you are."

"Hi, Jennifer," Penelope managed without sounding too disappointed at the interruption.

"Janie isn't shutting the movie down," Jennifer said, clearly very happy with the news.

"That's great," Penelope said with less enthusiasm.

"With one condition," Janie said, stepping forward.

"What's that?" Penelope said warily.

"I'm flying in a new writing team to work up a treatment of the story," Janie said.

"What story?" Penelope said, shifting forward on the sofa.

"The murder of Jordan Foster, and the murders of the Forrestville Five." Excitement clipped through Janie's words. "They'll have to interview you, of course, Penelope, since you have first-hand knowledge of everything that happened."

"Um," Penelope said. She looked at Jennifer's hopeful face. "Sure, whatever you need, Jennifer."

The women sat down at the bar behind them, discussing the project in hushed voices.

"I guess I'll be here a little longer," Penelope said.

"It's okay," Joey said, pulling her back against the sofa next to him.

"Did you want to have that talk now?" Penelope asked.

"Talk?"

"Yeah, you know, the levels you mentioned," Penelope urged.

"Right," Joey agreed, looking around the nearly empty room. "For me, the next level is for us to think about moving in together."

"Oh," Penelope said. "Yeah, but I have my arrangement with Arlena."

"You can still be her chef and not live there, right? My place is only twenty minutes away, and you're there a lot anyway," Joey said.

"Wow, that's a big level," Penelope said. "I like it."

Joey took her chin in his fingers and pulled her in for a kiss. "We can talk about the other levels when we're alone."

"Can you give me a hint?" Penelope asked, giving him another peck on the chin.

"You can guess, I think," Joey said. "I want you in my life. Permanently. How you feel about that, I'm not sure. I mean, I think I know...that's the next step for us in my mind."

Penelope's heart skipped and she kissed him again, freezing the moment in her mind, holding him close for as long as possible.

SHAWN REILLY
SIMMONS

Shawn Reilly Simmons was born in Indiana, grew up in Florida, and began her professional career in New York City as a sales executive after graduating from the University of Maryland with a BA in English. Since then Shawn has worked as a bookstore manager, fiction editor, convention organizer, wine consultant and caterer. She has been on the Board of Directors of Malice Domestic since 2003, and is a founding member of The Dames of Detection. Cooking behind the scenes on movie sets perfectly combined two of her great loves, movies and food, and provides the inspiration for her series.

**The Red Carpet Catering Mystery Series
by Shawn Reilly Simmons**

MURDER ON A SILVER PLATTER (#1)
MURDER ON THE HALF SHELL (#2)
MURDER ON A DESIGNER DIET (#3)
MURDER IS THE MAIN COURSE (#4)

Available at booksellers nationwide and online

Visit www.henerypress.com for details

Henery Press Mystery Books

And finally, before you go...
Here are a few other mysteries
you might enjoy:

A MUDDIED MURDER

Wendy Tyson

A Greenhouse Mystery (#1)

When Megan Sawyer gives up her big-city law career to care for her grandmother and run the family's organic farm and café, she expects to find peace and tranquility in her scenic hometown of Winsome, Pennsylvania. Instead, her goat goes missing, rain muddies her fields, the town denies her business permits, and her family's Colonial-era farm sucks up the remains of her savings.

Just when she thinks she's reached the bottom of the rain barrel, Megan and the town's hunky veterinarian discover the local zoning commissioner's battered body in her barn. Now Megan is thrust into the middle of a murder investigation—and she's the chief suspect. Can Megan dig through small-town secrets, local politics, and old grievances in time to find a killer before that killer strikes again?

Available at booksellers nationwide and online

Visit www.henerypress.com for details

FATAL BRUSHSTROKE

Sybil Johnson

An Aurora Anderson Mystery (#1)

A dead body in her garden and a homicide detective on her doorstep...

Computer programmer and tole-painting enthusiast Aurora (Rory) Anderson doesn't envision finding either when she steps outside to investigate the frenzied yipping coming from her own back yard. After all, she lives in Vista Beach, a quiet California beach community where violent crime is rare and murder even rarer.

Suspicion falls on Rory when the body buried in her flowerbed turns out to be someone she knows—her tole-painting teacher, Hester Bouquet. Just two weeks before, Rory attended one of Hester's weekend seminars, an unpleasant experience she vowed never to repeat. As evidence piles up against Rory, she embarks on a quest to identify the killer and clear her name. Can Rory unearth the truth before she encounters her own brush with death?

Available at booksellers nationwide and online

Visit www.henerypress.com for details

FINDING SKY

Susan O'Brien

A Nicki Valentine Mystery (#1)

Suburban widow and PI-in-training Nicki Valentine can barely keep track of her two kids, never mind anyone else. But when her best friend's adoption plan is jeopardized by the young birth mother's disappearance, Nicki is persuaded to help. Nearly everyone else believes the teenager ran away, but Nicki trusts her BFF's judgment, and the feeling is mutual.

The case leads where few moms go (teen parties, gang shootings) and places they can't avoid (preschool parties, OB-GYNs' offices). Nicki has everything to lose and much to gain—including the attention of her unnervingly hot PI instructor. Thankfully, Nicki is armed with her pesky conscience, occasional babysitters, a fully stocked minivan, and nature's best defense system: women's intuition.

Available at booksellers nationwide and online

Visit www.henerypress.com for details

CPSIA information can be obtained
at www.ICGtesting.com
Printed in the USA
LVOW13s0912040318
568590LV00011B/489/P